"What do you wish for in a wife, then?"

"I know it wasn't either one of my sisters, so apparently you do not want an intelligent, witty, charming partner." Her tone was mischievous, and he opened his mouth to reply, but realized he couldn't—not without insulting her sisters, himself, or her.

This hedgehog was far too prickly and intelligent to spar with. But she remained fascinating to him—when was the last time he was this engaged in a conversation?

"When I get married," he said, "which I will do, eventually—I want someone who is soft and gentle. Someone who will welcome me home at the end of a long day."

"You've just described either a fuzzy blanket or a pet, my lord."

He couldn't help but burst into laughter, and she joined him, both grinning at one another as though it were the most natural thing in the world.

By Megan Frampton

The Duke's Daughters

THE LADY IS DARING
LADY BE RECKLESS
LADY BE BAD

Dukes Behaving Badly

MY FAIR DUCHESS
WHY DO DUKES FALL IN LOVE?
ONE-EYED DUKES ARE WILD
NO GROOM AT THE INN (novella)
PUT UP YOUR DUKE
WHEN GOOD EARLS GO BAD (novella)
THE DUKE'S GUIDE TO CORRECT BEHAVIOR

MEGAN FRAMPTON

The LADY IS DARING

A DUKE'S DAUGHTERS NOVEL

AVONBOOKS

An Imprint of HarperCollinsPublishers

Excerpt from *Never a Bride* copyright © 2019 by Megan Frampton.

THE LADY IS DARING. Copyright © 2018 by Megan Frampton. All rights reserved. Printed in the United States of America. No part of this book may be used or reproduced in any manner whatsoever without written permission except in the case of brief quotations embodied in critical articles and reviews. For information, address HarperCollins Publishers, 195 Broadway, New York, NY 10007.

First Avon Books mass market printing: October 2018

Print Edition ISBN: 978-0-06-266667-3
Digital Edition ISBN: 978-0-06-266666-6

Cover illustration by Gregg Gulbronson
Cover photograph by Shirley Green Photography

FIRST EDITION

18 19 20 21 22   QGM   10 9 8 7 6 5 4 3 2 1

This is for all the women who've been shamed for being too smart.

Chapter 1

A dream is just an adventure not yet taken.

LADY IDA'S TIPS FOR THE
ADVENTUROUS LADY TRAVELER

1846, the Marquis of Wheatley's office

If given the choice between enduring twenty-four hours of amateur Shakespearean theatrics or speaking with his father for five minutes, Bennett, Lord Carson, would have only one thing to say.

Now is the winter of our discontent.

But Bennett hadn't been given the choice, so there would be no winter. Certainly not any glorious summer. Or any kind of escape at all.

"It was my understanding you were to be married to an heiress as soon as possible," the Marquis of Wheatley said, tapping the top of the desk. Bennett's desk.

The marquis had made a rare appearance at

his own home that afternoon, calling Bennett in to his office—the marquis's office only in name, since Bennett was the one who did all the work there—for what was certain to be an unpleasant encounter.

Most of Bennett's meetings with his father were unpleasant; the only topic on which it seemed they could agree was the weather. *Yes, sun is preferable to rain. Glad to have that settled.*

The office was normally a place of refuge for Bennett—after all, nobody else wanted to put in the work he did here—and the chair was adjusted to his height, not his father's. Likewise, the books closest at hand were mostly ones dealing with business and agriculture, although Bennett sometimes found time to dive into the latest works of Charles Dickens, although that author wrote faster than Bennett could read.

Which said more about Bennett's spare time than Mr. Dickens's output.

"And yet your younger brother Alexander snatched away the duke's daughter—"

"Lady Eleanor," Bennett supplied. "Your daughter-in-law," he said pointedly.

"And then that other one . . ."

"Lady Olivia."

"Was stolen by that bastard."

That bastard was also Bennett's best friend. "Edward. His name is Edward."

Bennett had long ago given up being resentful of having to bear the weight of the family's responsibilities; it didn't do any good, and it wouldn't help the many families and small businesses that depended on the Marquis's various holdings. Or provide funds for the care Bennett's invalid mother, the marquis's neglected wife, required.

The marquis waved his hand in dismissal. Because remembering people's names was far less important than maintaining the marquis's quality of life. "I've been to the bank, and even though Alexander's bride brought a dowry, it appears we are still in straitened circumstances."

Bennett clamped his jaw to prevent him saying what was on his mind—that his father was draining the funds to support his second family consisting of his mistress and her two children, that he was profligate in general, and that he hadn't shown an iota of interest in helping the family beyond marrying his heir off to a wealthy woman.

Had he thought he wasn't resentful? Never mind. He'd lied.

"It takes time to recover from the kinds of setbacks we've had." He was proud of his reasonable tone of voice. And for not pointing out that if his father didn't spend every penny that came in, the family finances would be much better.

Reinvestment, not constant spending, was the

key to a solid future. Something everybody but his father agreed on.

His father twisted on the chair, raising his feet to place them on the desk, disturbing the papers Bennett had been working on. "We don't have time. You'll need to sort this situation out as soon as possible."

As though finding the female with whom you'd spend the rest of your life was a situation to be sorted. Like choosing which coat to wear that day, or selecting one piece of horseflesh over another.

He'd seen firsthand the kind of marriages those types of business transactions resulted in, and he wanted no parts of that.

When Bennett allowed himself to think about what he *did* want—which wasn't often—he knew he wanted to fall in love. To marry a quiet, gentle lady, someone who would be a soft respite to come home to at the end of a long day.

But he didn't have the luxury of indulging his wants, since he spent his days working on business, and his nights at Society events drumming up support for more business ventures.

Business. Responsibility. Hard work. His life sounded as though it were the final directives of an instructive moral tale for children. And just as dull.

"You seem to be charming to the ladies," the marquis continued in a skeptical tone, as though he couldn't possibly see it himself, "so it shouldn't be too difficult for you to find someone to actually say yes. Unlike those other two," the marquis said with a harrumph.

If his father were less of a selfish solipsist—a redundant description, to be sure—Bennett would point out that the two Howlett sisters had fallen in love, and he was not going to stand in the way of true love. Especially when it happened to his brother and best friend, respectively.

But the marquis *was* a selfish solipsist, redundancy and all. Bennett would not let others suffer because of his father's blatant disregard for anything that didn't personally benefit him.

"So it's settled. You'll marry the wealthiest young lady you can persuade to have you. Perhaps you could try one of the other Howlett sisters. There's that other one's twin and that youngest one."

Of course, because it made sense to try to marry *all* of the sisters of one family. Not to mention all he knew about Olivia's twin, Pearl, was that she was continually active, unable to sit still for more than a few minutes, and would be ill-suited to be a Society wife, and that the youngest lady, Ida, had spent over half an hour at a Society party lecturing on recent innovations in gas lighting. Despite a clear indication from the people in attendance that they were totally and entirely bored.

A remarkable feat, to be sure, but he would not put "unable to stop spewing knowledge when most people wanted them to" on the list of his requirements for a wife.

"So you know what needs to be done," the marquis finished, getting up from the chair. Bennett's chair, damn him.

"Wonderful talk as always, Father," Bennett replied in as mild a tone as he could manage. "I'll consider your advice," he said, gesturing to the door of the room in obvious dismissal.

"You do that," the marquis said, stomping out of Bennett's office.

Bennett forced himself to breathe deeply, straightening the papers his father's boots had disarranged. It wouldn't be the first time—nor the last, unfortunately—that his father's discontent spoiled Bennett's summer, so to speak.

The only course to take was to roll up his sleeves—figuratively, since it wouldn't be proper to appear in public with his forearms showing—and find a way to sort the situation that didn't result in Bennett selling himself to the highest bidder.

Or to another lady in the Howlett family who absolutely did not want him as a husband.

"AND THEN I spent the rest of the night hiding behind a pillar." Ida leaned back in her chair and regarded her sisters Pearl and Eleanor, both of whom were smothering laughter. She gestured in their direction. "It's fine to find it humorous, I have to admit to doing so myself," she continued.

Both sisters burst out into peals of laughter, Ida joining them after a few moments. It felt good to laugh, to share a moment with her beloved sisters, even if they often did not understand one another.

"The pillar was not a good conversationalist. It looked at me stone-faced as I asked it questions," Ida continued, a wry grin on her face. Eleanor doubled over in laughter, Pearl holding her stomach. "It was a marble-ous evening," she finished, emphasizing the pun.

She took a sip of tea, smiling down into her cup as her sisters' laughter slowed. The praise washed over Ida, making her feel warm and nearly happy. "I do wish you'd let people see this side of you," Pearl continued in a soft voice. "Instead of seeing—"

Ida put her teacup down. "Ida the Sophist? Ida of the All-Consuming Knowledge? The lady with no sense of humor and an outsized sense of her own intelligence?" Ida sighed ruefully. "I know, I do try, but then I freeze up in public, and I end up blurting something out that sounds like I'm condescending to someone, or I get so excited to share the information I have that I just start talking, even if the other person is clearly bored by what I'm saying." Which was why she found it safer to hide during parties. Pillars did not judge.

"You do look rather ominous on occasion," Pearl admitted.

That shouldn't please her, but it did. "Even when I'm wearing debutante white?" Ida said, glancing down at her deplorably white gown. "Imagine what it would be like if I got to wear red or something equally striking."

"You would look spectacular in red," Eleanor said in an appreciative tone of voice, taking a sip of her tea. "Black hair, white skin, red gown, red lips."

Ida felt her cheeks heat at the compliment. Another one, in such a short period of time. Had that ever happened before?

Her sisters were all pretty in various ways, but she always felt as though, once again, she was the outlier—too pale, too dark-haired, too dramatic in her coloring.

They were all agreed in hating wearing white, however. If Ida hadn't seen Eleanor and her husband, Alexander, being all spoony over each other firsthand, she'd wonder if Eleanor wanted to get married just so she could wear actual colors.

The three sisters sat in Eleanor's parlor, Ida and Pearl having walked over with a maid from their parents' house. Unlike their mother the Duchess of Marymount's parlor, Eleanor's decorations were spare, chosen for their quality more than their quantity.

Apparently their mother had never seen a porcelain shepherdess she didn't like. And then purchased for her cluttered sitting room.

Their father, the duke, contrarily, seemed yet to find a daughter he *did* like, which meant the sisters had to rely entirely on each other for familial love.

Thankfully, that was in abundance.

The room suited Ida's aesthetic much more than her mother's parlor did. It felt like a place to exchange pleasantries or poke fun at oneself for trying to blend in with large marble columns.

"But you didn't want to dance at all?" Eleanor asked, peering at Ida from behind her spectacles. She had on a lovely blue gown with velvet trim. A matching piece of blue velvet was woven through her hair.

Not a speck of white in sight. Not a reason to get married, but definitely a bonus to entering into the institution. "I know Lord Bradford is a bit of a—" Eleanor paused as she pondered the word, waving her hands in the air.

"Numbskull?" Ida supplied with a grin. "He is, but he is so good-hearted I can't blame him for his lack of intelligence. It's his dancing I object to." She leaned forward to rub her foot. "Sometimes I think he has sworn not to actually touch the floor, only his partner's toes."

"And there was no one else who took your interest?" Eleanor asked. Since her older sister had gotten married, it seemed as though her sole goal in life was to ensure her other sisters did the same.

Except for Della. All four of the remaining duke's daughters were relieved that Della hadn't actually married the man she'd run away with; Mr. Baxter was a scoundrel, and—Ida often indignantly commented—he wasn't even that good a dancing instructor.

Ida shook her head. Trying to ignore the name— *Lord Carson*—that sprang to mind at Eleanor's words.

Lord Carson intrigued her, for some reason, and not just because of his handsomeness. Although his handsomeness helped, she had to admit.

It just seemed as though he was so kind, so thoughtful. Dancing with other young ladies who had made pillars their best friends too. Making certain everyone was as comfortable as they could be. Taking his responsibilities as a gentleman as seriously as it appeared he took his business. But she couldn't admit that, not to her sisters and barely to herself. Besides which, he'd already not married Eleanor and Olivia. Why would he ever pay attention to *her*?

"I don't want to find anyone who will take my interest," she said, surprising herself with her answer. And how she felt suddenly fierce and determined. Although that wasn't surprising; she often felt that way. Usually when sharing information nobody truly wanted to hear.

"I want to do something else," she announced.

"What else?" Pearl asked.

Ida rose to look out the window, putting her fingers on the glass. The people walking outside all seemed to have a purpose. Earning a living, running an errand, teaching a child. Helping somebody else.

She wanted to have a purpose too. Something beyond keeping pillars company. Wearing an endless succession of white gowns.

Or regarding her sisters' happiness wistfully, aware it would take a special gentleman to win her heart, and want her to win his in return.

She turned to face them. "I want to find Della."

Her sisters both drew in their breath. "But we don't know where she is," Pearl pointed out. "She's been very strategic in never including a return address whenever she writes."

"There has to be a way," Ida said, that welcome determination building inside her. "How can we just let her go? She's a part of us. And now she's had a daughter. How can we just give up?"

"If anyone could find her, you could," Pearl replied in a confident tone. She held her hands out, palms up, in a helpless gesture. "But even if you could figure out where she is, there's no possibility of you being able to go after her."

Why not? Ida wished she could ask.

But she knew the answer. She could probably recite it backward, were she to be challenged to: She was a young, unmarried lady. *Lady unmarried young a was she.*

It wasn't proper for her to walk two feet outside of her own door without some sort of chaperone, so the thought of her being able to go haring about the country in search of her sister was ludicrous. And scandalous. And befitting of the duke's disgraceful daughters.

So that meant she should consider it.

If only she had the slightest clue of how to begin.

Chapter 2

Adventure comes to those who search for it. A gentle hint: Searching for it means you have to venture out from behind large marble columns.

LADY IDA'S TIPS FOR THE
ADVENTUROUS LADY TRAVELER

"I'm sorry I, uh," Alexander said, a rueful smile on his face as he looked at Bennett, the breeze ruffling his hair.

"Sorry you went and fell in love with Eleanor?" Bennett punched Alex on the arm. "You're an idiot. You love her, she loves you, and that is all that matters."

"But if I hadn't—" Alex began.

"Then I still wouldn't have married Eleanor. I want what you and Edward have. I will not be bartered just to provide our father with funds." Bennett grimaced. "I think I know what it must feel like to be a young lady, having to entertain the possibility of marriage with every gentleman she meets."

The two brothers were walking in the park across from Alex's house, Bennett having gone there to consult with his brother about how to address their father's latest demand. Bennett had dragged Alex outside before his younger brother could protest. Bennett needed to walk, to burn off the agitation he felt after his father's visit.

He had the distinct worry that he could walk to China and he still wouldn't feel settled. Although then he would be half a world away, so that might be useful.

"At least you are the one making the offer," Alex pointed out. "Even if you don't want to."

"Except when Lady Olivia insisted that it was time we marry." Bennett grinned at the memory as he kicked a stone on their path. Eleanor's sister Olivia had believed herself to be madly in love with Bennett, and had made it clear on at least one memorable occasion. He'd narrowly missed being brained with some sort of objet d'art.

Thankfully, Bennett's best friend, Edward, had wound up being the true object of her love. The two were ridiculously happy, and Bennett and the world's collection of objets d'art were both relieved at the outcome.

"You do seem to be quite popular with ladies. If not the Howlett ladies specifically," Alex said with a grin. "If you were to even consider Father's demand."

Bennett grimaced. "Yes, it seems that having avoided being married to two ladies somehow makes me *more* appealing to the others."

"Woe is you," Alex said in a dry tone. Bennett punched his brother's arm again.

"My marital evasion is seen as a deliberate escape rather than a happy romantic accident," Bennett continued as Alex rubbed his arm pointedly. "Now all the eligible ladies behave as though I have a bull's-eye on my heart." He paused, considering. "Or on my title since how my heart feels doesn't seem to matter."

"Those determined Carson-hunters," Alex said with a grin. "It's the unfortunate side effect of being so damned charming, diplomatic, and handsome. See, if you were more like me," he began.

"An enormously tall rake with a penchant for blunt speaking?" Bennett finished, grinning at his brother.

"Ah, but now I am a tamed rake. I am only rakish with my wife," Alex said, his eyebrows wriggling.

"Forget that," Bennett replied hastily. He did not want to know anything about Alex and Eleanor's happiness in the bedroom. "The worst part of Father's request is that he is simply *wrong*. There is enough money, if he were to live reasonably, for me to take care of everything that needs to be done. Your marrying Eleanor brought the family her dowry, and that should have been more than enough."

"He's deplorable," Alex said in his usual abrupt way.

Alex was right.

His brother turned to regard him, a questioning look on his face. "What if you were to just leave? What would happen then?"

Bennett blinked. Just—*leave*?

"I owe you, Bennett," Alex said, his voice low. "Our family's survival is only due to your hard work and responsibility. Why not let me take over? Just for a little while?"

The thought hit Bennett like a punch to the gut. A good punch to the gut, but a punch nonetheless. That someone would offer to do that. That he hadn't considered anybody could possibly remove his burden. But that his brother had.

Alex continued, "You can ease up, for once, and it has the added benefit of making our father absolutely furious."

Because the marquis thought his second son was worthless. Alexander had thought that for a time himself, until Eleanor and her love had persuaded him otherwise.

"I can't." Bennett's words were clipped.

"You can. You *should*."

Bennett shook his head, the possibility of it making his shoulders feel lighter already. But only the possibility; he couldn't truly leave. Leave all of his responsibilities? Just leave?

Could he?

"Think about it," Alex said after a few moments. "Just think about it. It would be my honor to step in to assist. You know I can, it's just—"

"Just that Father has never allowed you anywhere near the family management."

"If you take the risk, Bennett," Alex said in a determined tone, "I will ensure nothing bad will happen to the family or the business. That's a risk you won't have to worry about. You have my word. Just think about it," he repeated.

BENNETT WAS THINKING about nothing else when the two men returned to Alex's house so Bennett could say hello to his sister-in-law. And avoid going home for another bit of time.

"The ladies are in the salon, my lord," the butler said as Bennett and Alex walked into the house.

"The ladies?" Bennett questioned.

"Yes, my lady has been joined by her sisters, Lady Pearl and Lady Ida."

"Come along then, Bennett," Alex said, a humorous twist on his lips. "Let us go visit with the only women who could be said are definitely not aiming their marital arrows at your heart."

Bennett felt his mouth twist into a smile. There was no possibility the two remaining Howlett sisters would be Carson-hunters. Lady Pearl could likely not slow herself down long enough to be courted, whereas Lady Ida would likely lecture him on all the ways he was courting her incorrectly, citing treatises and obscure Latin lectures to prove her point.

The thought, at least, made him smile.

IDA WAS NEARLY comfortable with her brother-in-law, but she felt that familiar frozen feeling when she saw his brother, Bennett, Lord Carson, accompanying him.

They'd met on quite a few occasions, although Ida wasn't certain he knew entirely who she was. But of course she knew who he was, him with all that thoughtful handsomeness. And not having married two of her sisters.

She'd dreamed, briefly, of him asking her to dance. Finding her behind the pillar and escorting her out to join the others.

Even though she did not dance. Insisting that was the truth made it easier when she was not invited to do so anyway.

But Lord Carson danced. And often. She'd watched him, all his sleek handsomeness, his long, lean form evoking thoughts of strength and purpose. When he said something, it was with such determination and authority that nearly everybody stopped and paid attention.

And not in the way people paid attention when Ida spoke; then people would barely suppress sighs of impatience, and she was acutely and sometimes painfully aware that they were simply not interested.

But everyone was interested in what Lord Carson had to say. She envied that.

"Good afternoon, Bennett," Eleanor said, rising from her seat to take both his hands in hers and present her cheek for a kiss. She spread her arms to indicate Pearl and Ida. "You have met my sisters?"

"Yes, a pleasure," Lord Carson said, and Ida had to marvel that it sounded as though he meant it.

Was he pretending sincerity? Or was it a facet of his ability to persuade? After all, he'd managed to persuade two of her sisters not to marry him, which hadn't been difficult in Eleanor's case, but was most definitely in Olivia's.

"Bennett and I were just talking about escape." Alexander's expression was sly, and Ida saw Lord Carson react, just for a moment, as though he were annoyed.

Interesting. So he couldn't entirely mask his natural emotions.

"What kind of escape, my lord?" Ida asked, her innate curiosity outweighing her potential mortification at being found too boring.

Bennett shot another glance at Alexander, who merely laughed, going to sit between his wife and Pearl, engaging them in conversation.

Lord Bennett sat beside her, stretching his long, lean legs out in front of him. He was immaculately garbed, of course, with a well-fitted dark green coat and buff-colored trousers. He was clean-shaven, showing the strong planes of his face, and his hair was smoothed back from his forehead.

At first it seemed as though he might not answer at all, and then he folded his arms over his chest and turned to look at her.

Had he ever looked so directly at her before?

She didn't think so. The prickly awareness she had of him when he was in the room became more intense than it had ever been.

It was likely all due to the unexpectedness of it. Nothing else.

Not his whiskey-colored eyes, or how one side of his mouth tilted up, as though he were constantly suppressing a smile.

Not that at all.

"My brother and I were talking about the allure of just leaving everything. Of escaping all one's responsibilities."

Ida felt her eyes widen. "Alexander isn't planning on leaving—"

Lord Carson started, his eyes wide, taking her hand in a fierce grip. A sincere and unexpected gesture that convinced her he was earnest. "No, of course not. I apologize for startling you, my lady." He gestured with the hand that still held hers. "Look at them, have you ever seen anything so—so—"

"Disgustingly happy?" Ida finished as she looked at Alexander and Eleanor, who were sharing a warm glance that indicated they were thinking of things that were definitely not teatime conversation.

He laughed, releasing her hand as he did so. "Yes, it is that, although I would never tell Alex."

"I am the sort of person who *would* say something," Ida admitted in a rueful tone. Lord Bennett looked surprised, but then his mouth curled up into a smile. Relief washed over her; he hadn't gone so far as to acknowledge her awkwardness, but he hadn't been disapproving about her words.

"I have noticed that about you, my lady," he said in a wry tone.

Ida felt alternately mortified and pleased that he'd noticed.

"But if you're not terrifying me about Alexander's future plans, explain more about escape."

She couldn't help how her voice sounded as though she were longing, almost plaintive, and she straightened in her seat to try to regain a measure of her equilibrium.

Hard to do when the most handsome gentleman of one's not-so-much-acquaintance was looking at you. And not as though you were an oddity.

"Escape." He made it sound just as much of a long-held desire as she had. Was it possible they had that in common? "There is something so intoxicating about the idea that one could just leave, just walk away from one's responsibilities, forget who you are and what you are supposed to do, even if just for a short time."

The idea was intoxicating, as he'd said. Ida felt almost light-headed at the prospect. As though she'd drunk a glass of champagne very quickly.

And then reality hit her.

"Gentlemen are able to do such things," she replied, hating how pedantic she sounded, but unable to stop the creeping tone of lecture in her voice. "Ladies are not. We aren't even given a purpose beyond marriage and children, much less the opportunity for any kind of escape," she finished.

It stung, to say it so directly. But Ida had never shied away from a truth, no matter how unpleasant, and she wouldn't begin now, no matter to whom she was speaking.

He regarded her with a thoughtful expression. Not as though he were judging her, or wishing she would stop talking, or even thinking of ways to rebut her statement.

Just as though he were . . . thinking about it. As though he were thinking about *her*.

Oh. That prickly feeling was like a monsoon of prickles. Not that that was an apt descriptor—it was a fairly poor one, if she were to be honest—but it felt that way.

"Ladies are not given the same sort of consideration gentlemen are," he replied at last, eliciting an unexpected snort from Ida.

She hadn't snorted. Had she? Damn it. She had. Wonderful. She'd *snorted* at him, which was almost as bad as lecturing him for hours on scientific method, the efficiency of gas lighting, or how she wished that for once people could eat dessert before their main course.

Just because no one could predict the future. And desserts were more delicious than what preceded them.

Because if someone could predict the future, if *she* could, she would have run from the room rather than emitting some sort of embarrassing sound in his general direction.

He didn't reel back from her in horror, however; in fact, his mouth twisted into another grin, and she felt an answering warmth inside at the sight.

He really did look good, she had to admit. No wonder two of her sisters had at least considered him as a husband.

"It was an asinine comment," he said, a half smile on his mouth. "Forgive me?" he asked, and she nodded.

And he could admit to a mistake.

"But if you could escape," he continued, this time in a lower, quieter tone, "where would you go?"

Words and images flew through her head in a tumult, so fast she couldn't even manage to speak for a few moments.

Where wouldn't she go if she could? If she had the same kind of freedom a gentleman had?

First she would find Della. And then she could escape, free from any obligations. Far away from the constrictions of Society, from feeling as though hiding behind a pillar was an acceptable response to mingling with people.

Honestly, it said a lot about how constrained she was now that even this conversation felt like an escape. A refuge from the usual discussions of the weather, a topic that always irked Ida; the only reason to discuss the weather was to decide what to wear or what to do, and most people in her world wouldn't stop going to parties and dancing and drinking tea with one another no matter what was happening outside. So what was the point of talking about it?

"I find that I am very interested in your answer, my lady," he said, making her realize she had yet to respond. "You have the rare ability, in our world at least, to speak the truth." He hitched his chair a fraction closer to hers, his eyes intent on her face, the expression in his gaze so obviously interested, and not judging, that her usual awkwardness slipped away, leaving her grateful for the relief.

WHEN HE'D FIRST met her, he hadn't paid much attention to the youngest of the duke's daughters. She was bookish, and firmly opinionated, and he had been too busy not marrying her sisters to notice her hardly at all, he had to admit.

Plus there was her tendency to declaim on complicated topics in polite Society.

But now those crises were safely averted, and now he couldn't help but notice her implacable, disconcertingly direct stare. Her opinions, which were given without her apparently worrying if they would be well received.

The way she made an inelegant noise in response to his ridiculously privileged comment. It was so unexpected, it was almost . . . adorable.

Just once, he wished he could behave like Lady Ida was now and say something without having to parse it through his own internal critic. To be so open about what she wanted and how much she longed for something.

What would it be like to long for something rather than long to escape from something?

"I think, my lord," she replied slowly, as though considering his question as thoroughly as possible, "that I would go somewhere that doesn't exist." Her eyes looked past him, dark in thought. "A place where it is acceptable to do what one wants. As long as you don't hurt anyone," she continued, her tone wistful, "it would be lovely to just be. It doesn't matter where, just as long as it wasn't—"

"Here," he said, finishing her sentence. "That sounds like a remarkable place, my lady."

"The thing is," she continued, "we're all trapped. And we know it, and we can't get out of it. If we're lucky, like Eleanor and Alexander and Olivia and Edward, we fall in love." She shook her head. "But that happens so very rarely. It certainly won't happen to me."

It won't happen to me. Bennett had to wonder why she was so certain, but then again, Lady Ida appeared to be certain about everything. She should have been born a man, or at least given the freedom to do and say what she wanted, like a man.

She could escape, and snort, and have the freedom to move as she wished, freedom he took for granted.

He was surprised to discover he liked Lady Ida. What was more, he *admired* her, which felt much rarer than mere liking; she said what she meant, and she didn't seem to care when her words—or her inarticulate noises—bothered people.

She was also severely and gloriously beautiful, almost too lovely to look at directly. How had he never noticed *that* before?

Her hair and eyebrows were as dark as her lashes, and her skin was ivory white, while her lips were dark red. Like the fairy story his mother had read to him when he was little about Snow White, before his mother had lost her energy.

She wore a gown that was lovely, he had to admit, but it just didn't suit her. It was white, and tasteful, and bland. She was vibrant, and fierce, and anything but bland.

There was something so enticing about her, beyond her beauty, even as everything about her seemed determined to push people away. Maybe that was the allure; to be the person she let into her closely guarded space. As she was letting him in now.

"You're lost in thought, my lord. Are you considering your own escape?"

Her voice intrigued him also; she didn't speak in the same high-pitched breathy way that other young ladies did. Her voice had a dark, smoky quality, like the best kind of brandy drunk late at night after a satisfying evening of some sort of indulgence.

"Envying yours, my lady," he replied, feeling almost vulnerable by making such an honest statement. One that, were she one of the Carson-hunters, would be tantamount to an invitation to chase him across London's landscape.

But he knew she had no interest in him that way.

Thank goodness. It was the only way he could allow himself to open up to her.

"Even though I am a lady, and so that kind of escape is impossible."

"I am sorry," he replied, meaning it. He had never really considered what it might mean for a young, curious lady to have to be so constrained.

"My lady?"

It was the butler, who'd walked into the room holding a silver salver. "A letter has arrived. I thought you would want to see it at once."

Eleanor gestured to him to bring it over. "Thank you, Mullins." She plucked it from the tray, her brow knitted as she turned it over. "It doesn't—oh!" she exclaimed, unfolding the paper. "It's from Della!" She glanced up and waved her sisters over. "Come, sit, we can read it together." Ida and Pearl sat on either side of their sister, their heads clustered together. He heard Ida take a deep breath, her finger pointing to something in the letter, and she raised her head to look at her sisters.

"That changes everything, doesn't it?" She sounded as though she'd made a great discovery.

The three were staring at one another as though in shock, Ida's expression one of triumph and fierce determination.

"We should go," Ida announced, getting up and pulling Pearl up with her. "Eleanor, we'll see you later." She curtseyed to Bennett. "A pleasure to see you, my lord."

"And you, my lady," Bennett replied, knowing he spoke the truth.

"Good day," she said as she and Pearl darted out the door, calling for their cloaks.

Bennett was most definitely intrigued—by her, by the conversation, and by whatever was in that letter.

Chapter 3

Open the door for adventure. It will always surprise you.

LADY IDA'S TIPS FOR THE
ADVENTUROUS LADY TRAVELER

"Let me see the letter again," Pearl said. They'd hurried home from Eleanor's soon after it had arrived, wanting to discuss what they'd found without the Carson gentlemen present. Of course Eleanor would tell Alexander, but it felt disloyal to discuss Della with anybody but the sisters.

Not to mention the distraction of Lord Carson's handsomeness making Ida all prickly, and unable to concentrate.

Ida took the letter out from her pocket, where she'd tucked it for safekeeping. They were in Pearl's bedroom—formerly Pearl and Olivia's bedroom, before Olivia escaped the house through marriage—hiding out from their mother, the duchess, who was entertaining the good-natured, albeit not so bright, Lord Bradford in her sitting room.

At least there wouldn't be dancing, so everyone's toes would be safe.

Ida pointed at the bottom of the letter. "You can see the barest outline of the letters, as though someone wrote on top of the paper. *Haltwhistle.* I'm sure Della didn't mean to send us a clue. It must be a town, although I've never heard of it."

"It is so clever of you to have seen it," Pearl said in an admiring tone. Ida squirmed in her chair, unused to praise that wasn't delivered grudgingly. As though it were her fault she was so intelligent.

Well, perhaps *that* wasn't her fault, but she did acknowledge that she didn't try to hide her intelligence, as many other people did.

Lectures about gas lighting innovation, for example, even though she'd done that for a distraction. But her ruse had worked, so everyone now thought she was even worse than she actually was.

But if she tried to explain, that would be more of the same, and would damn her in perpetuity.

It was a problem she didn't think even Sophocles could solve.

But none of that mattered. Not now. "I'll go to Mr. Beechcroft's house and consult his atlas tomorrow," Ida said in a decided tone. "He's got

much better atlases in his library than we do."
That her father, the duke, didn't see the point of
maintaining an excellent library was only one
of the many complaints Ida had about him. But
possibly the most egregious one.

"I wish she had told us herself," Pearl said as
she scanned the letter. She began to read aloud.

> *Dear Sisters,*
>
> *I hope you are well. I see that Olivia has mar-
> ried, I know that you would not allow her to wed
> if she wasn't head over ears in love. I am so happy
> for her.*
> *Little Nora has taken her first steps! I wish
> you could meet her. Perhaps someday, when all
> of you are honorably married . . .*

Ida raised her eyebrow. "Honorably married?
Eleanor married the brother of the man she was
supposed to marry, and Olivia married a gentleman whose parents were never married."

Pearl rolled her eyes. "At least they are both
actually married, and happily so. Even if the circumstances were not entirely usual. Della never
married Mr. Baxter, and she certainly sounds
grateful for that result."

"That is true," Ida admitted. *Happily married.*
It sounded like an impossibility, and yet two

of her sisters had achieved it. She felt that flutter of longing for the same thing, squashing it as soon as she acknowledged it. *Not now, Ida.* Maybe never?

She couldn't pursue that line of thought. Not when she needed all of her focus on the matter at hand.

Pearl continued reading:

Nora is talking up a storm! She reminds me a lot of Ida when she was little.

Pearl grinned. "So she shares an incredible amount of information?"

"That people may or may not want to hear?" Ida finished in a dry tone.

"She sounds delightful," Pearl said firmly. She shook her head and continued reading.

I wish you could meet her, she would love her aunts.

"Soon, little Nora," Ida promised. Pearl smiled, patting Ida on the arm. It felt like encouragement for what Ida knew she was going to do. As though Pearl believed in her.

I am sharing a small house with a friend, and we are giving lessons to some of the area's children. It feels wonderful to be able to provide for my daughter. I know it would shock most people, but I am grateful Mr. Baxter left rather than marry me. I knew it was a mistake nearly as soon as I left, and I miss you all so much.

"Oh Della," Ida sighed. She looked over at Pearl, whose eyes were moist.

"Once you find precisely where the town is, you're going after her," Pearl said. It wasn't a question. Pearl knew Ida too well for that.

"Of course I am," Ida replied. Although—if she were being honest—the thought of setting out on her own was a bit frightening, even for someone as fearless as Ida knew herself to be.

She couldn't take anyone with her; she wouldn't ask a servant to do something that might end in their termination. Not that there were servants in the duke's household she'd want on such an adventure anyway.

"And you could go at any time." Pearl looked at her sister, a knowing grin on her face. "I know you. It's not like you to wait to check with anybody first."

"I suppose," Ida admitted. There was something exhilarating about being thought to be impulsive, she supposed. Although others might call it headstrong and impetuous. And others had, for that matter.

"So as a practical matter, you should be prepared for any and all opportunities. Which means I will help you prepare."

Pearl got off the bed and opened up a small case on her bureau. "You're going to need funds. Here," she said as she dropped a pile of coins in Ida's hand. "Thankfully I have quite a lot of money. Mother forgot Olivia was with Edward, and accidentally gave me the money for our birthday she would normally have given to both of us." She shook her head. "I wonder if she remembers there are two of us."

The problems of being a twin with such a scattered mother. At least there was only one Ida to disappoint the duchess.

"I'll understand if you have to leave quickly, and can't let me know. I won't be frightened for you, I swear. But you have to promise to send regular updates of how you're doing just as soon as you possibly can." She wrinkled her nose. "And I'll have to figure out what to tell the duchess."

It was surprising that Pearl wasn't trying to talk her out of it. Even more surprising was that she seemed to be talking her into it. Even funding the trip, for goodness' sake. Ida took no small measure of pride in that—it meant that Pearl knew not only that Ida wouldn't be turned away from her resolve, but that Pearl trusted Ida could keep herself safe under any circumstances.

That awareness of her sister's confidence made Ida start to tear up herself, and she was crying before she realized it, which made Pearl sob and wrap her sister in a tight embrace.

"It's very brave, what you're going to do." Pearl patted Ida's back as she spoke.

"What if it doesn't work? What if I can't find this Haltwhistle?"

"You will find it and her. I have no doubt of it." Pearl's confident tone stiffened Ida's resolve. She would find Della.

She would find her, and bring her and her daughter home, where they should be.

This would be her adventure. Her escape, for the time being, at least.

She glanced at the clock, her heart sinking as she realized what time it was. "I have to get dressed for dinner." Pearl looked up also, nodding in agreement.

"You don't suppose Lord Bradford is still here, is he?" Ida continued.

Pearl shrugged. "He can't step on anybody's toes if he's seated at the dinner table." She grinned. "And he might share his opinion on whether he prefers dogs or cats."

Ida laughed, kissing Pearl's cheek. "Cats, of course," she said, dismissing the alternative. "Thank you, dear sister, for your confidence in me."

Pearl kissed Ida back. "You are welcome. We all want Della home where she belongs."

Everyone but their parents, Ida thought as she walked down the hallway to her own room. But she couldn't back down, no matter what consequences there were.

And if the duke and duchess refused to acknowledge their disgraceful daughter?

Well, Ida would deal with that when it happened. She had no doubt that her intellect could come up with some compromise that would result in honor on both sides. Even though at the moment she had no clue what that compromise might be.

But before all that, she had to actually figure out where Haltwhistle was, travel there safely, persuade Della to return to London, and then get the three of them safely back to London.

All without causing a scandal. Or too much of one, at least.

She didn't think she'd ever been presented with a more difficult problem. But instead of being daunted, she felt—vibrant. Alive with the exhilaration of it, of the adventure facing her.

And the end result would be Della back where she belonged. And then—then she could plan her own future. Her own escape.

She got dressed, putting Pearl's money into the pocket of the gown she was planning to wear

tomorrow to go to Mr. Beechcroft's library—
gray, not white, and what she thought of as her
library clothing. A gown that didn't define her
merely as a potential bride, but as someone who
was her own person.

"As if a gown can define you," she murmured
as she drew out the white gown she would wear
at dinner.

"Pardon?" the maid who'd come to assist her
into the gown commented.

"Nothing, never mind," Ida said in embarrassment.

Ida's mouth twisted as the dinner gong sounded
as the maid finished the buttons. Not only could
she not plan her own future or her own escape,
she was obliged to eat precisely when she was
told to. Not even considering if she was hungry
or it was convenient.

Although she was hungry, and it wasn't as
though she were doing anything else at the moment.

Hmph.

"Ida!" Ida froze at the sound of her mother's
voice coming from the second floor. It was the
day after the letter arrived, and far too early for
the duchess even to be awake; Ida had counted
on being able to go to Mr. Beechcroft's house to

consult his atlas without anyone noticing she was gone.

Drat.

She regretted not having already left, in fact; Pearl's money was safely in the pocket of her library gown, she was feeling more and more eager to get going, and she did not want to have to talk to her mother at the moment.

Granted, that last bit was always true. Still, she could not remember a time when she had less wanted to speak to the duchess.

She turned around slowly, raising her gaze to where her mother stood on the landing, her hair curling around her head, still in her dressing gown. The gown was another catastrophe of confusion, with flowers and leaves set amid a backdrop of plaid.

Some sort of nature-loving Scot, she presumed? At least it wasn't white, Ida thought wryly.

"What is it, Mother?" Ida gestured to where their butler stood, holding her cloak. "As you see, I was just going out."

"You're going to have to wait. Come up here," the duchess replied, whirling around to stalk back toward her bedroom.

"I shouldn't be long, you can just keep my cloak nearby," Ida said to the butler with a smile. He nodded as she followed her mother's path.

Ida strode up the stairs, not wasting any of her intelligence trying to figure out what her mother might possibly want. She'd given up long ago trying to make sense of that woman, whose feelings and opinions seemed to change with the wind.

Ida could usually analyze any kind of logical piece of information, but her mother would baffle even the most intelligent of scientists. Especially when presented with the evidence of the multitude of porcelain shepherdesses.

Linnaeus might even be forced to come up with a new species name for her: perhaps *Duchessum Irrationalis* or *Domina Confusus*.

Ida chuckled to herself, applying her fancy to herself. Maybe *Ida Adstutus* or *Cognitionum Idatum*.

She settled her face into its usual expression before walking into her mother's chamber, prepared for whatever the duchess might have to say.

Her mother was seated at her dressing table holding a piece of paper with a list of something written on it.

Notes on how Ida was the least malleable daughter? Or perhaps just a list of topics Ida would be allowed to discuss.

Sophocles, gas lighting innovation, Linnaeus, and the vital necessity of colored clothing were likely not there.

The room was overwhelmingly overwhelming.

Which is to say there were things everywhere, although the room was not untidy; just that wherever there was a surface there were things resting on top. Porcelain shepherdesses, jewelry, gloves, scarves, boxes of what Ida presumed was candy, pictures, and more.

It was like looking directly into her mother's mind, chockablock filled with things, with no rhyme or reason to the organization.

"Ida," her mother began, only to stop and make a face as she saw Ida standing behind her, catching her gaze in the glass. "For goodness' sake, sit down. We are having a conversation. I cannot have you hovering over me." She punctuated her words by waving her hands in the air, like a bird trying to fly.

Not yet having a conversation, since I haven't spoken, but then that is your idea of a conversation. At least I'm not having to read the list aloud.

Ida repressed a sigh as she sat herself on a low settee in front of the fireplace, moving a shawl to one side.

She couldn't let her mother become aware of how urgently Ida wished to leave, or she would take twice as long to say whatever it was she was going to say.

The Duchess Paradox, or some other intriguing name for how frustrating her mother could be.

"Ida," her mother began, swiveling around on

her bench to look at her daughter, "it is time for you to consider marriage."

Ida's mouth dropped open. Well. Her mother had wasted no time in saying *that*.

"To get married," the duchess clarified, because apparently it looked as though Ida had lost the ability to understand anything.

Mostly because she had.

"I had thought that you might attract *somebody*." Her mother made it sound as if it were so easy. Or wanted, for that matter. "Although you have made it difficult, what with your refusal to behave like the usual sort of young lady."

Thank God, Ida wished she could say. The last thing she wanted was to be the usual sort of young lady. *Puella Superficialis*, for example.

"What kind of girl doesn't want to dance or attend parties?" the duchess continued.

The kind of girl who is me. But you wouldn't know that, since you haven't the faintest idea of who I am. The pillar knows me better.

Perhaps she could marry the pillar? The downside would be many stony silences. The upside? That the pillar wouldn't try to control her.

And how sad was it that her most likely suitor was an inanimate object?

Her sisters, at least, knew her, a fact for which she was eternally grateful. Without them, without their love and support and yes, their uncanny ability to take her down a peg when she was being Ida the Insufferable, she would be lost.

"But never mind that," her mother said. Dismissing her daughter's own wishes as though they were meaningless. "If you will not take up the cause, I will have to. I have. It will be difficult, but I have managed to marry two off already," she continued.

Ida refrained from pointing out that neither of her sisters had married the men, or rather *man*, her parents had chosen for Eleanor and Olivia.

"Your father and I have reviewed a list of potential husbands," the duchess said, waving the paper. "And I am pleased to say that one of them, Lord Bradford, is coming to call. You'll need to be at home to wait for him."

Lord Bradford, the sweet but not so bright toe-stepper?

Oh, dear.

Lord Bradford who had once referred to foals as "horse kittens"?

Oh no.

"I . . . wasn't aware that Lord Bradford had a marked interest in me."

Her mother looked pleased as she shook her head. "No, he doesn't, and with any luck he won't get to know you until you're safely married. I've planned it all, you see."

Ida leapt off her chair, unable to sit any longer.

"I don't see, Mother. How can you already be planning my marriage to someone who barely knows me? Whom I barely know?"

Because if she were to be married off to a stranger, she might like to marry Kierkegaard, John Stuart Mill, or Charles Darwin. Maybe even Linnaeus, even though she knew him to be dead.

Not that she knew if any of those men were unmarried, but at least she knew they were intelligent. If not necessarily living.

"The best marriages are between people who barely know one another. Look at me and your father!" her mother said, making Ida's heart sink. She'd seen what kind of marriage they had. "You will be here today at five o'clock for tea, and you will not speak."

Never mind five o'clock, Ida couldn't speak *now*. She felt her cheeks start to burn as her emotions whirled inside her brain.

That piece of paper was far more dangerous than just proscribing Ida's behavior—it was a list that would determine her future.

She felt her stomach bottom out in real fear. What her mother lacked in common sense she more than made up for in determination.

If Ida didn't do something, she might very well end up accidentally married to Lord ToeStepper.

"You look delighted!" her mother observed, as if Ida's face turning bright red—as she presumed it had—was a good thing. "Just try to maintain that color. You are altogether too black and white. It is unfortunate you aren't less . . . stark," she said, her mouth turning down in disapproval.

"May I be excused?" Ida said quietly. Not wanting to engage her mother on how even her *coloring*—which wasn't under her control—was lacking.

Her mother smiled. "Of course, you will want to rest before meeting any potential husbands."

Ida curtseyed and fled, rushing downstairs to gather her cloak and head to Mr. Beechcroft's in a hackney as she'd originally intended. She would not wait while a carriage was summoned, and she would definitely not be resting.

A good researcher couldn't allow distracting news—news that your toes were going to be in permanent danger, for example, and that one's entire self was supposed to marry a gentle idiot— to keep one from an adventure.

She imagined Captain Cook, Henry Hudson, or even Lady Hester Stanhope had never had to evade marriage in pursuit of their true calling. Then again, none of those people had the duchess for their mother.

"LADY IDA," THE butler said, bowing. "Mr. Beechcroft had led me to understand you would be visiting. May I take your cloak?"

"Of course," Ida said, not waiting for the butler's assistance in removing it. "Thank you." She was halfway to the library before her cloak was completely in the butler's keeping. "Can you bring me some tea? With lemon? I might be a while," she said over her shoulder as she pushed open the door.

The sight of all the books in the library made Ida's breath catch in her throat, as always. She would never cease being excited at seeing so much information, entertainment, and *words* in one place.

If it were possible just to move her bed, she'd seriously consider just living in a library for the rest of her life. Marrying the books so she wouldn't have to marry any gentleman at all.

Perhaps then Della wouldn't be the most scandalous of the Duke's daughters. Because running away with the dancing master was one thing; wedding yourself to a bunch of leather-bound tomes would be beyond the boundaries of acceptable behavior.

She smiled at her own whimsy, pushing away any thoughts of what her parents wanted her future to look like as she walked to the section of the library that held the atlases.

Mr. Beechcroft had leased this townhouse from a family whose fortunes had suffered, so most of the books here had been purchased by the owners. The atlases, however, were Mr. Beechcroft's own; he had a passion for geography, although his business interests, and now his health, hadn't allowed him to travel.

Once he'd discovered that Ida was as fascinated as he, he'd left the books here for her use when he'd departed London for the country. She'd felt at home here as she didn't in her own house. And Mr. Beechcroft had come to seem like the father she'd never had—kind, and intelligent, and interested in what she had to say.

"Your tea, my lady." The butler had returned, and was placing the tea things on the table.

"Thank you," Ida said from in front of the shelves.

She kept reviewing the atlases until she picked out the one that appeared to be the most promising. It included detailed maps of England, and she brought it over to the long table that held the tea.

Its warm fragrance tickled her nose. If she were to move into a library, she'd have to add to her list of demands that she be served tea at least twice a day. With lemon, although she could forgo that if the circumstances required.

She chuckled at herself as she squeezed the wedge into the cup. She took a sip, sighing as the taste washed over her tongue, then put the teacup down on the table beside her, glancing around before she began the work.

This library was designed to be used. It was comfortable and welcoming, with low, well-worn chairs on either side of the table. A sofa was placed in front of the fireplace, which wasn't lit, but the room was warm nonetheless. Likely something to do with some new technology Edward had discovered. He and Mr. Beechcroft shared a passion for innovation.

Something they all had in common.

She flipped the book open to the index, scanning for the *H* section. Hableston, Hackford, and then there it was.

Haltwhistle.

"Aha!" she exclaimed. She had known it must be a town, but until she actually saw it on the page, she wasn't certain she would be able to locate it.

She traced her finger from London to Haltwhistle, feeling her stomach tighten at the distance.

At least a week's worth of travel.

And somehow, some way, she was going to get there.

Chapter 4

Always be prepared for something you haven't prepared for.

LADY IDA'S TIPS FOR THE
ADVENTUROUS LADY TRAVELER

*B*ennett hadn't figured out what he could do to help solve his problems, but he knew what he couldn't do: Marry a wealthy heiress just for her money, which would go directly into his father's pockets.

Now if only he could come up with another thousand or so ideas of what he couldn't do, perhaps he would stumble across the solution. There must be some mathematical formula that would help him calculate just how many wrong answers he'd need to come up with to find the right one. Perhaps the erudite Lady Ida would know.

Rob a bank, walk to China, create a scandal that would mean all the Carson-hunters found other prey.

Perhaps marry Lady Ida herself.

He smiled as he continued his walk, thinking about their conversation of the day before. He hadn't realized before how remarkable she was—he'd just seen the image he presumed she wanted to present: a terrifyingly intelligent woman who displayed herself entirely as she was, with no disguise. But he hadn't missed the vulnerability in her tone, nor had he missed how delightfully awkward she'd looked after she'd made that funny noise.

There was clearly more to her than mere intelligence.

"Watch yerself," a voice said, as Bennett swerved to avoid a trio of what appeared to be bakers. Their hats and fronts were coated in what looked like flour dust, and they were arguing amongst themselves about something. Bennett heard the words *yeast, rising,* and *punch* before their voices retreated into the distance.

He knew it was ludicrous to envy people like them—workers who likely had to save and scrounge every penny, who perhaps weren't even allowed to eat the fruits of their labors. He was warm, he was housed, he was fed. But he was also struggling against all the things that defined him. Who was he, when it came down to it?

It would take an escape for him to find out. An escape he wouldn't allow himself to take.

But no matter how desperate his situation felt, it was a relief to know that Alex supported him, no matter what he might choose to do. That Alex would step in to do whatever was needed. If it was needed.

"Lord Carson!" a voice called out, and Bennett stopped suddenly on the sidewalk, bumping into an older lady selling flowers. She glowered at him until he pulled out a coin and took one of her bouquets.

Then her glower turned to a smile. Of course. Money fixes everything, he thought ruefully. He plucked one of the flowers from the bouquet and put it in his buttonhole.

He shared another smile, this one a real smile, with the flower-seller. "Thank you, my lord," she said, giving him a quick once-over. "You look even finer."

Finally, he turned to where the voice came from on his other side.

"My lord, what were you thinking about?" It was Lord Mayweather, accompanied by what Bennett presumed was a Carson-hunter, judging by the hungry look in the young lady's eyes.

Or perhaps he was too suspicious, seeing a Carson-hunter with every flutter of an elegant skirt.

"This is my daughter, Frances," Lord May-weather said as his daughter dipped into a graceful curtsey. She kept her gaze on Bennett, however, so she was looking at him through her eyelashes, which might have looked flirtatious to another man, but to him appeared as though she wanted to pin him to a marriage board. Like a game of darts, but the bull's-eye was him. Skewered at the center.

Not too suspicious then.

"It is a pleasure to meet you, my lady," Bennett replied.

"You seemed so lost in thought," Lady Frances said in one of those soft debutante tones. "Father had to call your name three times to get your attention."

Bennett reflected that perhaps that might have indicated he was engrossed and didn't wish to be disturbed.

But he couldn't fault either one of them for thinking it was just good manners to say hello.

"Frances has just returned from finishing school," Lord Mayweather said, beaming down at his daughter. "It cost a pretty penny, but she is pretty worth it," he said, laughing at his own joke.

"Oh Father," Lady Frances said, lowering her gaze and shifting in a coquettish manner. "You make me blush." She raised her eyes to Bennett and batted her lashes. Had she been taught that at finishing school? Was there such a thing as a

Batting Lashes for Maximum Male Annihilation course of study?

"But I am hoping, my lord, that you will help me find my way in Society. I know so few people, you see," she said, lowering her gaze to his chest, presumably where the bull's-eye was.

"I would be pleased to do so," Bennett replied automatically. Wishing he could grimace as he realized what he'd just said.

No doubt Lady Frances was a perfectly charming young lady, imbued with all the graces a finishing school could instill. But it felt so artificial, this constant back and forth. He wished she could have just said what she meant—*Please ask me to dance at the next party so that other young unmarried men like you will know I am a reasonable person to pay attention to. Perhaps you would like to pay permanent attention to me*—only that would be scandalously shocking, to say what she actually meant.

In other words, he wished Lady Frances were more like Lady Ida.

Hmm. That surprised him, that he was already comparing other young ladies to that one. Thank goodness *she* was not among the ranks of Carson-hunters. Although that would be refreshing: "I wish you to propose, my lord. I have reason to believe you will annoy me less than most potential husbands."

He smothered a grin at the thought.

"Well, we will be looking forward to seeing you at the next event. If you will excuse us, my Frances has to drain my bank at the dressmaker's." Lord Mayweather chuckled as he spoke, and Bennett smiled wanly in return.

"Good day, my lady, my lord," Bennett said, turning on his heel to walk in the opposite direction.

He'd been joking when he'd thought of a bull's-eye, but as he walked away, he had the distinct impression Lady Frances was sizing him up for a ring and a yoke.

Escape was sounding better and better.

"Tell me again how difficult it is to be you. I want to laugh harder."

Bennett suppressed the urge to growl at his best friend, who sat opposite him at their club.

It wasn't precisely the escape he dreamt of, but he had taken a detour on his way home to stop inside for a drink and the company of gentlemen who had no wish to marry him.

It was a relief, although he knew he'd have to leave. Eventually.

Meanwhile, he'd been delighted to see Edward, who'd traveled up to London for the day to take care of some papers for his father, Mr. Beechcroft. Edward's wife, Olivia, had stayed at home with her father-in-law, although apparently she had sent Edward with several errands.

But they were completed, and Edward had a bit of time before he had to return, which was why they were here.

The two were in a dark corner of the club, as far away from anybody who might come to ask Bennett his opinion on a bill, urge him to marry one of their female relatives, or press him for investment advice.

The chairs were well-upholstered, and comfortable. Bennett felt himself relax just a tiny amount as he looked over at his friend.

"Another glass, my lord? Mr. Wolcott?"

And the club's servants were also impeccably trained to anticipate its members' wants. He wished he could just stay here for the rest of his life.

"Yes, thank you," Bennett replied before Edward could even open his mouth.

"You are desperate," Edward said, picking up his glass and draining it. "I've never seen you so—" He paused, tilting his head as he regarded his friend. "Morose? No, that's not it. You're not nearly as miserable as I would be in your position. Unsatisfied? Closer." He twisted his lips in thought. "Maybe restless. You seem restless."

Bennett shifted in his chair, bearing out just what his friend had said.

"Your wine, my lord, Mr. Wolcott," the servant said as he poured more into their glasses. Bennett leaned forward and took a long draught, relishing the way the liquid felt as it slid down his throat. The promise of oblivion only a few glasses away.

He'd wake up with a massive headache and with all of his problems still intact, but it would provide a temporary respite.

A bargain he would take, even though it wasn't good business.

The servant filled Edward's glass, then bowed.

"Just leave the bottle," Bennett said as the servant went to walk away.

The man bowed again, placing the wine on the table as Edward looked at him, one eyebrow raised.

"I've never known you to drink to excess. Or do anything to excess, actually," he said, knitting his brow. "This is serious, then." He picked up the bottle and topped Bennett's glass off.

Bennett explained the problems to Edward, who was sympathetic, even if he did spend a few moments mocking him, pointing out that he was the heir to a Marquessate, he was young, fit, responsible, and had an excellent best friend.

All of which were true, even the best friend part, but it didn't solve Bennett's concerns. Or his father's demand for funds.

"You could join a traveling circus," Edward

continued, after he'd stopped chuckling at his own jokes. Only it came out "you could join a circusing travel. Travel circusing." He shook his head in frustration.

Bennett and Edward had polished off one bottle of wine, and were making their way through a second. Bennett didn't feel any less hunted or trapped, but he had to admit he cared a bit less.

"As what?" Bennett said looking blearily at Edward. "I can balance account ledgers, manage grand estates, make money from investments, and partner young ladies in dancing." Bennett shook his head. "I don't think audiences would pay to see me doing any of those things."

Edward leaned his head back against the chair and laughed, the kind of exuberant chuckle that Bennett found he envied. His best friend, while still regarded as lesser because of the circumstances of his birth, was nonetheless incredibly wealthy and married to a woman with whom he was madly in love.

Bennett wanted that kind of happiness eventually. When it was the right time, which at the moment seemed as though it would be never.

"You could get a red coat and try as a ringmaster. You've got experience telling people what to do," Edward said, a humorous tone in his voice.

"I'd just be trading servants and farmers for lions and tigers," Bennett replied.

Edward pointed at Bennett. "But if one of the lions or tigers devours you, you wouldn't have these problems anymore."

"That's an excellent line of reasoning. Death solves all of it," Bennett said with a grin, draining his glass. Edward nodded in satisfaction as he regarded his friend.

A few drinks later, and Edward was on his way, leaving Bennett to contemplating his future and the bottom of the wine bottle.

"Lord Carson!"

Bennett turned around at hearing his name, wobbling just a tiny bit. He'd relished the peace and quiet of the club for precisely this reason—nobody coming up to talk to him.

Damn. Lord Mayweather, the father of the Desperate Debutante, stood behind him regarding him as though he were a fox run to ground. A proxy Carson-hunter, it seemed.

Bennett was not as drunk as he'd like, but still muzzy enough to have dulled the edges of his responsibility.

"Yes, my lord?"

"I am so glad to run into you this evening." Lord Mayweather moved closer, his expression making Bennett brace himself for what the man was about to say. He doubted Lord Mayweather was going to offer to do anything but add to his problems.

"You see, Frances—my daughter—and I were

hoping that you could come to dine with us. Frances knows so few people in town, you see. I believe you are just the third person she's met since she returned. It would help immensely if one of Society's most respected members were to be known as a particular acquaintance."

Bennett blinked at Lord Mayweather, his wine-addled brain taking a longer time than usual to process the words.

So perhaps he had had enough to drink after all.

"And then if it were an evening where there is a party, we could all arrive together," Lord Mayweather said in a disingenuous tone. As though it wouldn't be seen as an indication of Bennett's intentions toward Lady Frances for him to squire her to a party.

How clueless did Lord Mayweather and his daughter think he was?

"And since my leg—the gout, you know—makes it impossible for me to dance, you can take her out onto the floor for her first dance in Society."

Very clueless.

"Yes, erm, well, yes. I do like food."

Bennett wished he could smack himself in the face at his reply. *I do like food?* Who was he to call anyone clueless? At least he hadn't added he also liked dancing. Even though he did.

He should not have had so much wine. Damn his father and his own responsibilities.

At the moment, he'd welcome a chance to engage in a battle of wills with a feline predator. Even if the lion or tiger ended up devouring him. Presumably, after all, the predator also liked food. So they would have that in common.

"Excellent! I shall send an invitation over."

Lord Mayweather's expression made it appear as though he'd not only caught the fox, but had also snagged a salmon and bagged a pheasant. If Bennett was the fox, salmon, and pheasant, respectively.

Now he had a menagerie running through his mind.

He really was drunk. And perhaps he should think about the zoo as a potential escape plan.

"Good evening, my lord," Bennett said, walking the rest of the way down the stairs. If he didn't exit quickly, he might start asking Lord Mayweather his favorite type of sport so that Bennett could get the appropriate garb in which to be hunted.

He ambled for a bit, then realized he'd been walking instinctively toward Edward's house, although Edward was already heading back to the country.

Edward's father, Mr. Beechcroft, was a kind, generous man, a marked difference to Bennett's own father. No wonder Bennett would want to take refuge at that house rather than his own. It felt far more like home than his own home did.

He paused on the sidewalk before the house, staring up at the few glimmers of light within, the indication that the servants were still about.

"Thank you, Smithton," he heard a voice say behind him. He turned to see an older woman walking up the steps to the house, a few large bundles in her hand. A coachman walked up just behind her, while a young servant stood by the carriage from which the woman—probably the housekeeper—had emerged.

"Do come in for a cup of tea," the woman said. "It's the least I can do for taking me to the shops."

"The horses needed exercise," the man replied. "But I'll take a cuppa anyway," he said as they stepped inside the house.

Bennett glanced toward the carriage, realizing he was suddenly very tired. And that there was a carriage right there, with seats and everything.

Nobody could hunt him to ground in the carriage, could they? If he could just rest for a bit, he could return home and make his plans. Plans that did not include marriage or him spending his life making money to fund his father's lifestyle.

Good luck with that, a voice said inside his head.

Shut up, another voice replied. Likely the voice that had drunk all the wine.

Bennett moved to the side of the carriage, waiting until the boy who held the horses was on the other side, engaged in whistling some sort of tune.

He opened the door and slid inside, conscious of not making too much noise.

The carriage was indeed sumptuous, with plush red velvet cushioning that looked perfect for Bennett's head, which had started to ache.

He now knew why he never drank to excess.

He lay down on the cushion, propping his feet up against the carriage door, contorting his frame so as to get more comfortable.

The next thing he knew, he felt a rumble as the carriage started to move.

Chapter 5

Even teatime can bring an adventure.

LADY IDA'S TIPS FOR THE
ADVENTUROUS LADY TRAVELER

*I*da closed the atlas and leaned back in the chair. She'd finished her tea long ago, and she knew it was past time for her to go home, but her mind was still spinning with all the possibilities.

Should she try to reach Haltwhistle by train?

The only impediment there was that she was a young single lady who had no idea how to navigate any kind of transportation that wasn't her father's carriage.

Ida Ignoramus, species *Anglia Dux*. But she was intelligent, so she could figure it out if she needed to.

Although that did seem daunting. And dangerous. And likely many other words that started with *D*.

Disastrous, daring, doubtful.

But she was *dauntless*. And domineering, on occasion. As her sisters would affirm. As well as determined.

She could also write directly to Della and send her the funds Pearl had given her so she and Nora could return to London.

But since Della had given no indication that she wanted to return home, that could mean that instead of coming to London, Della would just leave Haltwhistle with all the money to set up somewhere else and the search would have to start all over again.

If she were to write a letter directly to Della, let her know how much they all missed her, then their sister might agree to come back. But Ida couldn't risk the chance of Della just haring off when she realized that they knew where she was.

She could take her horse out riding one day and then just keep going. But what would happen when she had to stop? Or if her horse threw a shoe, or had some other mishap that Ida couldn't possibly fix?

She was a fine horsewoman, and could drive a carriage well, for that matter, but she had never paid attention to any horse maintenance issues. How did they sleep? Did they eat anything but grass?

She'd need to look into that later.

Plus, there was the fact that a young lady who rode anywhere but the park was in clear danger.

And she couldn't carry a weapon, what with being on horseback and all. That would draw comment. Never mind she didn't own any weapons, unless one were to count a particularly egregious hat pin that was her sworn enemy.

She rose from the chair slowly, wishing she could just stay locked in Mr. Beechcroft's library. But that wouldn't help get Della back either.

She needed to go home and think some more. Until something brilliant and obvious occurred to her.

"Leaving, my lady?" the butler said as she opened the door, stepping out into the hallway. The hallway, unlike the library, was ablaze in candles, and Ida felt blinded for a moment.

"I will call someone to escort you home," the butler continued, snapping his fingers.

It was on Ida's lips to say not to bother, but that was foolhardy. She'd rarely ever ventured anywhere on her own; she should not be traipsing about London with her head filled with escape plans.

At the very least there should be a servant with her as she traipsed about London with her head filled with escape plans.

Much safer.

Ida the Practical Escape Artist strikes again. She smiled at her own wry thought.

"Miss Calder will take you home in Mr. Beechcroft's carriage," the butler said, gesturing to an older woman who was clearly the housekeeper walking into the hallway.

"Thank you," Ida replied.

The two walked outside, where Ida saw the carriage waiting. A boy held the horses' heads.

"Go find Smithton, he should be in the stables. I'll mind the horses," the housekeeper directed. "It will be just a few moments, my lady," she said to Ida.

The two waited, Ida's mind churning with thoughts and plans of what to do. It was one thing to know one's sisters were fully confident she was going to do *something*; it was another thing entirely to know just what to do.

There was also now the added complication of Lord Bradford. Her mother was usually haphazard about tracking Ida's whereabouts, but now that there was a potential husband to be snagged, she would likely want Ida to be at home to welcome her suitor. She knew it was close to five o'clock, the time Lord Bradford was supposed to come to tea.

She needed to find Della. And she needed to escape her mother's machinations.

And she needed to sort out her own future.

Plus, she had her sisters' confidence and her sister's money. And time was of the essence.

"I can't find him." The boy had returned, out of breath from running.

"Well. I imagine he might have returned to the kitchen." The housekeeper glanced at Ida as though unsure what to do.

"I'll wait here. I know it won't be long," Ida said in a reassuring tone, though her head was spinning.

"Fine, I'll just go find him. Tom, you hold the horses."

"Yes, ma'am," the boy said.

The housekeeper walked back up the steps and entered.

The boy walked to the other side of the carriage so that Ida couldn't see him any longer. And then she turned her exciting, dangerous, and altogether scandalous idea into an actual escape.

SHE'D DONE IT. She had taken the carriage, navigated her way out of town, and was heading north. To Della. She had funds, she had a warm cloak on, she had a purpose, and she was alone. Escaping.

It was marvelous.

Only her marvel turned swiftly to fright when she heard the first thump.

Followed by another thump. And another.

Thump, thump, thump.

The sound was coming from inside the carriage. Inside. The. Carriage.

She was not alone after all.

What in goodness' name was there inside? A large dog? A particularly rambunctious cat?

A person?

Please don't let it be a person, she thought. She'd far rather try to subdue an animal than speak to an actual person.

She glanced around, her spine tingling as fear raced through her entire body. Very much regretting she hadn't grabbed a weapon—even something as ineffectual as a hat pin. The sky was dark. It was probably very close to five o'clock.

Was Lord Bradford already at her parents' house? Waiting for her so she could not speak or otherwise reveal her personality?

And was it preferable to be taking tea with the toe-stepper—knowing he was about to propose—or be on your own in the impending darkness as an unknown thing made loud thumping noises?

And how terrible was it that she might prefer the latter?

She slowed the carriage to a stop, looking around for any kind of possible weapon.

Unless she were able to remove one of the

horses' bridles and loop it over the thing, what-ever it was, she did not have anything with which to defend herself. Only her sharp wit.

But she hardly thought a long-winded expla-nation of Linnaeus's *Systema Naturae* would do much to dissuade a potential assailant. Unless she were able to actually bore him until he ex-pired. Cause of death? *Taedium Mortem.*

The door opened, and she braced herself, grip-ping the side of the seat on either side of her.

A figure tumbled out, a person who did not seem intent on attack, at least. More in need of a good brushing.

"Lord Carson!" she exclaimed as she saw who had emerged.

He stared up at her as though in shock—*well, that makes two of us*, she thought—his hair ruf-fled, his cravat loose, his jacket rumpled.

He still looked undeniably handsome, just less sleek. Definitely more confused.

Still handsome. How did he manage that?

"What are you doing here?" he asked, making her mouth drop open.

"What am *I* doing here?" She waved toward the horses and the road. "I am driving this car-riage, as you can see, but I have no idea how you came to be inside it." She stiffened as she considered it. "Did my family send you?"

That would be the most humiliating possibility, if that were true. Sending the one gentleman who had dodged the Howlett marriage bullet after her? *Mother, you wouldn't*, she thought.

Lord Carson looked confused, then his face cleared and he made a rueful noise. Not quite a snort, but something expressing derision.

She should be relieved he hadn't been sent specifically after her. Yes, she should. That she wasn't entirely relieved felt disturbing.

"No, of course not," he said, his tone revealing just how ludicrous an idea it was. She suppressed an urge to cringe at his scorn. "Why would they? You and I are Lord Carson and a Howlett daughter, you know how well those pairings have worked out."

Ida folded her arms over her chest, her heart slowing as her brain assessed the possible danger to her person. *None.* Lord Carson was a gentleman. A gentleman who had never paid attention to her until yesterday. "Never mind that. The thing is, you have to leave." She made a shooing gesture. "Return to London."

He put his hands on his hips and leaned back to regard her, his expression clearly argumentative. "No, I do not have to leave. And I will not." He gestured toward her, his arm making a sweeping motion that managed to convey both incredulity and disdain.

She'd be impressed if she weren't so startled by his presence.

"You are clearly doing something you should not be." His firm tone made her feel suddenly guilty, and then she was annoyed at herself for feeling that way. He was not in authority over her. He just needed to recognize that, and the fact that he had no responsibility toward her. "You are my sister-in-law, and a young lady, and it is my duty to protect you."

He sounded so sure of himself, and for a moment Ida almost agreed with him—damn his persuasiveness—but she stopped herself, instead hearing the words pouring like a tumult from her mouth.

"I have no need of your protection, my lord, and I am certain you have far better things to do than accompany me to where I am going. We are only about ten miles from town. It should not be difficult for you to find your way back."

The last thing she wanted on this dangerous and thrilling adventure was a gentleman to tell her how it should be done. This was *her* adventure, damn it, not his.

He didn't answer, not right away. He did, however, grab hold of the carriage and swing himself up onto the seat beside her. She started at him, openmouthed. Had he not heard anything she'd said?

She might as well ask him. It wasn't as though she cared at all what he thought about her. Or that her reputation hadn't preceded her.

"Have you not heard anything I've said?" she said in an outraged tone. "The part where you should return to London and I will continue on my journey?"

He stretched out in the seat, folding his arms over his chest and regarding her with an amused stare. A look that made it clear he might've heard about her, but he would not be intimidated.

Oddly, that made her feel better. "I heard you, but I will not be leaving your side." He shrugged. "I could not live with myself if I knew you to be out here on your own." He lifted a questioning brow. "I suppose I cannot persuade you to return to London with me?" He made a show of glancing at the horses and the side of the carriage. "Because I am fairly certain neither the horses nor the carriage belong to you, and I know you don't want the scandal of having purloined someone else's property."

"If the only thing keeping you out here is your fear that I be arrested for theft, I assure you that Mr. Beechcroft would have gladly lent me his carriage if he knew I was in need of it."

"But he didn't," Lord Carson pointed out, truthfully if also annoyingly. "And I am also concerned about your safety. As I mentioned just a few moments ago." *Do keep up, Lady Ida.* He hadn't said those words, but he might as well have.

Had anyone ever intimated that Ida was not capable of following a conversation? Nobody had ever even dared to suggest she was not the most intelligent lady in the room.

Hmph.

"I appreciate that, my lord," Ida said slowly, trying to remain calm in the face of his implacable refusal, "but what I want most is for you to get out of this carriage." She could not risk anyone from their world seeing them together, given their family's history. She would be damned if she'd risk everything to find Della, just to end up married to Lord *Marital Evadus* here. "You don't have to return to London, if you're bent on escape." She paused as another suggestion occurred to her. "I can even give you a lift to the next village, if that is your desire. But you cannot accompany me for the entirety of this trip." There. She'd presented some options, acknowledged that his goals were valid, and stated her own wishes quite firmly.

Aristotle would be proud of her argument.

"Fine."

He'd capitulated far too easily. He hadn't asked what trip she was on, why she was alone, and how long she was planning on being out. Driving a carriage she'd clearly stolen.

"Fine?" she echoed, hearing the suspicion in her tone.

"Fine." He sounded sincere. But then again, he was renowned for his ability to get along with anyone, if it meant he could persuade them to do something for him.

With the notable exception of Ida's sisters. She'd just have to remind him of the possible danger to his marital status if he continued to insist on accompanying her. That would definitely do the trick.

She brightened at just how quickly he'd desert her once she reminded him of who he was, and how close he was to marrying yet another Howlett sister, something it seemed was the absolute last thing he wished to do.

Thank goodness I am so unmarriageable, she thought ruefully.

Yes, his presence would mean she was safer—but it would also mean she would never be able to escape. Because he was ridiculously honorable and responsible, and he'd insist on marrying her, even though neither one of them wanted that.

She would prefer to try to protect herself rather than barter her future for the next week or so of safety.

"Do you need me to drive?" he asked in a mild tone.

"No, thank you," she said. "I can do it by my-self." *I have been doing it until you woke up, or what-ever it was you were doing in there.*

"Of course you can," he replied in an amused tone of voice.

"How did you learn anyway?" he asked in a conversational tone.

She picked up the reins, shot him one last glowering look—not that he seemed to notice, drat it all—and urged the horses forward.

"I know a great many things, my lord," she said vaguely. It was not an explanation, but it was an answer.

"That you do," he replied, and it did not sound like a compliment. How on earth did she wind up here with him, of all people?

The sooner they came to a town, the sooner she could be rid of him. If he wouldn't leave on his own volition, she'd make sure he understood the risk he'd be taking.

LADY IDA DIDN'T sound as though she trusted his answer when he'd agreed to leave her company, nor had she explained just how she came to be such a good driver. A smart woman not to trust him—she shouldn't, not when Bennett had no intention of allowing her to continue her trip without him. Whether or not she had excellent driving skills.

Even though he had no idea where she was headed or why she would do something so foolhardy in the first place. He'd agreed to her so quickly because he could forecast that otherwise they'd be stuck in the road arguing rather than moving forward.

"Was this your reaction to our conversation about escape?" he said after a few moments of silence. Apparently she could remain quiet, even though it was clear she was agitated. Most people would continue to argue.

She seemed to have many unusual talents, not least of which was the ability to speak her mind directly and do something as rash and brazen as steal a carriage. Or not speak her mind when she could tell it wouldn't make an iota of difference to the outcome.

He admired that. He knew firsthand how difficult it was to veer from one's chosen course, and for a young lady, that veering must be even more difficult. That she'd emerged from it so wholly her own person spoke to her strength and her character.

She made one of those snorting noises again. "Hardly. I've longed for escape for as long as I've been aware of who I am and the world I live in." She glanced at him, the hint of an amused smile on her face. Apparently now that she thought she might be getting rid of him she could afford to be amused. "But I have to ask you the same question. Were you escaping from something, my lord? Spurred on perhaps by our conversation of yesterday?"

He thought of Lord Mayweather and his daughter, thought of all the Carson-hunters who had him in their sights.

"Yes," he replied. "My brother Alexander—"

"I know who your brother is, my lord," she interrupted. As though he were an idiot. He wanted to grin at how dismissive she sounded. "He is my brother-in-law as well. Actually, he is more my brother-in-law than you are. You are the brother to my brother-in-law, so I don't believe saying you are my brother-in-law is at all correct."

"So what are we then?" he asked. Wondering how Lady Ida—whom he was quickly beginning to think of as a prickly hedgehog—would respond.

"We are acquaintances who happen to share some connections." She paused. "And we happen to, through extraordinary circumstances, appear to be traveling together for the moment."

"About that," Bennett began, "how did you come to borrow Mr. Beechcroft's carriage?" he asked, stressing the word *borrow*. "And where are you going?"

"I will answer your questions when you have

answered mine," she said, nodding toward him. "I saw a sign right before you started thumping—"

"I was not *thumping*, I was knocking to get your attention. Hedgehog," he muttered, unable to keep himself from saying the word. She was all prickly, but attractive, and definitely impossible to ignore, once you'd seen her. Plus, she tended to assume a defensive protective posture whenever someone seemed like they were getting too close.

"Knocking, thumping, whatever you wish to call it." She waved her hand in the air in dismissal. "That is not the point. The point is I saw a sign right before you made your presence known, and it indicated that there was a town in another seven miles or so. We will have to make conversation, especially since you seem so determined to ask questions. And don't think I didn't notice you referred to me as a hedgehog," she said, hurriedly, as though she didn't want to admit he'd even uttered the word. "We will eschew nicknames, if you please," she said firmly. "So if you answer my questions—which, I will point out, I asked first—then I will answer yours. And then we should be at the village."

"And then what?" So prickly. How had he never noticed her before yesterday? He'd known who she was, of course, but had never paid her much mind. She was just sort of there, hovering near her sisters, like a storm cloud thundering out lectures.

"Another question, my lord?" Her tone was reproving. "Mine first, if you please."

He grinned at how bossy she sounded. *Hedgehog*.

"My father is urging me to marry," he began after a moment of thought. He wouldn't insult her by prevaricating. "And there are several young ladies who wish the same for me. Alex calls them Carson-hunters."

She snorted again, this time lifting a hand to her mouth to smother the noise. "Carson-hunters. Armed with debutante lace and batting of lashes to conquer their prey?"

Bennett laughed. "Exactly. Instead of arrows they've got dainty feet and fluttering fans and doting fathers."

"I have to say I have an image of you scampering away from a phalanx of determined ladies wearing white."

"*You* wear white," he pointed out.

"But the difference is that I do not like it."

"And I do not *scamper*," Bennett said with a grin.

"Nor do you thump." He could almost hear her rolling her eyes. "Duly noted, my lord. And none of these ladies suit you? You must be very particular."

"I'm not!" he retorted, wondering just how they came to be having such a ridiculous conversation.

Oh, of course. She'd asked him things, he'd asked her, and he'd seemed amenable to answering her questions if she'd answer his.

"What do you wish for in a wife, then? I know it wasn't either one of my sisters, so apparently you do not want an intelligent, witty, charming partner." Her tone was mischievous, and he opened his mouth to reply, but realized he couldn't—not without insulting her sisters, himself, or her.

This hedgehog was far too prickly and intelligent to spar with. But she remained fascinating to him—when was the last time he was this engaged in a conversation?

"When I get married," he said, "which I will do, eventually—I want someone who is soft and gentle. Someone who will welcome me home at the end of a long day."

"You've just described either a fuzzy blanket or a pet, my lord."

He couldn't help but burst into laughter, and she joined him, both grinning at one another as though it were the most natural thing in the world.

He had never laughed with a lady like this before. He'd only ever laughed this hard with Edward, in fact. And Edward wasn't a stunningly beautiful hedgehog on some crazy adventure in a stolen carriage.

Chapter 6

Do not mistake adventure for risk.

LADY IDA'S TIPS FOR THE
ADVENTUROUS LADY TRAVELER

So you sought refuge in Mr. Beechcroft's carriage?"

His mouth twisted into an embarrassed grin. "I hadn't intended it to be a permanent solution. I had—I had a bit to drink, since Edward was in town."

"He is most definitely my brother-in-law also."

He arched a brow. "Touché, my lady hedgehog."

"I am not a hedgehog."

"Prickly."

Hmph.

"I've answered your questions," he said after a few moments. "Now you have to tell me. Where are you going?"

"I'm trying to find my sister."

"Ah," he said in an understanding tone as he realized to whom she was referring. "Your sister who—?" He paused delicately.

"Yes. Della." Ida hadn't spoken her name to anyone who wasn't related to her in so long. It felt odd to say it aloud.

"I didn't realize you didn't know where she was." He took a deep breath. "I'm sorry, I should have."

Ida shrugged, as though it didn't matter, when of course it did. "There's no reason you should have. It is not as though we discuss it even in the family." Because neither the duke nor duchess would allow Della's name to be spoken at home, so the sisters had grown accustomed to making oblique references to her, even when they were not at home.

"Most people didn't spare a thought about her," she continued, "or where she'd gone. The only thing they wanted to talk about was how it would affect the rest of her sisters."

"And how has it affected you?"

He was sensitive enough to ask. To ask how she felt, how this cataclysmic event had affected her. That touched her.

Even though she could not wait to be rid of him.

Sophocles would definitely be baffled by this lapse of logic.

"Besides having everyone in Society think all the duke's daughters are bound to be disgraceful?" She pondered. "Not that they're wrong, though Pearl and I have yet to do anything too scandalous."

"Of course, since stealing a carriage and heading off for parts unknown all by oneself is entirely within bounds." His tone was dry.

She just barely suppressed yet another snort. *Good work, Ida. At this rate he'll think you're a rare sort of pig.* Porcus Idatus.

"I meant until today," Ida replied, rolling her eyes. "But the thing is, I found out where Della is living, and I am going to get her."

"Won't her husband have something to say about that?"

"Della never did marry that Mr. Baxter." Silence as he absorbed that bit of gossip. Gossip that apparently hadn't reached his ears. "And it's a good thing they didn't marry, since we discovered what a blackguard he was after they eloped."

"Because of the eloping, one assumes," he said in that same dry tone. He folded his arms over his chest, completely at ease. Once again revealing just how comfortable he was at all times.

She laughed at his comment. He had a delightful sense of humor when he wasn't asking intrusive questions. And sometimes even then.

"Not just that, although of course that was the impetus for us finding all about Mr. Baxter's checkered past."

If she had been in charge of hiring tutors, she would have discovered all of this before the man even entered the house. But the duchess saw a handsome man who was light on his feet and let him in the house to teach her daughters how to dance. As far as Ida knew, he hadn't even had to show his letters of recommendation.

"What did Mr. Baxter do?"

Ida shook her head at the memory of all they'd come to learn about him. "He stole a few of mother's jewels, then managed to pin the blame on one of our scullery maids. She came very close to losing her position, of course, but she denied taking them. I believed her, and I persuaded my mother to give her a second chance."

"How did you discover the truth?"

"It was only after he and Della had left. We found receipts for the stolen items, items he pawned in order to make their escape."

"And by then it was too late."

"The worst part of it was he really was not a good dancer!" she added scornfully. "Even I could tell that, and I do not dance."

"You have not danced with me." His tone was commanding, as though he knew—absolutely *knew*—she would enjoy dancing with him.

And that commanding tone made her know that too. As if she hadn't already imagined it.

A fact that both irked and intrigued her. As *he* did.

"WE'LL BE GOING our separate ways soon, my lord," she said, slowing the carriage as they made their way into the small town. "I will have to let you return to evading the Carson-hunters."

"You know I can't let you go on your own."

"I know that," she replied. "Of course I know that. Just as I know that I must continue by myself." She stopped the carriage, glancing about at the buildings that surrounded them. "I see one inn there. If there isn't another we can go in separately."

She was impossible. "Do you have any money?"

She made another one of those noises. "Of course I do. Do you think I'd run off without any kind of funds?"

"Well, I don't know," Bennett replied. "Since you're foolish enough to believe you can just walk into an inn and hire a room without notice."

"I am wearing my library clothing," she said, as though that were an actual thing, "and nobody will look twice at me if I pull my hood down and pay in cash. If anyone asks, I'll tell them I am a governess traveling for my next assignment."

It wasn't a terrible idea, and he had a moment of admiration that she'd thought it through.

A thought struck him. "I don't see any luggage. So you have money, but you didn't pack any items for travel?"

She frowned as she considered it. "I did not. I came rather suddenly."

Even more impossible. "And just what is 'library clothing'?" he asked.

She made a noise indicating it was a foolish question. Even though of course it wasn't. Since he was asking it. "It is clothing I wear to the library. Clothing meant for comfort, and study, and long hours in a chair." She smoothed her hand down her arm. "You cannot see it, but this gown is in a very serviceable color. Definitely not white."

Baffling. "What is a serviceable color?"

She heaved an exasperated sigh. "A serviceable color, Mr. Brummell, is a color that holds up to use. Drab colors. My gown, for example, is gray. Library clothing."

He agreed that she would be less noticeable in her chosen garb, but his leaving her, no matter what kind of disguise she'd done herself up in, would still mean she was left vulnerable, alone to any kind of danger.

And she was a duke's daughter; she wouldn't have the first idea about what could happen to a young lady traveling alone. No matter how she'd created this idea of a set of clothing that could render her invisible to possible attackers.

Drab garb would not save her.

Bennett knew he wanted to run from responsibility—hence the drinking and the hiding out in his club—but he could not run from this particular duty.

Nor did he wish to; he wanted to accompany Ida on her adventure, her escape, even though he would be participating by proxy. Eventually he would have to return home and resume being the dutiful son, looking back on this moment with no small amount of wonder that he'd been able to be free for even this short a period of time.

"You're not going into that inn on your own," he said. He dismounted from the carriage and held his arms out to her so she could descend safely. "If you refuse to accept my assistance, I'll march behind you and announce just who you are and what you are doing. The news will reach London probably faster even than Mr. Beechcroft's fine horses can travel."

"You wouldn't dare." She glared at him from the carriage. "Then we would be forced into marriage, and you know full well I am neither soft nor welcoming. I am not the wife you want. You would not."

"I would. Come down," he said, gesturing to her. Would she call his bluff?

She didn't reply, but lifted one foot down, sliding into his arms, stiff and angry. Whew.

Not welcoming, perhaps, but definitely soft. Hardly the prickles he'd been expecting. Oh. Well then. His cravat suddenly felt tight around his neck.

She stepped away from him as soon as her feet touched the ground, adjusting her cloak so it completely hid her gown and most of her face.

"Since you refuse to listen to sense, what will we say?" She lifted her eyebrow and looked him up and down. "You cannot be a governess as well." Her eyes widened. "And we cannot pose as a married couple." She sounded so horrified by the idea that he had to laugh.

He held his hands up in surrender. "I understand, Lady Ida. You do not wish to marry me, even as a ruse. I have to say, my ego is taking a substantial blow this evening." Bennett accompanied his words with a chuckle, and she gave a tentative smile in response.

He was surprised by how relieved he was that she was apparently not one to hold a grudge. Even if she was vehemently opposed to a marital subterfuge. "We can be brother and sister, and our servants are delayed by a broken wheel or something."

"Very clever," she said admiringly, and he bowed in acknowledgement of the compliment.

"Are you looking for a room?" a woman's voice called as they walked toward the inn. A worn sign proclaiming it to be The Goose's Egg swung back and forth in front of the door.

"Yes, we are. Two rooms," Bennett clarified.

"Well, we have them. Not adjoining, though." The innkeeper stepped forward, peering at them from a broad, friendly face. She wore an apron over a gown in what appeared to be a serviceable color.

"That is fine," Lady Ida said quickly. Likely hatching a plan to escape when he wasn't paying attention. As though he would be so easily duped.

"You'll want something to eat." It wasn't a question. She turned to the door and swung it wide, poking her head in. "Eustace! Come out here."

Bennett took Ida's arm and looped it through his, walking her inside.

The inn was bustling, surprising given the late hour.

Eustace, presumably, emerged from the kitchen and nodded to the innkeeper and to Bennett and Ida. He was tall and broad, an apron on over his clothing, his cheeks flushed. "Bags are in the back?" he said in a broad country accent.

"Actually, we don't have any, our servants—"

he began, but Eustace was already out of earshot.

"Just put the carriage away," Eustace's mother called. "And feed the horses.

"Sit down over there. Clark, clear out," the innkeeper said, shooing a man from one of the far tables.

He picked up his glass and went and joined another group who were clearly celebrating something.

"We just had a wedding," the innkeeper explained. "And the guests don't want to stop the party tonight. Good for business. Hope you can sleep through the ruckus."

"I'm sure we'll be fine," Bennett said, helping Ida into her seat. The small round wooden table was pitted with evidence of its use, but the innkeeper brought a lantern over and placed it in the center, the light casting a warm, golden glow.

"I'm Mrs. Hastings, I own this place. I'll bring you two slices of my meat pie, the best in the village, and two ales, unless you want something else? Not that we have anything else but some hard cheese and bread."

"Meat pie sounds heavenly," Ida said. "Thank you."

Her words were accompanied by a low, distinctive growl, and Bennett tried not to laugh as she clutched her stomach.

Mrs. Hastings nodded as she took herself back to the kitchen, which was when Bennett noticed the nearby group was staring at them.

"A round of ale for the wedding guests, too," he called out to the innkeeper's retreating back. The group cheered, and returned their attention to themselves, as he'd wanted.

"Very clever of you," Ida remarked in that low, smoky voice of hers. "Though perhaps I should return the question—do you have funds? I am not paying for your largesse," she said tartly.

He ignored her question. He had no idea how much she had in her possession, and he didn't want her to get any ideas about taking his. She'd stolen a carriage, after all. What was to prevent her from taking his money?

"Well, if you spend as much time as I do with people, people of all types, you learn how to handle them."

She leaned back, her eyebrow raised. "That sounds awfully condescending of you."

Bennett opened his mouth to deny what she was saying, then took a moment to think. Damn it. She was right.

"I apologize," he said in a low tone. "It sounds worse than I meant it, but of course that doesn't matter. I like to believe I can find something in common with anyone, no matter how different we might seem on the outside."

"What do you suppose we have in common, then?" she asked, her expression curious. And not just pretending to be interested—he'd seen enough of the Carson-hunters' expressions to be able to tell when someone was truly interested. She was.

He felt more than a flicker of interest in her himself.

"Well," he began, "I suppose we have the urge to cast off our proscribed roles in search of adventure."

She sighed, looking almost wistful. "I have always wanted an adventure," she said. "Something where it didn't matter that I was a duke's daughter. Something that asked me to do something because of who I am, not"—and then she hesitated, a funny look on her face—"who I am."

She sat up, giving him a sharp look. "Is that what you mean when you say you wish you could escape? That you want to be seen for yourself, not who you are supposed to be?"

He nodded. She understood. She knew what it was like.

"Absolutely. But then—as Edward reminds me—I am the heir to a Marquessate, anybody would envy my position."

"But they don't understand it," she said softly.

"So we do have that in common."

She swallowed, as though it were a difficult truth for her to reconcile. That she had something in common with him, the gentleman who had most definitely not married her sisters.

He needed to make her feel more comfortable. His mind scrabbled around for a topic that would ease this odd feeling of closeness.

"What else do we have in common?" he asked. "What is your favorite book?"

Her eyes lit up. "In history, philosophy, scientific studies, novels, or poetry?"

"Not novels or poetry, but the rest, yes."

"Oh, that is so difficult to answer!" She sounded delighted. Far more pleased than if he had told her he admired her lovely face, or that her dancing was divine.

Not that they'd danced together. He wished he had asked her. They had to have been at some of the same social functions.

"I have lately been classifying people," she said in a voice that sounded almost embarrassed. "So I suppose Linnaeus's *Systema Naturae*."

"Classifying people—?" he began, entirely intrigued.

"Yes," she said with a wry smile. "Like your Carson-hunters. They might be *Debutantum Desperatus*, for example."

He burst into laughter, making a few of the people near them stare. "And I am *Pradeam Carsonus*, then?"

She looked startled. "You speak Latin."

"I think it's more surprising that I remember any of it at all, given how long ago it was."

"True." She bit her lip. "I forgot that you are a gentleman, so of course you would be taught Latin. I had to learn it myself, purloining books from my father's library. Not that he noticed," she said.

"What about fiction?" he asked.

She drew her eyebrows together in thought. "I think I like anything written by Charles Dickens. There's not one specific piece of his writing, just—just all of it."

"Hmm. I haven't read much Dickens myself," he admitted. "What is it you like about him?"

She considered it. He liked it, that she thought about things. *Cogitatare Idatum.*

"I like how he writes about people. That they're more than just what job they have, or where they come from. That people, all people, should be given an opportunity."

"Very egalitarian of you," he teased. He saw the innkeeper's son walking toward them with a tray. "And I think all those people, no matter who they are or where they come from, would enjoy a glass of ale at the end of a lovely day."

"Lovely, was it?" she said with a grin. "Even though I tried to make you return to London and refused your help and accused you of being sent by my family? Not in that order," she corrected.

"It was lovely," he replied in a firm tone.

"I suppose it was a lovely day," she conceded. "Not that I've ever had any ale," she said, turning as she heard the boy approach the table.

"Your ale," Eustace said, placing both glasses on the table. "My mam will lead you up after dinner."

"Thank you," Bennett said, reaching into his pocket.

"Here you go," Ida said, placing a coin into Eustace's palm as she gave him a dazzling smile.

"I will not be obliged to you," she said in a quiet tone of voice as the boy stepped away.

So prickly.

Bennett raised his glass, holding it in the middle of the table. Ida picked hers up as well, giving him a questioning look.

"To adventure," he said, clicking his glass gently against hers.

"To adventure," she echoed, then took a hesitant sip.

Bennett drank a healthy swallow of his ale.

She held the glass in front of her, appraising it before she took a sip. "This is not terrible," she said in a surprised tone of voice.

"Now you sound condescending," he replied in a sly tone.

"I do," she admitted. "And also inexperienced. That seems like a dreadful combination." Her tone was wry. She took another, larger sip. "I like it, even."

"Slow down," Bennett warned, conscious of his own recent encounter with too much alcohol. At least being distracted with Lady Ida had kept him from noticing how much of a headache he had.

Replacing his alcohol headache with the headache of Lady Ida seemed like a good exchange.

She put the glass down as the innkeeper arrived with their food. "It's a bit hot, so be careful," the innkeeper warned as she set the plates down. She drew cutlery and linen from her pocket and placed them on the table, too. "It's the best."

"So we've heard," Bennett replied, winking at Ida, who smothered a laugh by putting her hand over her mouth.

"You'll let me know what you think," Mrs. Hastings said as she walked away.

Ida picked up her fork and poked at the pie, causing steam to emerge from the top. "It looks wonderful," she said as she picked a piece up, bringing it to her mouth. She ate the forkful, her eyes widening at the taste. And then moaned in satisfaction, making Bennett even more mesmerized. "This is so good," she said as she took another bite. "Mmm."

Bennett had never seen a lady enjoy her food so wholeheartedly before. It made him envy her all over again. To display so much pure enjoyment, to reveal emotion, wasn't something he was able to do. Or had impetus to do either. He was too busy running the estate, seeing to his various business interests, concerned about his mother's health, and a myriad of things that occupied his brain to indulge in something as simple as relishing a good dinner.

Damn, how had his life come to this?

"Are you all right? You're not eating."

Bennett hastily took too big a bite, swallowing hard against the tightness of his throat. "Mmm, yes, I was just thinking about how long we should plan to travel tomorrow." Which of course was not at all what he was thinking about, but he wasn't about to reveal himself too much to her.

"You're operating under the assumption that we will be traveling together tomorrow."

She laid her fork down and glared at him. Which would be intimidating if she didn't have a bit of sauce on her mouth, and her eyes weren't bright from the ale, and she was less incredibly beautiful.

He reached forward and wiped her lips with his napkin, her eyes widening as his fingers touched her skin.

"Oh," she said in a soft voice as he withdrew the napkin, showing her the spot he'd wiped from her face.

His hands felt shaky. And also as though they wanted to touch her again. Push his hands into her hair to see if it was as silky as it looked. Run his fingers over her eyebrows, those extremely expressive eyebrows. Slide his hand down to her jaw, cupping her face as he lowered his mouth to—

"Well," she began in an entirely different tone of voice. As though she knew what he was thinking and was determined to shake him free of it. "You do know that if you accompany me on this trip, you will be forced to ask for my hand in marriage when we return." She spread her hands out in explanation. "You have successfully evaded two of my sisters. And I assure you, my lord, I am not another Carson-hunter."

"That is clear," Bennett said in a wry tone.

"And I will not be known as the only Howlett sister who was unable to escape you." He raised his eyebrows in disbelief. Had she just insulted him?

"So unless you wish to spend the rest of your life in dismal matrimony to me," she continued, "I suggest we go our separate ways tomorrow." She nodded her head in finality, as though they'd reached an agreement.

"No."

Her eyes shot up to his face. Her mouth dropped open. "No?" she echoed. "But you don't—I don't— we don't," she sputtered.

"I know the conjugations for do not, my lady. I speak Latin, remember?" he said wryly. "And we do not, we can agree on that. It is a risk I am willing to take to keep you safe." He shrugged. "Besides which, you can always refuse my suit. You must know that running off like this has already damaged your reputation. A refusal to marry the man who has theoretically compromised you will not do much more harm."

Her mouth opened and closed, rather like a fish gasping for air. A lady grasping at straws. An exceedingly intelligent person outsmarted.

Got you, he thought. *Capturam Domina.*

"But wouldn't you rather just be rid of me?"

It made him hurt for her that that was her first response—that someone would rather not be with her than keep her safe. No wonder she was so bent on escape. If she were constantly with people who didn't appreciate her—? Her intelligence, her wit, her courage?

He had to admire her all over again for her resilience, for pushing back against anyone who would try to keep her in her prescribed box.

"I would not," he said simply.

"I will consider what you say," she said slowly, getting up from the table.

"You're finished, then?" the innkeeper said, stepping out from behind the bar. "I'll show you to your rooms. Was the food good?"

"It was incredible," Ida replied. "I don't think I've ever had a meat pie as good as that one."

"I wonder if you've ever had a meat pie," Bennett murmured behind her as they walked up the stairs. She swatted behind her, and he caught her wrist, clasping her hand.

He couldn't explain what made him want to touch her. Well, beyond the fact that she was beautiful and they were together. He had never felt this urgency, even with other nearly as beautiful women.

But Lady Ida was special. She was a gorgeous, vibrant, intelligent woman wrapped up in her hedgehog disguise and her library clothing, pushing people away with her honest emotion and frank opinions.

He didn't want to be pushed away. He wanted to pull her close. To let himself go and lose himself with her, both of them expressing just what they felt. All their emotion on display with one another.

That kind of freedom felt impossible just yesterday, and yet now it was a possibility. A remote possibility, to be fair, but something that was more than just an unrealized dream.

She was holding his hand. She hadn't pushed him away.

What did it mean, that she hadn't pushed him away?

Chapter 7

*T*his room is for the young lady," Mrs. Hastings said, opening the second door on the right-hand side.

Ida looked inside, almost unable to process what she was viewing as the tumult of emotions swirled inside her brain. She shook her head, trying to clear the fog of whatever it was she was feeling.

He'd held her hand. And she had held his.

Her skin tingled where they'd touched.

And he'd joked with her. *In Latin*. No wonder she was all tingly.

The room was small, but tidy, the bed in the center made up with a floral counterpane. There was a table beside the bed, a screen in the corner, and a chair in front of one of the two windows.

"It's not much, but it's quiet," the innkeeper said. "I'll send someone up to help you with your gown, since your own servant hasn't arrived yet. Do you expect them tonight, my lord?" she said, twisting to look at Bennett.

"Likely not. I told them to find lodgings elsewhere if they could not get here by this evening."

"Ah, then you'll be needing my Mary's help. She's Eustace's younger sister, and she's been helping out in the inn."

"That would be excellent. Thank you for thinking of it," Ida replied. She drew a coin from her purse and began to hold it to the innkeeper, who waved it aside.

"You'll pay me tomorrow morning for the food and rooms. You can save that for Mary, if she serves well enough. And you'll let me know if she doesn't."

The innkeeper stepped back out into the hallway. "I'll show you your room, my lord, and then wish you and your sister good-night. It's just two doors away," she continued, gesturing to a door on the opposite side. "If you need anything in the night."

He would be leaving her. Alone.

"Good night, Ida," Bennett said. He stepped forward and gazed down at her face, an intense expression on his face.

Dear lord.

"Good night," she replied abruptly, shutting the door as she spoke.

She leaned against the door, her shoulders sagging. In fatigue? Relief?

Frustration?

For a moment, he'd looked at her as though he . . . appreciated her.

In a way she'd never been appreciated before.

In a way that looked as though he wanted to kiss her.

Ida had never been kissed. *Obviously.* Not only that, but she'd never even had the opportunity—she had yet to meet a gentleman she'd like to kiss, much less had one want to kiss her.

But she could imagine, just for a moment, what it would feel like to have Lord Carson kiss her.

To have all that sleek handsomeness focused on her, on her mouth, on her reactions to what their lips were doing.

She hadn't been kissed, but she did know the mechanics of it all. She'd taken a peek at some naughty books her older sister Eleanor had in her possession, and had done some further research when Eleanor had turned bright red and refused to explain.

So she knew technically what it entailed, but she knew full well that knowing something and experiencing something were two entirely different things.

For example, one could describe the deliciousness of strawberry shortcake covered with freshly whipped cream, but one couldn't understand just how delicious it was until one had tasted it.

Lord Carson wasn't precisely strawberry shortcake. But Ida had the worrisome thought that kissing him would be altogether far more enjoyable.

Shortcake left crumbs, and there was never the correct balance between cake, fruit, and cream.

Lord Carson would likely know how to achieve the best balance in kissing. And there'd be no crumbs.

She jumped as there was a knock on the door. She turned to open it, hoping she wasn't blushing.

It was him. Of course it was him. Lord Shortcake.

"Oh," Ida said in what she hoped sounded like a surprised voice. "I thought it would be the girl come to help me with my gown."

"I wanted to—look, might I come in for a moment?" he said, glancing down the hallway. "Just for a moment," he repeated as she held the door open wider for him to step inside.

"Of course." She closed the door. And then they were alone. Again. In the room that was technically, for this evening at least, her bedroom.

Nothing she had ever read could have prepared her for how much she felt. She felt everything at this moment, so keenly alive and aware of the distance between them, how his eyes were focused on her, how much she longed to launch herself into his arms.

No launching, Ida, she admonished herself.

He leaned against the door, similar to her own position just moments before. "I just wanted to ask if you have everything you need to be comfortable." He frowned in thought. "You don't have any clothing with you, do you? What will you sleep in?"

Ida felt her cheeks heat. A gentleman was inquiring about her nightclothes.

Somehow, that felt more shocking than stealing a carriage and running away in search of an errant sister.

So much for her personal perspective.

"I'll just—" she began, and gestured toward her body.

"We'll buy clothing tomorrow. And not library clothing either," he said with a grin.

She tried to laugh—she did find him humorous—but her mind was too engrossed in the current situation to actually emit any kind of chuckle at all.

Because she wanted, quite desperately, to kiss him.

Well. There it was.

And so here she was. And he was right there, so why shouldn't she?

IDA'S FIRST THOUGHT should have been, *What am I doing?*

But it wasn't.

It should also have been the second, third, and fourth.

But it wasn't.

Why haven't I done this before? was what went through her mind as her mouth found his.

Dear lord, so this was kissing. She relished the warmth of his lips, of how it felt as though they were connected, not just there, but *everywhere*, as though sparks were traveling between them and they were enclosed in their own Faraday cage.

You're thinking too much, a voice admonished inside her head. *Feel.*

And so she did, pushing everything away but how it felt, how her body seemed to be melting, leaning toward him, her very skin tingling with awareness.

And then he moved his mouth, opened his lips, and his tongue licked her, slid along the seam of her mouth, and she gasped, opening her lips as she did.

At which point his tongue went inside her mouth.

She knew that was how kissing worked, but she hadn't expected it to be so—so fraught with feeling.

It felt as though she were a normal female, not Ida the Judgmental and Prickly Hedgehog. An apt description, if she were being honest with herself.

But now it felt as though she were a woman who could engage in this kind of activity without having it be something she was ashamed or embarrassed about.

Or something that anyone else was ashamed and embarrassed to do with her, either.

Dear god, don't let him be ashamed.

But she could tell it wasn't shame he was feeling as his tongue explored her mouth, tangled with her tongue, his breathing coming harsh and ragged on her face. It was an entirely different emotion.

His hand was on her arm, sliding up to grip her shoulder, moving so his palm was at the back of her head and he was pressing her closer, even though they were already connected at the mouth, and how much farther could she possibly go?

Without ending up on his lap, that is.

Did he want her on his lap?

But we're standing, she reminded herself.

Thinking too much still, Ida, that voice reminded her.

Right. Keep kissing, stop thinking.

And then it was impossible to think as he intensified the kiss, even though she wasn't certain how. Just that everything was more intense—it felt as though there were colors exploding inside her head, and her whole body felt languorous and at the same time as though she wanted to jump out of her skin.

She heard a noise, and realized it was she, and it was a moan. She was *moaning*, and now the hand not cupping her head was at her neck, fingers sliding over bare skin. She wanted to arch into his hand, place her body in his care, curl inside him and forget about thinking ever again.

It felt wonderful to be kissed. And to kiss. She found herself mirroring his action, brushing her tongue against his, wanting to make him react as strongly as she had.

"Nggh," he said, removing his lips even though his hands were still on her. He leaned his forehead against hers, breathing heavily.

I did this, Ida thought in triumph. *I rendered him inarticulate.*

Before remembering that he was an unwanted encumbrance on her journey, him and his sleek handsomeness, his responsibility apparently extending to making sure she was safe, even though she'd told him she would be fine.

Although she had to admit that was thoughtful of him.

"Ida, you—" he began, then shook his head. He removed first one hand, then the other, and Ida wanted to beg him to put them back. To kiss her some more.

Did she really just think that?

Yes. She couldn't deny the truth of what she wanted, even though she was entirely conflicted and had just made an irrational choice, which wasn't something she ever thought she'd do.

First time kissing someone. First time being irrational.

"Well," she said, stepping back from him, "that was educational."

She heard his intake of breath, and wondered if she had said the wrong thing. All of her studying had not mentioned the correct thing to say after someone had put his tongue inside her mouth, and vice versa.

Perhaps she could make a study of that. Although she didn't want to kiss any other gentlemen to have a control. That should alarm her, but she was too unsettled to be alarmed.

"Educational?" he echoed, sounding displeased.

Apparently *educational* was not to be on the list of post-kissing descriptors. Somehow his displeasure pleased her, which was another entirely irrational thing.

But if saying it made her less vulnerable, less prone to wanting to start it all over again—

which she knew she shouldn't, this was Lord Carson, after all, the gentleman who desired a soft, welcoming respite at the end of the day, of all things.

Definitely nothing close to Ida.

"Precisely." She spoke in as sprightly a tone as she could manage, although it still sounded rather breathless.

"Hedgehog," he said in an amused tone. As though he knew what she was doing.

Not only not dull, but intelligent and incisive to boot.

Drat.

"Thank you for that educational interlude, Lady Ida," he continued. "There remains nothing more but to wish you good-night. Again."

She froze for a moment, then nodded in agreement. "Good night," she murmured.

She would not be discomfited by him, no matter how nonplussed, and yes, discomfited she was.

One kiss had rendered her oxymoronic.

She could not let it happen again. Even though she had been the one to instigate it in the first place.

BENNETT WALKED SLOWLY down the hall to his own room.

Had what just happened just . . . happen?

He rubbed his hand over his face, still feeling

the imprint of her mouth on his lips. Her hand clutching his arm.

He glanced around the hallway, relieved nobody was there to witness his obvious befuddlement. And his erection.

He pushed the door open, taking a deep breath as he did so.

His room was similar to Ida's, with what appeared to be a large, comfortable bed, a chair, one window instead of two, and a desk. Mrs. Hastings had set a candle on the bedside table. The room was lit with a flickering glow that made it look very homey, and suddenly Bennett realized just how tired he was.

And how much he wanted to return to her room and continue what they'd started. Not finish it, he wouldn't risk that situation, knowing she wouldn't want that herself.

But if he could just touch her. Caress her skin, and kiss her mouth, and make her make those low humming noises he'd heard from her when they kissed.

The reality of it brought him up short. *Lady Ida.* Lady Ida the Prickly Hedgehog had kissed him. She'd begun it, and she'd seemed to truly enjoy it. Lady Ida. And him.

"You are ridiculous," he muttered to himself as he drew his shirt over his head. He ran his hand absentmindedly across his chest, then paused as yet another thought that did not belong in his usually practical brain appeared—what if it were her touching his chest? Sliding her fingers over his stomach, through the hair on his upper body, down to there?

His cock throbbed at the thought.

No. He couldn't think about that. It wasn't right. No matter how enthusiastic his cock was at the idea.

He folded his shirt and put it on the chair, then took his boots and trousers off so he was just in his smallclothes.

He hadn't planned on taking this trip, so of course he didn't have anything to sleep in. Like her. Was she sleeping in her chemise? Just a thin scrap of fabric over her body?

Or wearing nothing at all.

Stop thinking, Bennett, he thought as he got into bed.

He closed his eyes firmly, placing his arms on top of the covers and willing himself to think of anything but her.

Bills for equipment, the average life cycle of barley, the correct spelling of "clandestine."

There. That should do it.

And if he ended up staying awake all night in a torment of suspended sexual frustration, well then, he would be so exhausted he wouldn't be able to muster any kinds of thoughts at all—either salacious or appropriate.

Wonderful. Frustration or fatigue, with the distinct possibility that it would likely be both.

"GOOD MORNING," HE called out as he reached the bottom floor, relieved to see her already sitting downstairs.

He'd wondered if she would try to leave without him, but short of sitting outside her door all evening—which would provide its own different temptation—he couldn't control that.

"Good morning," she replied in that low voice of hers, one he couldn't help imagining saying dangerous things close in his ear. "Did you sleep well?"

No, I lay awake trying not to pleasure myself as I thought of you.

He'd finally managed to drift off around three o'clock, only to wake up a few hours later as the other guests in the inn started stirring.

They were back downstairs in the public area, a few other people staring blearily at the wooden tables at which they were seated. They looked as bad as he felt.

"Absolutely," he lied. "And you?"

She lifted her chin as though daring him to refute her. "Yes, wonderfully."

She had to have spent at least some of the night thinking about it, even if it was only weighing its educational value.

"I'm surprised to see you this morning," he said, leaning back in his chair.

Her expression shifted into that prickly defensive one that seemed to be her default. "Why?"

"I thought you might have tried to leave without me."

She swallowed, and glanced away. *Aha!* She had thought about it, at least.

"Why didn't you?" he continued.

Then she did look at him. "Well, I did consider it, of course. You knew I would. But your reasoning makes sense, and I judged it better to run the risk of utter scandalous ruin by traveling with you rather than run the risk of utter scandalous ruin by traveling on my own. With whatever dangers there are out there."

He felt himself exhale in relief. "Thank goodness. You are not as stubborn as it first seemed."

"I am too!" she said, making him burst into laughter.

She hesitated, and then she started to laugh too. "Oh, I've just proven . . . something," she said, smiling.

"Now that that is settled, we'll need to discuss the terms of the journey," he began. "We were fortunate this time to secure two rooms. But as we proceed, if I believe that it would be safer for us to share a room during our journey, we will. And I will also say that you cannot argue the point if I make that judgment. You have to trust me."

"I think I do," she said in a wondering tone. "I trust so few people, it's remarkable."

He was struck by the sincerity in her tone.

"I am delighted that you do trust me, although I'm not certain I've earned that trust. All I've done is not marry your sisters. Hardly something worth trusting another person for."

"If not marrying my sisters were something to trust a person over, that would mean I would only distrust two gentlemen in the world." She lifted her gaze to him, and he was caught by the intensity of her expression. "And I have to say, I *do* trust those gentlemen. As I do you."

"That is settled, then," he replied, feeling the warmth of her words—her trust—wash over him.

"What'll you have this morning?" Mrs. Hastings said as she approached the table. "We've got tea, oatmeal, eggs, and toast. Nothing else."

"Tea and oatmeal, please," Ida said. "With lemon, if you have it."

"Tea and eggs."

Mrs. Hastings placed napkins and cutlery on the table.

"So," she began, after Mrs. Hastings had bustled

away. "About last night." And then she turned bright red, but he couldn't laugh at her, not with her feeling so clearly vulnerable.

"So . . . ?" he said.

He could practically see her brain clicking and whirring as she processed her thoughts. He liked watching her think.

"Are you all right?" he asked, unable to resist poking his hedgehog.

Wait, not his. The hedgehog with whom he happened to be keeping company. And kissing.

"I am fine, thank you," she replied stiffly. "We cannot—that is, I do not—" She faltered.

He stretched his hand out to place it on top of hers. She looked at him then, her eyes wide, her expression almost confused.

The confused hedgehog. Not quite as prickly, but just as adorable.

He did not think she would appreciate the adjective.

"Do not what? If you wish to apologize for kissing me, that is fine, but no apology is necessary. I quite enjoyed it," he said, winking at her for good measure.

Her cheeks flushed red, and her eyes sparkled with a militant light. *There you are, Ida*, he thought. *There's my girl.*

"I was not going to apologize," she sputtered, and then he almost laughed aloud, although he knew she would likely storm off, and that would be awkward, since he would have no choice but to chase after her. "I was going to say," she continued exaggeratedly, "that I will understand if I have made you uncomfortable."

"In other words, you want to apologize," he said. Wicked, he knew, but he just couldn't resist teasing her.

"I—well, I—I suppose, yes. I am sorry." Her tone was sincere, and he squeezed her hand in response.

"There is no need. I am not uncomfortable. It was a kiss. You were curious about what it would be like to kiss me, I presume." He shrugged, looking at her from out of the corners of his eyes. "And now you know, so we may proceed."

He smothered a smile as he heard her mutter some sort of disgruntled noise, then withdrew his hand and glanced around the room, pointedly not looking at her. This was definitely the most fun he'd ever had.

And it had only been one kiss.

What would it feel like if there were more?

Chapter 8

Do not worry about what you are wearing.
Adventure has no regard for fashion.

LADY IDA'S TIPS FOR THE
ADVENTUROUS LADY TRAVELER

Shouldn't we be going?" Ida asked, glancing up at the sky, which was not helpful. The sun was covered by clouds, so she couldn't figure out what time it was. Just that it was after breakfast, and Della was out there somewhere, and now that she'd decided to let Lord Carson accompany her, she wanted them to be on their way. She'd thought the trip might take a week, but what if it took more?

"Soon, Lady Impatient. We need clothes. Unless you wish to wear your library clothing for the duration of the trip?"

Ida hesitated. She'd never worn the same dress two days in a row, never mind having worn the same underthings. Why hadn't she considered that when embarking on the journey?

Oh, yes. Because she'd impulsively stolen a carriage and run away from London in search of her sister, leaving Lord Lapdog and her mother's plans behind. And she was a duke's daughter who had never had to consider anything like a change of clothing. Things were just done for her, and she'd accepted them as a matter of course.

Well, then.

"I suppose so," she said grudgingly.

"I knew you would see reason," he said in a smug tone.

"Hmph." That was as close as she would come to admitting he was right.

He took her arm. "Mrs. Hastings told me there is an adequate shop for ladies, and the men's clothing store is just across the street."

"Do you have enough money for all of this?" she asked. Because she was fairly certain she did not—not that she knew how much anything cost, but she couldn't imagine Pearl's birthday money would stretch to accommodate the cost of a new wardrobe and traveling funds. There was a limit to the duchess's generosity.

"I do." She didn't doubt it, he sounded so positive. Then again, he had the ability to sound persuasive about anything.

"Stop making those noises," he said.

"What noises?"

"Those disapproving noises. You're thinking again. I can tell."

"I'm always thinking," she replied in a reproving tone.

"Can't you just stop? Or maybe only think about what kind of clothing you wish to purchase?" They'd stopped in front of a small shop with a sign indicating it was Mrs. Battle's Boutique, and he pushed the door open, a welcoming bell tinkling overhead. "Be like most other ladies, as far as I can tell?"

"I can't." It was as close to a confession as she could manage.

"No, of course not." She braced herself for what else he might say, how he might make her feel odd and strange. As she usually did.

"That's because you are so intelligent and honest. Not to mention foolhardy and impetuous."

It didn't sound as though he were judging her poorly. Almost the opposite, in fact, despite the last couple of words. But she had no opportunity to ask him to clarify, since they were now inside the shop.

Just that his words made her tingle all over again, as though his words were kisses. Verbal kisses that sparked something inside.

"Can I help you?" A lady stepped toward them,

a look of surprise on her face. The shop was filled to overflowing with bolts of fabrics, dress forms, and ribbon hanging from the ceiling. Luckily the proprietress was short in stature, or she would be perpetually pushing ribbons off her face.

Ida was not short, so she held a piece of dark purple ribbon to one side as she looked around the shop.

"Mrs. Battle?" Bennett asked. The woman nodded. "Yes, we're hoping you can help us. Our luggage is with our other coach," Bennett said smoothly, as though he dissembled everyday. He likely did. "And my sister is in need of a few things in case the coach does not catch up with us."

"Of course," Mrs. Battle replied. "I was wondering why two such fine gentlefolk would be patronizing my shop. But I assure you, the quality is just as good as you would find in the best shops in London."

"I am certain it is," Bennett said reassuringly, and the woman smiled in response.

He was very good at that charm thing.

"Did you stay at The Goose's Egg? Mrs. Hastings's meat pie is wonderful."

"Yes, it is." Ida smothered a giggle as Bennett shared a knowing look with her.

"Let me just pull some things out. I do keep some ready-made gowns in the shop for some of

the local girls, as long as you don't mind wearing
serviceable colors."

Ida arched a brow toward Bennett, who looked
chagrined.

"Serviceable colors will suit me perfectly," she
said. "Thank you, Mrs. Battle."

It didn't take long for Ida to select a few gowns
and other necessities, unfortunately having to
pass over the purple ribbon, which didn't go with
anything else Ida had chosen. Mrs. Battle didn't
have that much of a selection, but as she'd promised, the gowns were well-made and in serviceable colors like dark green and leaf-brown, and
soon they were out the door, looking across the
street to where Holdings' Haberdashery stood
directly opposite Mrs. Battle's Boutique.

"Do you suppose the town has nothing but
alliterative shops?" Ida asked in a low, amused
voice.

"No, if that were the case The Goose's Egg
would be The Goose's Gegg, or something like
that."

"Mrs. Hastings's Hotpies and Hotelier."

"Meatpie and Manor."

"The Goose's Egg is hardly a manor," Ida
pointed out.

Bennett waved his hand as they crossed the
street. "Artistic license. For the alliteration and
all."

Ida had a smile on her face as they entered the haberdashery, and she realized she had never had twenty-four hours filled with so much smiling. And conversation, and sparring, and remarks on her general prickliness.

Not to mention the kissing.

She liked it. She felt as though she were finally escaping, even though it wasn't truly an escape, at least not for long—she'd be returning to London eventually, if only to bring Della back and reunite all the sisters.

And then face the scandal of being yet another duke's daughter who'd run headfirst into danger.

"Good morning." A salesman greeted them as they walked in. Like in Mrs. Battle's shop, Holding's Haberdashery was small and cluttered, with an assortment of hats and handkerchiefs on one side, and fabric on the other.

"Good morning. I am in need of some essentials, if you please."

"Of course." The salesman—Mr. Holding, Ida presumed—looked Bennett up and down. "I believe we have some things that will fit you." He glanced at Ida. "And perhaps while we discuss the specifics, your—?"

"Sister," Ida supplied.

"Sister will want to have a cup of tea in our waiting area? Mabel!" he called, and a young girl emerged from behind a white fabric curtain, a questioning look on her face that cleared when she saw who was there.

"Mabel, please take the lady into the back and make her a nice cup of tea."

Mabel nodded, and gestured toward the place she had just come from, Ida walking forward as Mr. Holding approached Bennett.

TWENTY MINUTES LATER, Bennett reappeared, a package in his arms and a new hat on his head. "Are you ready, sister?" he said with a grin.

"Thank you, Mabel," Ida said as she stood, placing the teacup on the table beside her. "I appreciate your keeping me company while my brother shopped."

"It was no problem, miss," the girl said, staring at Bennett.

And why shouldn't she stare? He truly was glorious, all long limbs and confident grin and smiling whiskey-colored eyes.

The only thing that wasn't perfect about him was the hint of stubble on his face, and even that only made him more attractive.

Hmm. She hadn't noticed the feel of the stubble when she'd kissed him. She'd have to make a note to pay attention the next time.

Oh no. No, there would be no next time. Hadn't she said just that this morning? Apologized for kissing him, and he'd treated it as though it were nothing? Which made her feel odd, and not in her usual feeling like Odd Ida way.

"You're thinking again," he said, squeezing the arm he held.

"I'm thinking we should be on our way," she said brusquely. *Not about how the stubble on your face might feel on my mouth.* "We don't know how long it will take to get there."

"The carriage is waiting, my lady," he said, gesturing toward where Eustace stood holding the horses.

Ida took his hand as she stepped back up onto the carriage seat.

"Ouch!" she exclaimed as she sat. Her bottom was sore, and she sprang up, glaring at the seat. She had never sat on a carriage seat for so long in her entire life as she had the previous day.

She almost missed her mother's sitting room with all of its overstuffed chairs.

He shook his head in mock dismay, then swung up and sat down, making an exaggerated noise that indicated how comfortable he was.

"Hmph," she said as she placed her bottom gingerly down again.

"We could stay here a bit longer," he said, "if you need to rest your delicate self."

She didn't reply, just glared at him. He, of course, laughed.

"I'd give you something to sit on, but you kidnapped me before I could pack a bag," he continued.

"You just bought things!" she said.

"I didn't think to purchase a cushion for your—" He paused, and looked down.

"Besides which, I did not kidnap you," she replied in a prim voice, feeling her lips start to curl up in a smile, even though she was trying to remain serious. "On the contrary, you are a stowaway on this particular adventure."

He picked up the reins and urged the horses into motion, causing the carriage—and her—to lurch forward.

She felt his hand at her waist, steadying her, and she tried not to think about how welcome and lovely his touch made her feel.

He's just making certain you don't fall onto the road, she told herself. Even though she knew full well that he had already shown that he liked to touch her—hadn't he taken her hand going up the stairs? And held her as they kissed?

Ida the Omniscient now felt as though she knew nothing at all. And she wanted to know everything. Especially about kissing.

BENNETT'S FINGERS TINGLED from where he had touched Ida. But that was disingenuous; his whole body felt as though it tingled, every fiber of his being wanting that contact with her again.

He wanted to kiss her so badly it hurt.

Focus. Focus on anything else. Things like—

"My God. I never even asked. Where are we going anyway? Where does your sister live?"

He felt her shift in the seat beside him. She cleared her throat, and he could almost hear her thoughts—*Should I tell him? What if I decide I want to go on my own after all? What if someone finds us, and asks where we are going, and he tells them? Is it safer for me to be quiet?*

"A town called Haltwhistle," she answered at last.

"I've never heard of it," he replied.

"Hardly surprising. It is tiny, so small, it took a lot of searching in the atlas to find it."

"Ah, which is why you were at Mr. Beechcroft's."

"Yes." She paused. "And—and there was not wanting to be at home."

She was confiding in him. Like before, when she'd said she couldn't be like other women. He could hear it in the hesitancy of her voice, so different from her usual confident tone. He didn't want to startle her, but he wanted to know more.

"Why did you not wish to be at home?" he asked, keeping his tone mild.

"Well. You know my mother, the duchess—"

Thoughts of the Duchess of Marymount practically forcing him into marriage with no fewer than two of her daughters came to mind.

"Yes, I am acquainted with her, of course. She is quite . . . insistent."

"That is one way of putting it." She sighed. "My goodness, you truly are diplomatic. I envy that ability. I cannot seem to temper my words when I speak."

"But your mother—?" Bennett prompted.

"She has decided I am to be married. *Was* to be married. After this adventure, I don't think anyone will want to marry me." She sounded pleased.

"Not to me, I would have heard about it, I presume," he said with a chuckle. "At least, I don't think so."

"No, not you. Far, far worse than you."

"How could there be anyone worse than me?" he said in mock horror.

She nudged him with her elbow. "Silly. You know you are splendid in many ways."

He wanted to hear more about that, but first . . . "So who did the duchess deem worthy of marriage to her most intelligent daughter?"

She made an embarrassed noise, and he smothered a grin. Lady Ida was not immune to compliments, it seemed, especially if they were about her intelligence.

"Lord Bradford."

Bennett frowned as he searched his recollection.

Lord Bradford, Lord Brad—"No. He is pleasant enough, but he is . . ."

"A nitwit? Yes. A perfectly pleasant nitwit, but a nitwit, nonetheless."

How could the duchess possibly think Lady Ida would be at all happy with Lord Bradford? How little did her mother know her daughter?

And how much must that hurt Lady Ida? That her parent didn't know her enough to know who would be the worst possible match for her?

"Do you know Lord Bradford informed me horses go twice as fast as humans because they have four legs, whereas we have only two?" She sounded outraged.

"Well, at least he is interested in nature?" Bennett said, trying not to laugh. "And he can count?"

She nudged him in the side again. "That is not the basis of a marriage, and you know it. Oh wait, never mind. You don't at all. You said you wanted someone *soft* and *welcoming*." Her words were accusing, and he wondered if he'd insulted her when he said that. Never mind, he knew. He had insulted her, even though she had no desire—as she'd said several times now—of wanting to marry him.

Wait, had she stung his pride? Damn it, she had.

They did not wish to marry one another. That

had been firmly established. He did not want to hear her announce it in that particular Lady Ida way anymore.

But he *did* want to kiss her again. And he had the distinct impression that she wanted the same thing.

The two could coexist, could they not? In some sort of parallel theorem?

He did not want to sidetrack her into geometry, however, so he would not ask.

She continued. "Lord Bradford would be soft and welcoming." Her tone was sprightly. "Perhaps you should consider marriage to him yourself. He's very similar to a lapdog. I imagine he would fetch your slippers, if you rewarded him with a treat."

Bennett burst out laughing. She was funny, unexpectedly so. "I could take him out for walks, let him sleep at the foot of my bed. It sounds ideal."

"For you, obviously."

"And for you? What do you want?"

A moment where she hesitated, and he wondered if he had gone too far, pushed too much, been too inquisitive.

"That's like asking me where I wish to escape to," she began, in a voice so soft he instinctively slowed the horses so he could hear her better. "I don't know who that person might be. I don't know if that person exists. Just that I want someone who can accept me, who I am. How I am, more accurately." That last bit said with a rueful sigh, as though she were acutely aware of how she was perceived.

"It sounds as though you want someone welcoming."

"Perhaps," she said. "Perhaps I do. I think it might be more difficult to find someone who would welcome me."

Damn it. He wanted to stop the carriage, turn to her, and pull her into his lap, kissing her senseless. Anything to show her that she would be welcomed, by the right gentleman. Someone who could appreciate not only her stark, glorious beauty, but who could also appreciate her strong, gorgeous brain.

That person could not be him, however. He didn't want to be encumbered, and he did not want a wife who would challenge him at every turn. In conversation, in life, in bed.

Did he?

THIS WHOLE CONVERSATION, the past twenty-four hours, felt so intimate. Ida felt raw, exposed, vulnerable. She'd always been able to hide behind things, either a literal pillar or a pillar constructed by her own blunt condescension, tempered by her intelligence and complete disinterest in what most "normal women" were interested in.

It was a large imaginary pillar, to be sure. One that was able to hide all the varying parts of her. Something she'd grown accustomed to drawing over herself, like a blanket.

Not the fuzzy blanket it seemed he desired; a blanket that was more like a shroud, designed to hide what was underneath.

But he was plucking at the fabric enclosing her, luring her from behind her pillar, making her say so many things she hadn't realized she'd thought, much less felt.

And then there was that kiss. She had to do something to stop thinking about it, about him, and how he'd held her. How he'd made her feel so precious and yet so powerful.

Her mind chased itself in circles looking for something. Anything.

"Why did you compare me to a hedgehog?" she blurted after a few moments of silence.

"Well," he said in a thoughtful tone, "I suppose at first it was because you were all prickly, and yet also adorable."

"I am not—not *adorable*!" she sputtered.

"So you say."

"Did you always think like that? Or is it only after embarking on this—whatever it is," she said, gesturing toward the carriage.

"Would it insult you if I said that I hadn't paid

much attention to you before? Before that day at Alex and Eleanor's house?"

It didn't insult her. Nor did it surprise her. "No, not at all. I know how I appear to people," she began.

"How?" he asked, his tone genuinely curious.

"Well," she said, hearing the wry humor in her voice, "you likely only saw me when I was lecturing about something or another. I tend to do that, go on and on about a subject even if my audience doesn't necessarily appreciate it."

"Like the gas lighting incident," he said. "But you did that for a reason, didn't you?"

That he knew, that he might understand, made her warm inside.

"Although I didn't realize that until I got to know you."

She shifted on the seat, trying to get comfortable. "Yes. It was the only way I could think of to distract everyone so as to allow Eleanor to speak with our father the duke."

"So you used your knowledge for good."

Definitely warm.

"Thank you." She looked off into the distance in thought. "It wasn't anything I'd planned—"

"Much as you didn't plan stealing Mr. Beechcroft's carriage, I wager."

She laughed. "Yes, much the same."

"I admire that, you know."

She held her breath, waiting for him to say more.

"That you launch yourself into the fray without worrying about how you will be perceived. You have this innate honesty that shines through." He chuckled. *"Sincerus Idaterum."*

She smiled, pleased he had taken up her classification game.

It wasn't often anybody actually spoke her language; not in the literal way, but in a communicative way. He did. He understood what she was trying to do and say, and he seemed to appreciate it.

That connection felt so special, so unique, she wanted to hold onto it with all of her strength. Even though it wasn't her future, she knew that.

"But back to me calling you a hedgehog," he continued, still in that amused tone. "You're so much more than that, I realize," he continued, taking one hand from the reins and wrapping it across her shoulders, drawing her body closer to his. "You are an intricate, layered person, Ida. I have to admit I never met anyone like you before."

"Thank you." Her throat was tight. "You know most people don't find me intricate at all. Usually they find me annoying. Or boring. Or both."

"Or hedgehog-like," he added slyly.

"But it seems hedgehogs are intricate creatures."

If he was going to compliment her, albeit oddly, she should at least embrace the comparison.

"It takes great maturity to admit your similarity to the animal," he said, teasing.

"What kind of animal would you be, then?" she demanded.

Silence. She could hear him thinking, though, which was comforting. That he was seriously considering her question instead of just dismissing her, or teasing her some more.

Not that she didn't like being teased—it turned out she did, especially when he did it—but this wasn't the moment, and he seemed to know that. Seemed to know her.

WHAT KIND OF animal was he? One that was steadfast, and persevered through difficult times, and was also governed by routine.

"I think I might be a cow," he said, aware of how ridiculous he sounded. But not caring. Not with her. Not after the past twenty-four hours or so of conversation. "Cows are very useful animals. They are essential for life if you are fond of milk and cheese."

"I love cheese," she said. Another item in the column of facts about Ida. He wouldn't have expected her to have a preference of foodstuffs beyond pure sustenance. And yet it seemed she did.

"But cows are dull, aren't they?" he continued. "I don't want to be a dull animal."

"I think you'd be a leopard," she said in a musing tone. "All sleek and powerful and blending into the background until you see them and then realize just how beautiful they are."

Her words left him speechless, but his other body parts responded quite well. It took a moment before he could speak.

"Th-thank you," he managed to say at last. "Being a leopard sounds as though it would be far more fun than being a Bennett."

"What is the worst thing about being a Bennett?" she asked, her tone curious.

He exhaled as he thought about it. "I suppose it's never being able to relax. Never being able to just let go of something and know it will be taken care of. I'm the one who takes care of things, and now everyone expects it of me. I'm the one who does things. Nobody else takes initiative and does things on their own."

"You do seem to be quite engaged and responsible."

"Is that how you first saw me? It sounds very dull."

"I suppose it could be seen as dull, if one were unimaginative."

Oh. She most definitely was not unimaginative. She continued. "It takes a lot of concentrated effort not to marry someone, especially with someone else like my mother so determined to make it happen." Her tone was rueful. How hard must it be for Ida to have the duchess as her parent? "That you didn't want it, but that you didn't end up hurting anybody—that told me you were caring and thoughtful as well as utterly responsible."

It didn't sound so dull when she said it.

"Thank you. I believe that is also why I always end up taking charge of things—because otherwise, people will get hurt." His mother, his brother, his father's tenants and the other people whose livelihoods depended on his family. "Which actually is why I asked Alexander originally to spend time with Eleanor. If I cannot commit to something entirely, I cannot do it in good faith."

"Oh," she said with a sharp intake of breath. Was she thinking of him entirely committing to something? In some other context?

He should not be thinking of that now.

"But you said—you said you would like it if someone else could take charge once in a while? Oh no!" she exclaimed, twisting in the seat to look at him. "Who is handling your business affairs while you are away? Dear lord, I never even thought of that! I am so sorry. I could not live with myself if people suffered for all of this."

He gave a reassuring smile. "Alexander offered to help, should I need to escape. I didn't expect to take him up on his offer so soon, but I assure you, nobody will suffer."

"Oh, thank goodness," she replied. "What will happen when you return? Will you be able to relinquish some control so you can finally take some time for yourself? Would you be able to let someone take initiative?"

The thought brought all kinds of images to his mind, pictures of her telling him what to do in that bossy tone. Demanding that he kiss her, or touch her in very specific spots.

But then reality intruded. She'd asked about what would happen now that he'd left; what about her?

"Does anyone know where you've gone? Much less that you left?"

Her quick, sharp inhale told him what he needed to know. *Ida, you impetuous carriage-stealer.* He spoke in a firm tone of voice. "We will stop in the next village. We need to send letters letting everyone know we are safe."

"Everyone but Pearl and Eleanor are going to think we've eloped," she said in a resigned tone.

"We should tell them that," he said.

She swung herself on the seat to stare at him, and he turned to look at her face. He was surprised to see just how shocked an expression she had.

"It's the only way," he explained. "If our families believe that we have eloped, they will both be pleased at the outcome, just not the process. My father wants me to marry, as does your mother. I assume I am a better catch for you than Lord FourFeet, and so your family won't chase after you."

"Likely if my mother considered it, she'd realize that I might not be sufficiently compromised, so she should leave me be." Ida spoke in a flat tone of voice, making him hurt for her. He knew why the duchess didn't understand her youngest daughter—she was far too complicated and intelligent—but why couldn't the duchess just love her?

She deserved to be loved.

"That's settled then," he replied, turning back to face the road. Not wanting to face his own desires. "We'll stop at the next village to write our letters, and we might as well stop there for the night as well."

IDA KNEW SHE owed Pearl a letter—she'd promised, after all—but she hadn't anticipated her letter would include:

I have run away with Lord Carson, the gentleman that nobody in our family has married yet.

Pearl would be aghast. The Ida of three days ago would be aghast as well. The Ida of today?

Well, she was discovering that she liked being adventurous, and daring, and speaking her mind. Sharing her thoughts.

Her sisters loved her, but they didn't always understand her. Reasonable, since it seemed Ida didn't always understand herself—why was she so determined to hide behind pillars? Why couldn't she imagine a happy future for herself?

This Ida, the one at this very moment, was happy, even though the future was still uncertain, and Della was still missing, and Ida had no idea what would happen when she and Bennett returned to London.

"Well," she said, wanting to share her happiness, but not entirely certain how. Or if he would want to hear her. Or if he would understand her. Or anything at all, really.

Was this how it felt to be a normal woman?

Hmm.

"Yes?"

"Now that we've been on the road for over a day."

"Meaning we're seasoned travelers?" he said in an amused voice.

She swatted his arm. "Not precisely. But it is very different from how we were just a few days ago."

"How does it feel to you?" he asked.

She sighed. But not in an unhappy way. "It is an

adventure. It is an escape, and it feels dangerous, and exhilarating, and wonderful."

"And serviceable," he teased.

"Yes, that. Service in finding my sister, after all."

"About that—are you certain she wants to be found?"

"Uh . . ." Ida began.

"You're not." He did not sound surprised. "So you are saying that you took off in Mr. Beechcroft's carriage heading for this tiny village called Halt-something."

"Haltwhistle."

"And you're not certain your sister will even want to see you."

Ida shifted in her seat. "That's right."

"Ida." She had to admit to feeling a thrill at how forceful he sounded. What was wrong with her?

"My lord?"

"What happens if she won't return with you? If she refuses to see you?"

"That won't happen."

He made one of her snorting noises. Had he always done that, or had he picked them up from her?

"It won't happen because, and I know you can corroborate this, I am too stubborn to allow it to happen. Della will have to see me. I need to persuade her to return to London so we can be a part of Nora's life."

"Nora? Who is Nora? Another sister?"

Ida chuckled. "No, I believe five is plenty."

"More than enough," he murmured. She ignored him.

"Nora is Della's daughter."

"Her daughter?" He sounded surprised. "But you said your sister never mar—oh!"

"Precisely."

"So not only are you planning on returning to London with your scandalous sister, you are also planning on returning with her natural-born daughter? And you are going to refuse my proposal?"

Ida nodded. "Yes. All of that."

"What do you think will happen? Do you think you'll just be able to pick up your life where it was? Because you're an intelligent woman, Ida, I know you cannot think that is true. Society won't allow it."

"I know." And it felt so freeing to admit it. "I expect I will be a pariah, as will Della. No honorable man will have me, and so my parents will be forced to send us both away. Perhaps I'll be able to go live in a cottage somewhere, me and Della. And Pearl, if she wants to come."

"You'd be happy there?" He sounded wistful. As though he wished to escape. Not necessarily with her, she wasn't so presumptuous to think that—it was just one kiss, after all—but strike out on his own.

"I think so." A few days ago she would have been more confident in her answer. But now the layers of herself were starting to peel, and perhaps she wanted more than she knew. "At the very least, I would like the freedom to try."

"Freedom." The word sounded as though he'd been forbidden to say it, whispering it in a quiet tone as though afraid of being overheard. "It is something we have, to some extent, and that we also take for granted."

Her heart hurt at how aching his tone was.

She put her hand on his arm and rested her head against his shoulder. No, it wasn't proper, but none of this was. And if she could give comfort to someone she was realizing might actually be a friend—a very attractive friend whose long, confident stride made her breath hitch—then she would.

He placed his hand on top of hers, squeezing her fingers.

They drove like that for a while, him caressing her hand as she breathed in his scent, a blend of soap and clean linen.

Surprising, since it had to have been some time since he last bathed. Even his cleanliness was perfect.

"What?" he asked as she shook her head.

I can't admit I was thinking about how you smell.

"You've told me about your father, and his wishes for you," she said, raising her head off his shoulder. But keeping her hand on his arm. "What about your mother?"

"My MOTHER IS an invalid."

"I am so sorry," Ida replied. Her hand was still on his arm, from before; odd that he hadn't realized it until now. It felt so right, that felt odd too. But in a right kind of way. "I'd like to know more about her. If you want to talk about her."

"I do. I will." He took a deep breath. "My mother used to be very active. She was involved with my and Alexander's upbringing, supervising our tutors, and spending time with us when we weren't at our lessons. Our father was often absent, but it's rare to find fathers who aren't, in our world, at least."

"And in the world of men who have to work long hours to support their families," she added.

"Yes, of course, I was thoughtless."

"That wasn't what I wanted to point out. Your thoughtlessness. I think I am more guilty than you of focusing solely on myself—my wishes, my feelings, my thoughts. I know that I was blindsided by Della's departure. I wish I had paid more attention. Maybe she would still be with us if I had."

And then I wouldn't be here with you. But that was the most selfish thought of all—that he was at all happy to be benefiting from her family upset was inexcusable. Even if it was true.

"But I started talking about myself. I want to hear more about your mother. What is the nature of her illness?"

Her tone was matter-of-fact, not pitying or overly curious. Just as though she honestly wished to hear the answer, and wouldn't use his response to be falsely sympathetic or tell anybody else.

The idea, honestly, of her being falsely sympathetic was so ludicrous he nearly laughed aloud.

"The doctors aren't precisely sure. Except that—except that her decline began around the same time she discovered my father's second family." He took a deep breath, relieved that she hadn't immediately peppered him with questions. As though she knew he would tell her everything, but that it would take time.

And since they were traveling to an unknown village where they may or may not have a mailbox or a place to sleep, apparently they had a substantial amount of time.

"My father has a mistress. Like so many men of our world." He nudged her in the shoulder. "That is one circumstance where I think we can agree it is limited to our world."

She laughed abruptly, and then her hand shot

up to her mouth as though she'd surprised even herself.

"And he has two children with this woman. I've never met them." That hurt more than he would admit, even to himself. "I'd like to, but I don't want to make my mother more upset, if she were to find out. But I wonder about them—they're about ten years younger than Alex and me, and my father is not the most—well, he's not very affectionate. And Alex and I, we have our mother, and the security of our position. I don't know anything about their mother. I just hope they're happy."

She leaned into him, curling her hand more around his arm. "When we return with Della, I would like to assist you in meeting your half siblings. I know how important it is to have the support and love from your family, especially if your parents aren't . . . well, you know."

He thought of her mother, and her obvious machinations to marry him off to at least one of her daughters, and he nodded. "I do know. We both know. I hope that when I have children I will be as kind to them as my mother was to me."

"You will be," she replied immediately. "You cannot help but be honorable and kind and thoughtful."

"Thank you," he said in a quiet voice.

Chapter 9

Don't concern yourself with maintaining "ladylike" behavior. You are a traveler first, a lady second.

LADY IDA'S TIPS FOR THE
ADVENTUROUS LADY TRAVELER

*H*e had siblings he didn't even know. Imagine if she didn't know Pearl, or Eleanor, or even Olivia, who could be annoyingly bossy, but who would drop everything to help if she suspected possible danger.

And Della, whom Ida was risking everything to find.

She knew Bennett was as loyal to Alexander as she was to her sisters. And how much he likely wished he could protect and help his other siblings, the ones his father couldn't possibly introduce him to.

Her heart ached for him.

"It's fine," he said, as though reading her mind.

He was so empathetic; no wonder he was so persuasive in his sincerity. He was sincere. He was just that honorable and responsible, far more than likely most people were.

"How much longer until the next village? Did you see a sign or anything?" she asked. She hoped she could wait to find the facilities, since her bladder was starting to make itself known.

"Another hour or so. Hopefully the town will have a post office. I saw a sign a ways back."

"As long as there is meat pie," she said. "And ale."

"And for the letters—are you going to tell your family everything?"

"Most everything," she said in a prim tone. Everything except that the most responsible aristocrat, Lord Carson, was so much more than he first appeared to be. That he was kind, and thoughtful, and sincere, and his emotions were deep and heartfelt.

And she was altogether far too swoony about him, damn it.

"Ah, so you won't be mentioning the kiss?" he teased.

She felt herself blush. "I will not. And besides, we weren't going to discuss it again."

"Such a prickly hedgehog," he said in a humorous tone.

"Prickly rhymes with tickly," she said, digging

her fingers into his side. "Are you ticklish, Bennett?"

Why she even thought of that she couldn't answer to herself. Just that even mentioning the kiss seemed to bring out a whole different side of Ida.

Plus, it seemed he was quite ticklish indeed.

He leapt in his seat and squirmed, his hand on her wrist as he attempted—unsuccessfully—to loosen her hold.

She edged over to get a better grip on him, putting both hands on him now, laughing as he twisted to try to get away.

And then he clamped his arm around her and dragged her body onto his as he stopped the horses, and there they were, she on top of him, his face lit with laughter, his eyes gleaming dangerously.

So of course she had to stop tickling him and start kissing him.

And of course he had to kiss her back.

As soon as their mouths met, Bennett had to say that outdoor kissing was possibly the best kissing experience ever. The sun was warm on his face, her body was molded into his, and there was no one about, but the possibility that someone could stumble across them merely increased the excitement.

He had not known he was a fan of exhibitionism. And yet here he was. Out here. With her.

He slid his fingers into her hair as he thrust his tongue into her mouth, shifting so her body lay between his legs, his hardening cock pressing against her.

"Mmm," she moaned, that low sound that made him forget to think—not that he was able to think anyway, not with her kissing him like this.

Her hands were on his shoulders, holding herself up against him, and then she wiggled to get herself more firmly situated, then moving her hand to his cravat, which she began to unwind.

All while still kissing him. She was very efficient.

He yanked a few pins out of her hair, feeling the tumble of it come down on his skin, then moved his hands lower. Down her back, gripping her arse with his hand, then caressing its soft fullness.

He hadn't known before, women's fashion being what it was, but her arse was tremendous. Lush, and full, and round. He wanted to bite into it like a juicy peach. But that would mean having to stop kissing her, which he was not willing to do.

He gathered a handful of fabric in his hand and began to draw it up, imagining how it must look. His cock thickening at the image in his head: Her legs getting slowly bared as her dress moved up and up and up, until eventually he was able to gather the fabric up and bunch it at her waist, leaving her entire lower body exposed.

He opened his eyes but was momentarily unable to see because of the dark fall of hair around them, caging them in together. It was a welcome refuge, one where only they existed, where he could kiss her until neither of them could see, much less think.

But he wanted to see her body, so he reached up and swept her hair to one side, looking over her shoulder to what he'd revealed by lifting her gown.

Oh lord. It was so much better than his imagination.

She raised her mouth, her eyebrow arched in that questioning way he was coming to adore. "This is not at all an equitable situation," she murmured in her low, husky voice. She shifted so she could yank his cravat entirely off his neck, dropping it onto the seat. Her gaze focused on his neck, intent, her fingers beginning to slide the buttons through their holes as her fingers touched his skin.

And then she smiled, a wicked half smile as she started to rake her nails over his bare skin.

It was intoxicating, it was delicious torment, even more than when she'd been tickling him.

And the view.

He could see the pale globes of her arse, round and lush as he'd felt. She'd moved so her feet were on the seat, and her legs were on either side of his body, all that soft skin so close to his hands.

"You're gorgeous," he said in a growl, clamping his hand on her buttock. His eyes nearly rolled back in his head at the feel of her bare skin on his palm, squeezing its soft roundness, his cock hard and pressed against her.

"Thank you," she murmured in reply, straightening to push his coat off his shoulders. "I would say the same to you, but I need to see more of what I'm assessing." And she slid her palm under his shirt, caressing his chest, her fingers on his nipple, raking it with her fingernail, making him arch under her touch.

He couldn't take it any longer; he put his other hand on the back of her head and dragged her face down to his so he could kiss her, both of their mouths widening to accommodate the other, tongue, and teeth, and lips all meeting in a glorious clash of passion.

Her breasts were pushed up against his chest, and it was awkward, but he couldn't resist moving his hand from the back of her head to between their two bodies, his fingers wiggling down, finding the neckline of her gown, then sliding down farther to discover her skin.

At least women's fashions had already fore-warned him about her bosom; as round and full as her arse, and he squeezed it, making her moan all over again against his mouth.

"We have to stop," she said after a few long minutes of kissing.

"Yes, we shouldn't keep—" he began, but she shook her head, placing her hand against his mouth.

"Not because of that. I need to—" she started, then glanced away, biting her lip. "I need to pay a visit to the trees."

"What?" he asked, confused, then realized what she was really saying. "Oh. Right." He hadn't thought about the practical bodily functions they'd have to take care of while traveling.

"I'll just go over there," she said, twisting so she was no longer on top of him, shaking the skirts of her gown down as she did so. He missed the sight of her bare arse already.

"I'll just wait right here," he replied, shifting to adjust his erection. He saw her eyes dip over, then right back to his face, her cheeks flushed. Was she blushing because of what they'd just done, what she'd just said, or what he looked like at the moment?

So many things that might possibly cause embarrassment, and yet he didn't feel ashamed at all.

In fact, he wanted to do it again, only with more energy and time.

IF IDA WERE a different sort of woman, she might have felt awkward about admitting that she needed to tend to some lady business out in the woods. And she did feel awkward, but not about that; it was that she'd practically climbed into his lap. She *had* climbed into his lap. And done other things to him while he did things to her, and they were in the outdoors where anybody could see them.

And she didn't seem to care.

So it was that she felt awkward about the lack of awkwardness she felt, which made no sense at all, which definitely bothered her. Lady Ida of the Hard and Factual Truths always made sense. Except when swept away by Lord Short-cake, who was an exciting travel companion, an excellent kisser (at least in her test experience of two kisses), and a splendid conversationalist.

She walked deeper into the woods, looking back every so often to make sure she kept her bearings. She did not want to be Lady Ida the Lost. At last, she found a quiet, shaded place and took care of her bladder, then walked back, her mind reviewing everything that had happened.

One: She'd tickled him. And then kissed him.

Two: He'd kissed her back.

Three: He'd bared her to the waist, and then she knew he'd looked, so he'd seen more of her than any other person in the entire world.

Four: She'd touched his bare chest with her bare hand, and it felt wonderful and entirely different from her own body.

Five: All of that made her more curious about what might happen next.

Six: They were still traveling together alone, and neither of them knew how long that would last.

Seven: She had no idea what might happen.

And Eight: She couldn't wait to find out what else might happen.

"ALL TAKEN CARE of?" he asked as she returned, his expression carefully neutral. It seemed he might be feeling awkward as well, although she didn't know if it was because she'd had to mention something ladies normally did not discuss with gentlemen, or that they'd been indulging in some very scandalous behavior.

Either way, she thought with a shrug, it didn't matter. At least he was being polite.

"Yes, thank you," she replied. She gathered her skirts and stepped up on the rail of the carriage, settling herself on the seat.

He swung up beside her. She found herself disappointed that he'd wrapped his cravat around his neck again; she liked being able to see his bare throat, his strong neck.

"About before," he began, his voice strained.

"Yes, I should not have tickled you."

He barked out a surprised laugh. "Not that. But you know that."

"Yes. About before."

"I—I don't want you to feel as though you have to do anything. If you don't want to. Just because I am here with you and everything."

She frowned in confusion, then realized what he'd implied. "Do you think that I would ever possibly feel as though I had to do something? If I didn't want to?" She shook her head. "You do not know me at all, Bennett."

"Hold on, there," he expostulated. "I didn't mean—"

"Yes, it sounds as though you did." She turned halfway on the seat to face him. "I very much like kissing you, Bennett, and I also very much like it when I touch you and you touch me. This has been an unexpected benefit to us traveling together, and it is a learning experience. For me, at least. I presume you have done all this before," she said, waving her hands in the air between them to indicate their activity.

"Not with you," he replied, a wry smirk on his lips. "The experience has been very different for me, I assure you."

It was on the tip of her tongue to ask what the difference was, for curiosity's sake, but then she realized, oddly enough, that she most definitely did not want to hear about his doing these things with any other ladies.

Was she jealous?

She'd never felt jealousy before, so she wasn't certain, but she strongly suspected she was. But it did reassure her that he said the experience was very different when with her. Which brought her a feeling of satisfaction, one she definitely had never had before, only because he was her first kiss.

Hmm. Another surprising element of this adventure they were on—discovering emotions she didn't know she had.

"But thank you. I didn't mean to imply you were merely grateful. I have too much respect for your own self-worth to believe that. I just wanted to be certain."

She waved her hand airily. Trying to maintain an attitude that wouldn't ask too much of him, and of this situation. "Well, do not worry about it. It is quite enjoyable, and I am gaining quite a bit of knowledge I never had before."

"So that is all it is to you? Knowledge gathering? *Educational?*" He sounded aggrieved, which made her surprisingly pleased.

She turned back in her seat to face forward again. "Isn't that the ideal for a gentleman? Not to have to promise anything but reap the benefits of the activity? Neither one of us has any expectation that it means any more than it does." Not that that made sense, but it *sounded* as though it did.

"Hmph," was all he replied.

She smothered a laugh. Not that it was humorous, necessarily, but it felt wonderful to be able to take the initiative in whatever was to happen between them next.

She didn't think he'd appreciate it if she pointed that out.

"WHAT ARE YOU saying in yours?" Ida asked as she peered over at his paper.

Bennett shielded the letter, making a shooing gesture. "You are not allowed to comment on my letter. Not on my penmanship, my choice of words, or what I say."

They sat at a round wooden table in a small, anonymous pub. They'd found the stationer's, located the postbox, and had gotten ale, much to Ida's delight.

Now they were seated beside one another writing their respective letters. Only, it seemed, his critical Ida wanted to oversee what he was writing as well.

Wait. *His?* No, she wasn't his. She would never be his, entirely because she wouldn't allow it. She was her own person, she was too exuberant and vibrant and intelligent to be in anybody else's shadow.

She was like a meteor shower, a stunning event that one could view, but never replicate on one's own.

She was *stellar*. He wished he could point out the pun to her, but the explanation would be too convoluted, and she'd likely raise one of those dark eyebrows because he took too long to get to the point. Or argue with him that a star was nothing like a meteor shower, despite both being in the sky.

She could be pedantic and argumentative, no matter how delightful he found her.

"Let me see," she said, tugging the paper in front of her.

And persistent.

Dear Alex,

"Well, that is fine, I don't know what you would think I would have to say about that," she said, looking up at him with a grin. And then taking another sip of ale before she continued.

Lady Ida and I are on a rescue mission.

"That will pique his interest, for certain," she said.

I am not certain when we will return.

She drew back from the paper, her mouth twisted in disapproval.

"What?" he asked, feeling defensive. "I haven't signed my name yet, if that is your complaint. I was just about to get to it when you snatched it from me."

She tapped the paper, ignoring his comment. "This is the beginning and the end, but there is no middle. Where are we on a rescue mission to? Do we have enough funds, are we safe, did we plan on taking this journey together?" She shook her head. "You would not be a good novelist. It is a good thing you have a good head for business, because you cannot tease out a reader's excitement at all."

"Can I not?" Bennett allowed his gaze to drop to her mouth, sensing a challenge he would enjoy. That mouth he'd kissed just a few hours before. Her lips parted, and he saw her tongue dart out.

"How should I tease out the information, then?" he continued, putting his fingers on top of her hand. Starting to rub her skin gently, edging his chair closer to hers so their shoulders were only a few inches apart. He leaned over to speak in a soft whisper.

"Should I tell Alex that we have formed a

particular bond while traveling together?" He heard her breath hitch. "That I am discovering hidden depths in my not-exactly sister-in-law? That when we kiss, it is like being scorched by a glorious fire?" He leaned in closer, so close he could touch her ear with his lips.

So he did.

She jumped, gripping her left hand as he continued rubbing the right.

"You are a tease," she said in that low, husky voice. The voice he wanted to hear call his name.

He already knew she was passionate; what would she look like as she climaxed? What spots in particular would make her writhe in pleasure?

He desperately wanted to find out. But if he continued to think about it, he'd end up tossing her over his shoulder and taking her to a room, any room, to ravish her thoroughly.

And they had relatives to inform and letters to critique. He needed to focus. And not on her, or her luscious mouth, or the way she might cry out in passion.

"What will your letter say?" He drew back, but draped his left hand over the back of her chair, letting his fingers rest at the nape of her neck. There was only so much focusing he could do with her this close. "Dear Sister," he said as he winked at her, "I have escaped the tedium of my existence with the most exciting gentleman of my acquaintance. You might be surprised to hear who it is—"

"That is an understatement," she said wryly.

"But I assure you, he is devoted and concerned about the safety and care of my person. Particularly my—"

"Stop!" she said, biting her lip as she spoke. "Stop, or we'll never make the post."

He shrugged in mock obedience, returning his chair to its former place. "I will be certain to incorporate your suggestions into my letter. I do like it when you tell me what to do."

"Oh," she said on an intake of breath.

"You are welcome to order me to do anything you wish," he said, noting the heightened color on her cheeks.

YOU ARE WELCOME to order me to do anything you wish.

The words were so mild, but the impact of them sent her mind into a tumult, her brain conjuring up all sorts of things she hadn't realized were possible. Well, she did know they were possible—she'd seen some of Eleanor's naughty books—but she hadn't realized that they would pique her own interest.

"Have you finished your letter?" Bennett asked, interrupting her thoughts. Only it was him, and he was a substantial part of her thoughts, so it wasn't necessarily interrupting. Augmenting, perhaps.

"Uh—just about," she said, picking up her fountain pen.

What should she say? For all that she'd critiqued Bennett's words, she had no idea how to tell Pearl everything she might need to know.

Safe.

Della.

Lord Carson.

Back soon.

She shrugged, beginning to write, hoping Pearl would be satisfied both as to her safety and to her retrieval of Della. Taking the last swallow of her ale as she wrote, feeling as though right now, in this quiet pub, with him, was the closest she had ever come to pure happiness.

That was a terrifying thought, wasn't it? The man whom she'd promised multiple times not to marry was the one who made her feel safe, and happy, and appreciated.

Damn it, Ida. What are you doing?

She shook her head at herself, finishing the letter, folding it up as he waited, his own letter in front of him.

"You'll appreciate that I did not critique your letter as you did mine," Bennett said with a smile. He looked so much more casual and relaxed than she had ever noticed before—as though he'd stop shouldering, just for the moment, all the burdens he habitually carried around with him.

"That is because my letter has a plot, my lord," she said in mock severity. "A beginning, a middle, and a satisfying ending."

"I am sure your ending is very satisfying," he replied in a sly tone.

She did not know specifically to what he was referring, but she could discern it was something salacious—primarily because she was starting to blush, even though she had no idea why.

"It is so much fun to tease you," he said. And then his expression grew serious. "But of course anytime you do not wish to be teased, you will tell me? You can order me to stop as much as you can order me to not stop."

She felt her throat tighten. That he was aware of the constraints of being her, a female, prone in this situation. That he was so very concerned about her consent, about what she might want. Or not want.

"I know that." She stretched her hand across the table and took his. "I know that, and I thank you for it."

He squeezed her fingers, a sincere look on his face. "Thank you."

Chapter 10

While it can be exhilarating to embark on an adventure, it is important to keep in mind your ultimate purpose, whatever that might be.

LADY IDA'S TIPS FOR THE
ADVENTUROUS LADY TRAVELER

*S*o your sister doesn't know you are coming."

Ida shook her head as she chewed.

Bennett waited impatiently for her to finish. Why would anything be simple with this woman? *But if it were simple, you wouldn't be here.*

Fine. He wished it were less complicated, then.

"She doesn't. But I have a plan." Ida placed her spoon down on the table. They were eating at the same pub they'd written their letters in—it turned out it also served as the local inn, and so they'd managed to hire two rooms for the evening.

The food wasn't as good as Mrs. Hastings's meat pies, they both agreed, but it was warm and filling.

The staff had lit a fire in the fireplace near where they were seated, and the warmth of the fire along with the strength of the ale and the hot food combined to make Bennett feel as comfortable as he thought he might have ever been.

Although that could have been attributed to her as well. But actually no—he wasn't comfortable around her, necessarily; he was uncomfortable, but in a very pleasant way. Keenly aware of how passionate she was, what noises she made in the back of her throat when they kissed.

How she snapped back at him, not deferring just because he was who he was. She was most definitely not a Carson-hunter, and yet he felt as though he'd been ensnared. In her intelligence, her refreshing honesty, her vibrant enthusiasm for ale and meat pies and adventure.

"What is your plan, then?" Bennett inquired.

"I will find out where she is in Haltwhistle. Then I will persuade her to return with me. She has to, she cannot raise Nora without her child knowing who her relations are."

Bennett wanted to ask if the duke and duchess felt the same, only he thought he knew the answer.

"What if she refuses?"

Ida's mouth tightened. "I do not anticipate her saying no."

"Like you didn't anticipate me coming along

for the journey, or you going on the journey at all at that particular time?"

She glared at him, and he raised his eyebrows in question in return. A standoff that ended when she threw her hands up in the air.

"Fine. She could refuse. That is a possibility. One I do not believe will happen."

"As long as you admit you can be wrong, hedgehog."

"Many more times than before, thanks to you, leopard," she retorted.

He grinned, picking up his spoon and eating some more of the stew. The warmth of the fire, the warmth of her personality, the open-ended question of how long it would take and what would happen when they got there. He had truly escaped, hadn't he?

But he knew he couldn't escape forever. Eventually he would have to return. Eventually.

Meanwhile, he had this moment to savor. Ale to drink, and a gorgeous woman to look at and speak with.

"How would you go about persuading her? If you were me, that is?" she asked.

And now he felt even warmer—that Ida the Intelligent was asking his opinion on what to do was astounding. He knew she wouldn't ask unless she truly wanted to know. And she wouldn't want to know unless she trusted him, and his opinion.

He thought for a moment, keenly aware that he couldn't just toss out any idea. That he had to think about it, because she'd honored him by asking.

"I suppose I would tell her how much you and her other sisters miss her. That family means more than reputation."

She nodded, and he felt encouraged to continue.

"That her daughter should have that same sense of family. Also that your sister Olivia has access to all of Edward's money—which is substantial—so she wouldn't have to worry about her or her daughter's future."

"I don't think Della will want to be dependent on anyone," Ida commented.

"But at least knowing it is there, if she does need it, would be reassuring."

"True. What else?"

"If all else fails, you can tell her that unless she returns with you that your reputation will be irreparably damaged. Whereas if Society has the opportunity to think that you have just done a good deed by finding your sister, rather than running away with me, that they might reward you rather than scorn you."

"Especially since you were passed around my sisters like a plate of biscuits," she added.

"Ouch!" he said, reeling back in mock hurt.

"You certainly know how to wound a man's pride."

"Oh hush," she replied. "At least you were passed around. I was offered to someone with the assurance that he wouldn't get to know me before we got married in case he decided to refuse after all." She looked up at him, shaking her head. "Can you imagine how that makes me feel? I don't want anyone to ever feel as though they're not wanted."

"Which is why you're going after your sister," he said in understanding. "You want her to know that no matter what she does, you love her."

"Within reason. I mean, if she were to repudiate Linnaeus, for example, in favor of some lesser system . . ." she said, her voice trailing off.

"You'd classify her as *Idiotus Sisterum*?" he said with a smirk.

"Exactly." She beamed at him, and he basked in the glow of her smile.

"Is THERE ANYTHING else I can do for you, miss?" the maidservant asked.

The room was not quite as clean and tidy as Mrs. Hastings's offerings, but it was warm and cozy. Or perhaps that was just Ida, since she'd had a few more ales sitting downstairs with Bennett.

He was down the hall, and she resisted the

urge to go to his room, to discover what other kinds of things they could do together.

"Thank you, I am fine."

The servant nodded, and left the room, leaving Mary in her chemise. They'd purchased a night rail at the shop, so she withdrew it from the bag and laid it on the bed.

She felt restless and oddly unsatisfied, but not in an unhappy way; just as though there was something else she could be doing, and wanted to be doing, and wasn't.

You know what that is, a voice said inside her head.

I do, she admitted.

Before she removed her chemise, she put her hands on her upper chest, then over her breasts, then down to *there*, where it hadn't stopped aching. But in a good, entirely uncomfortable way.

She pressed against there with the heel of her hand, relieving some of the ache. Hmm. That felt interesting.

She raised one of her hands and put it back onto her breast, feeling how her nipple was hard and her breasts felt heavy. She ran her palm over her breast and sighed at the sensation. This was what it might feel like if he touched her. Here. There. Everywhere.

It felt good. She continued to press against her mound with her other hand, wanting more, and then she got onto the bed, twisting onto her back and dragging the bottom of her chemise up to her waist.

She brushed her fingers against herself, gasping at how it felt—so good, but there was definitely something more. Bennett would know what to do if he were here. How to find the something more she craved.

She put her finger right there, right where it ached the most, and then, tentatively, began to rub, her back arching as the pleasure spread throughout her body.

Meanwhile, she rubbed and squeezed her breasts, kneading them and feeling the hard nipple press against her palm.

She added more fingers to where she was rubbing down below, and that seemed to do something even more intense.

"Oh God," she whispered as she kept rubbing, thinking of him, and his hard body pressed against her, his hands pinning her against the door.

His mouth plundering hers as he kissed her, and she kissed him back, her hands in his sleekly styled hair, mussing it up.

And then she felt the moment when everything broke, and she spasmed down below, a warm rush of pleasure washing through her body, leaving her limp and satisfied.

Not as satisfied as if it had been him, but definitely satisfying nonetheless.

She sat up and removed her chemise, regarding her night rail with displeasure. She would sleep without anything on tonight, just to feel what it was like. This was an adventure, and the point of the adventure was to try new things. Things like kissing a man she was not intending to marry, and rubbing oneself to extreme pleasure, and sleeping nude.

She slid under the covers, gasping at how it felt for her skin to be directly touching the sheets. She'd never been so raw and exposed before. In so many ways.

Hmm. This was the satisfying ending he'd referenced, wasn't it?

How much more satisfying would it be if it were with him?

"You look well-rested this morning," Bennett said as she came to the table.

She blushed and nodded. "Yes, I slept quite well, thank you."

She was wearing one of her new gowns, in dark green with very little ornamentation. Serviceable. The severity of the gown's cut only highlighted just how beautiful she was, her dark hair pulled back from her pale, delicate face, her dark eyes holding a warm glint of laughter as she sat down.

Oh, he was besotted, wasn't he? Damn it.

"The maid came to help me get dressed this morning," she said. "And I asked her if she knew where Haltwhistle was. She said she thought it was only a few days from here. But that we're headed in the right direction. When I first looked at the atlas in Mr. Beechcroft's library, I thought it would be at least a week. It will be less than that, at least. You must be wanting to return home to London."

Not at all.

"I suppose," Bennett said, gesturing to one of the passing barmaids.

"Yes, sir?" she asked.

"Tea and whatever you have for breakfast, please," he replied.

"No ale?" Ida asked in a wistful tone.

He chuckled. "When you return to your parents' house, you'll have to ask them to serve up ale at their dinner parties."

"I highly doubt I will be in the position of making any demands when I return home," Ida replied, a rueful look on her face. "I wonder if I will be allowed to stay in the house, actually. I was hoping for some brilliant solution to spring into my brain, but so far my ideas for the future include moving into Mr. Beechcroft's library, Della and I opening some sort of home for scandalous women, or me getting banished to the country."

"The offer stands, you know."

She glanced away, biting her lip.

"I know you don't want to, but you could marry me if that is your only choice. I won't have you suffer because of this adventure. I promise I would leave you to live your own life."

Even though it would be the most difficult thing he had ever done.

"You're doing the right thing, you know," he continued. "Going to find Della, even if you don't know that she wants to be rescued."

"A damsel in distress who might not be in distress after all?" She uttered a derisive noise. "I won't be the cause of you not having a choice in your life. It would be hypocritical of me to even consider it, given how much I chafe against it in my own life."

What if I want to choose you?

But he couldn't say that to her. Not now, not without losing that trust he'd gained. And more than that, they had become friends. Friends who kissed at times, but friends nonetheless.

He wouldn't risk losing that friendship.

Even though he felt as though he were in danger of losing his heart.

"I'M STARVING," SHE said after an hour or so of not speaking.

Not that it was an awkward silence; it actually felt comfortable, as though they were at peace with themselves and one another.

Every so often, they'd pass another carriage, or see cows in a nearby field, and meet one another's eyes.

"We should be able to find a place to stop soon," he answered. Only a few more days of travel with her. Only a few more days to glory in the splendor of her, her wit, her kindness, her fierce intelligence.

It already hurt. Bennett focused on driving the carriage, not allowing himself to think too much about it. Just about the road ahead, and keeping his eye out for a place to stop for the night.

They drove past a few cottages, then followed a road that appeared to lead into a village, which was confirmed within a mile or so. This village looked smaller than the two others, and he glanced around at the few people who were walking around, looks of open curiosity tempered with suspicion on their faces.

"Which way to the inn?" he asked one of the pedestrians. The man didn't answer, just pointed down the road and kept walking.

"Taciturn group," Bennett said, keeping the horses on the road the man had pointed down.

The inn came into view a few minutes later, and Bennett regarded it with a critical eye, conscious of how Ida was glancing around them with interest. No doubt more learning experiences to add to her knowledge.

The inn was shabby, a few chickens strutting about in front. It appeared to be the only option, however, which meant he'd have to make a decision that would be more difficult for him than for her. "We'll say we're husband and wife," he said in a low voice. "I don't want you to sleep in your own room at this place."

"Yes, I agree," she said, and he exhaled in relief. And nearly as much anticipation.

"Can we help you?" an older grizzled man asked as he stepped out into the light from the inn, wincing as he did. That did not bode well for the inn's potential airiness.

"Yes, my wife and I will need a room for the night," Bennett replied, deliberately eschewing his normal aristocratic tones. He had found he was a good mimic, so it wasn't difficult for him to adopt the speech patterns of his London merchant acquaintances.

"We've got a room, if you're certain," the man said in a skeptical tone, glancing between the two of them. Apparently they did not look like the inn's usual clientele, which made Bennett even more determined that they would share a room, despite its potential for far more frustration.

"We are," Ida said, altering her own voice. Bennett looked over at her, surprised at her adept reading of the situation as well as her own ability with a different accent.

"Then we'll get your horses taken care of and show you up to your room." The man whistled, and a young boy ran up, his eyes wide at seeing the carriage. "Take the carriage round to the back, and water and feed the horses," the man ordered. "If you'll step this way, we'll see what we can do about some food."

He did not sound confident.

Matching Bennett's own thoughts.

Bennett took Ida's hand in his, drawing her close to his side.

It was dark inside, as Bennett had expected, and there were a few patrons who already seemed the worse for wear.

"Sit there," the innkeeper commanded. Not the pleasantly bossy tones of Mrs. Hastings.

Bennett helped Ida into her seat—even though she didn't need any help—and took the chair opposite, aware that the inn's inhabitants were staring at them.

"Good evening, everyone," he said, gesturing broadly. "My wife and I are here for the night.

We are heading to Haltwhistle. Does anyone happen to know its whereabouts? My wife"—and then he leaned forward and chucked Ida on the chin, delighting in her look of stifled outrage—"lost the map." Silence. "Of course I will buy a round for the room, if anyone has the information."

"I do," a voice said from the far corner. A broad man dressed in plain farmers' clothing walked toward them, removing his cap as he did. "It's only about ten miles from here, you can just follow that road you came in on."

"Oh, excellent!" Ida blurted out, forgetting to unculture her tone.

Bennett shot her a warning glance, and she clapped her hand over her mouth. "Thank you," he replied, rising. "A round of drinks for everyone here, if you please," he called out. The innkeeper nodded as the room's inhabitants cheered.

"Ten miles," Bennett said to Ida as he lowered himself back into his chair. "It shouldn't take more than half a day. We can be there tomorrow afternoon."

They both sat in silence, Bennett wishing the man had said it was at least another week's worth of travel.

"I can't believe it was that easy," she said at last in an awed tone.

Bennett raised his eyebrows. "So easy. You merely had to steal a carriage with me inside, drive north together, spend a few nights at some of England's finest lodgings, agree not to get married, and hope that nobody from our world would see us."

She narrowed her gaze at him, folding her arms over her chest. "Hmph," she said. "I think it feels as though it were easy because it was—it was so pleasant." Her cheeks were flushed, as though she were confiding in him again.

He had to admit to liking how that felt.

"It was pleasant," he agreed. "But it's not finished yet, not by a mile. Or ten," he added with a smirk. "And once we get there, you'll need to persuade your sister to return. And then hope we make it back to London without anybody from our world seeing us. Then we might have a chance of you not having to move into Mr. Beechcroft's library."

"Food." The innkeeper placed two wooden bowls on the table sharply, making both of them jump in their seats. "You owe me for the food, the drinks, and the lodging. I'll take that now, if you don't mind."

Bennett wanted to retort at the innkeeper's belligerent tone, but shut his mouth when he saw Ida shaking her head slowly, as though she knew he wanted to engage.

"Here," Ida said, withdrawing the money from within her gown somewhere. She placed it into the innkeeper's outstretched palm, then bestowed a patently false smile. Not that the innkeeper was paying attention; he was staring down at the coins in his hand and walked off without acknowledging the payment.

"Not quite up to Mrs. Hastings's standards," Ida said, picking up her spoon. She dipped it into the bowl and brought it to her mouth, then wrinkled her nose and took a bite of whatever it was.

What was it?

Bennett debated picking up his own spoon and eating, but judging by the play of expressions on her face—surprise, contemplation, and then a dawning horror—he decided he'd probably rather go hungry.

"That is awful," she said, confirming what he'd seen on her face.

"We should just head up to bed," Bennett said, glancing around their surroundings. The other inhabitants had gotten less interested in what they were doing, but it seemed that they had gotten more interested in whatever alcohol the innkeeper was serving them. "I doubt this clientele is here for the food, so they must be here for the drink."

"Of course," Ida replied. "We should go to bed." And then her eyes widened as she realized what she'd said, and she licked her lips, which only made Bennett think about it more.

Damn it, he wished he weren't so honorable. Because if he weren't, he wouldn't have a moment's hesitation about what they might possibly do together, alone, with a bed in the room.

But he was honorable. Even if his cock had risen to the occasion, making him wince as he rose as well.

Hoping she didn't notice.

Chapter 11

*S*he couldn't help but notice what was happening there as he stood. If she were another kind of woman, she'd probably be horrified and appalled that his body had reacted to her words with such—alacrity.

Instead, she wished she could ask him about it. Did it hurt? What would the inevitable result of it be?

But for once she didn't just ask questions in pursuit of knowledge. Not because she wasn't curious—of course she was—but because she had to imagine that it would be a difficult thing to discuss.

"I took our bags up myself," Bennett said as he walked close behind her. She could feel his presence at her back, which made her feel all tingly.

"I will wait in the hallway while you change. Just call out when you are under the covers."

He opened a door at the end of the hall, gesturing for her to step inside. She hadn't had strong expectations of the quality of the room, given the exterior and the inedible food, and her expectations, low that they were, were met. The bed dominated the room, its coverlet a jarringly cheery red color in the midst of mismatched dark furniture and smoky windows.

Their bags were at the foot of the bed, and she turned her head to nod at him. "I won't take long."

He nodded. "I wouldn't expect you would," he replied, closing the door.

She withdrew her night rail and twisted her hands behind her so she could undo her buttons. Thank goodness she was flexible enough to do it herself; she did not want to ask him for help. It was awkward enough, having seen his . . . alacrity downstairs in the public room.

She got dressed quickly, launching herself toward the bed and pulling the cover up to her chin. "I'm in bed," she called, then winced as she realized what she'd just yelled.

Hopefully only he had heard her.

He stepped inside, closing the door firmly behind him. He glanced toward her, then cleared his throat as he looked away, moving to crouch on the floor in front of his bag.

"If you don't mind closing your eyes for a minute," he said in a strained tone.

She felt a giggle lurking in her chest, but suppressed it. He would not appreciate being laughed at. Or he would appreciate it, and then they would both be laughing, and then other things would happen. As they had in the carriage.

Although she had to be honest, that was entirely her doing.

She squeezed her eyes shut, hearing the noises of fabric shifting. Squeezing her eyes more tightly when she was tempted to open them to see what he might look like with less clothing on.

"Here," he said, and she felt a thump as something landed on the bed. Not him, fortunately. Or unfortunately, she couldn't say which she'd prefer.

Drat. That wasn't something she should even be admitting to herself.

He'd tossed his coat on the bed, and she looked at it, and then at him. "Are you expecting me to go out?" she asked in a haughty tone.

He shook his head, chuckling, then drew the coat so it lay in a straight line right in the middle of the bed. "So I had heard of this practice from the Americas. It is called bundling." He gestured toward the coat. "It's a way for courting couples to spend time together without being compromised."

"By placing a coat between them." She arched an eyebrow at him to accompany her skeptical tone of voice.

"Not a coat, hedgehog. I am improvising. But, yes, the point is that there be some sort of physical barrier between two people as they share a common space. Like the walls of Jericho, only neither of us has a trumpet."

Of course. The walls of Jericho. "Oh."

"You're not convinced."

She shrugged. "If you want to have an artificial barrier to protect yourself from my advances . . ."

He heaved an exasperated sigh as he got into the bed. She felt the mattress dip with his weight.

"It's not your advances I'm concerned about, Ida." The way he said her name—it made her body heat, and she couldn't help but wriggle her feet in some sort of bizarre dissociative response.

"It's mine." He leaned up to blow out the candle he'd placed on the nightstand on his side of the bed, plunging them into darkness. Oh, she wished it didn't feel quite so intimate. "I know that you and I—that we agreed about the future, but when I kiss you . . . When I touch you, I can't seem to remember that." His voice lowered, and it felt as though the world had shrunk to just the two of them, alone and adrift in the darkness. "I want you, Ida. And it would be a terrible mistake."

Just when she'd been considering reaching over to touch him. Just then, he'd said it—"a terrible mistake." Of course. Because they'd agreed that neither one of them wanted the other. He wanted someone soft as a wife, even if he might want her now as—as something else.

"Yes. It would be." She was proud of herself that she hadn't let any emotion color her voice—that he had no idea what she was thinking.

Even though she wished he did know what she was thinking. That he often seemed to guess correctly what she was thinking was remarkable.

Come to think of it.

And then she had to grin at her own illogic, even though finding illogic amusing was not at all her way. It was . . . illogical, in fact.

"Are you laughing?" He sounded incredulous.

Of course he would be. He'd just admitted that he wanted her, in a dark, hopefully depraved and passionate way, and she apparently found that amusing.

Well, that likely made him want her a bit less. Which could only help the situation.

"No, it wasn't—that is, yes I was laughing, but not at you. I promise."

He was silent for a moment, and she caught her breath, hoping he would understand. Or at least be willing to overlook her inappropriate behavior.

Which wasn't nearly as inappropriate as what it seemed he wished to do with her.

But she couldn't think about that.

But it seemed it was all she could think about after all.

"You mentioned before that I was welcome to order you to do anything I wish. That you usually were the one to take an initiative. That you wanted someone else to take charge."

HE HEARD THE movement of fabric, and then the unmistakable sound of a body shifting, and then she was on top of him, her hands in his hair, her warm mouth pressed on his.

So much for the walls of Jericho.

She urged his mouth open with her lips, sliding her tongue inside, her nails raking on his scalp, making him feel as though his entire world had just reduced to this moment, this dark room, her body on his, separated by the coverlet as his arms wrapped around her, his hands settling at her lower back.

So close to her arse. He stroked her back up and down as she kissed him. And it was her kissing him; she took the lead and he surrendered it gratefully, letting her set the pace of their kiss, relishing the feel of not being in charge. *For once.*

She was responding to his words, of course. She was taking initiative, doing things on her own, not waiting for him to begin.

She moved her mouth from his lips to his jaw, bestowing tiny kisses as she worked her way down to his neck, licking his skin, her hands tugging on his hair, her body moving on top of his.

His cock was hard, aching for the brief contacts her body made with it. He heard a groan, and realized it was him. She chuckled softly, and he felt her laughter on his skin.

"I want to see you," she said, moving her body so she was straddling him. She leaned over him, and he could feel the movement of her, and it was even more alluring that her breast was so close to him, likely barely covered by her night rail.

His throat thickened, as did his cock.

He heard the strike of the match, then the flame of the candle, setting a soft glow where they were.

His eager eyes could gaze at her in the candlelight, the flicker of the flame causing intriguing shadows around her body.

She made a satisfied noise, then eased herself back down so she still straddled him, but her face was slightly below his.

He reached for her, but she swatted his hands

away as she shook her head. "You said you wanted someone else to do the work. So now I am," she remonstrated, placing his hands firmly on the coverlet on either side of his body.

Oh. This was very interesting indeed. He'd never been in such a submissive position before. Not out of bed, and certainly not in it.

This was nothing like he'd ever experienced before. And he most definitely liked it.

She was sitting on her heels, just looking at him as though pondering what to do next.

"You said you wanted to see me?" he asked in a ragged voice. One roughened by need and passion.

"I do." And then she leaned forward, undoing the buttons of his nightshirt as she pressed her lips to his exposed skin.

Her fingers slid underneath the fabric, onto his upper chest, her fingertips surveying his body as though it were an atlas and she was a very interested explorer.

And then she lowered her mouth to him, kissing his chest, dragging her teeth over his skin, all the while making soft noises deep in her throat.

She rested her body on top of his again, and he felt even more blissfully and agonizingly trapped.

"Your skin feels so different from mine," she murmured.

"I wouldn't know that, since I haven't been able to touch you," he replied reproachfully.

"Patience, leopard," she said, drawing the coverlet down to his waist, wrapping her fist in the fabric of his nightshirt. "Just be. Just for right now."

And she yanked her hand down, shredding his nightshirt and separating the two halves, placing her palms on her thighs as she gazed at him, her tongue emerging to lick her lips.

He had never been in such acutely painful ecstasy in his life.

And then she put her hands back on him, sliding her palms over his nipples as he shuddered at her touch. "I like this," she said in a low voice as she ran her fingers through his chest hair, tugging a little bit as she lifted her fingers to drag one fingertip from his breastbone down to his abdomen, making him inhale sharply.

"Does this feel good?" she asked.

"It does," he said through gritted teeth. His hands twitched on the coverlet, desperate to touch her, but not wanting to disturb her explorations.

"Mmm," she replied, lowering her mouth to one nipple, licking it before closing her mouth over it. He bucked underneath her, jostling her, his cock straining to bury itself inside her.

"Ida," he said, hearing the pleading in his voice, but not sure what he was asking for.

She chuckled against his skin, sliding her body down so she could bring her tongue from his nipple to underneath his pectoral muscle, down to the top of the hair that led down to the thatch of hair around his cock.

"What do you want me to do now?" she asked. It wasn't a rhetorical question, and he knew she would welcome an honest answer.

"I want you to touch me. There." He punctuated his word with a thrust of his hips, and she nodded, wriggling down the bed farther as she slid the coverlet down so it was below where he throbbed.

She sat up to rest on her heels again, her hands clasping the fabric of his nightshirt, dragging it up to rest on his lower belly.

His cock rose proud and straight in front of her, and her eyes widened, making him both pleased and anxious. He knew she hadn't seen a male member before, and he hoped she wasn't horrified.

"How does that do that?" she asked wonderingly before placing her palm on it to grip his shaft.

He groaned at her touch. Not horrified, thank god.

"Now what do I do?"

"Stroke it. Up and down," he said, willing himself not to move, not to touch her, as he so desperately wished to do.

She caught her lip with her teeth, then began to do as he'd said, sliding her hand up and down his cock, her expression entirely focused on the matter at hand. So to speak.

He didn't think it was possible to get even harder, but he could feel himself thickening under her touch.

"Is this right?" she asked.

"Yes, God, Ida, it is so right." He could barely speak.

She kept stroking, sliding her fingers over the top of his cock before bringing her palm down again.

"A little faster," he urged, and she did, her breath coming out in short, wicked gasps that filled the room.

He could see she was shifting as well, likely because her sweet nub needed the friction her hand was currently giving him.

"I need to touch you," he said, and he didn't wait for her permission, but put his palm right there, right where her night rail was bunched up, his fingers finding her wet and slick. Making him even more lust-crazed.

He slid his fingers along her slit, his thumb on her small pearl, rubbing gently.

"Ohh," she moaned, widening her legs to allow him better access. "It feels much better when you do it," she said.

"You've done this to yourself?" he asked, images immediately coming to mind. "I want to see you climax, Ida."

"Is that what it's called? That explosion?" She'd slowed the speed of her hand, and he rolled his hips to remind her that there were more important things than etymological questions.

"Yes, climax. A little death," he added, sliding his finger inside her where she was tight and wet.

"Ohh," she said again, stroking her hand faster on his cock.

And then he was coming, his back arching, everything forgotten but how good it felt. She gasped as he spilled onto his belly, and she released her hold of him, staring at him from under heavy lids.

He waited until the pulse of his cock lessened, and then he began to work her again, rubbing her nub as he slid his finger in and out of her, adding a second finger as she began to writhe on top of him.

"God, Bennett," she gasped as he felt her spasm under his hand, watching her face as she closed her eyes and tilted her head back, her hands fisted.

It was glorious to watch her climax. He felt ridiculously proud of having brought her to that point just by watching her reactions and timing his touch accordingly. And, still, she remained entirely in charge of all of it, of their pleasure, and it was unlike anything he'd ever experienced before.

He didn't want this moment ever to end—both of their climaxes subsiding, the feelings leaving a soft, luxurious well-pleasured sensation. Alone in the dark together with nobody knowing where they were.

"That was amazing," she said as she got off his body to lie against him, one arm thrown over his chest.

"And you took the lead. As you knew I wanted, but I didn't know myself." He picked up her hand and kissed her fingers. "Thank you."

"You are welcome," she said as she yawned.

He grabbed the edge of his nightshirt and wiped away his seed, then sat up partway to remove it, dropping it on the floor.

"And all it took was one ruined nightshirt," he said as he lay back down.

"Your coat didn't do its job very well," she observed, yanking the coat out from under herself and tossing it to the other side of the bed.

"That's because it had a very determined opponent," he replied, gathering her in his arms. "You are far more powerful than a mere trumpet."

"Whatever that means," she said sleepily. "But thank you," she said in a pleased voice.

Chapter 12

Sometimes you have to compromise.

LADY IDA'S TIPS FOR THE
ADVENTUROUS LADY TRAVELER

*G*ood morning." The rumble of Bennett's voice echoed through Ida's head, and she realized she was lying on his chest, her body pressed up against his.

It felt warm, and delicious, and utterly sinful.

"Good morning," she replied, stretching. "Oh!" she said, scrambling to a seated position, "we are so close to finding Della! We should get moving," and she got off the bed, looking around frantically for her clothing.

It shouldn't have felt so natural to be here with him in the morning. Especially since she had insisted on having her own bedroom when she was five years old, and hadn't shared with anyone since.

But that didn't seem to matter. It just felt right.

She heard the rustle of movement behind her, and froze; should she turn around or stay as she was, so she wouldn't see him getting dressed? And why was all of her clothing tossed around the floor? She never thought she'd miss having a lady's maid, and yet she could have used some tidying up.

It seemed like a ridiculous notion to worry about turning around or not, since she had seen—and touched—most of him the previous night. But still. There was something about activities done in the middle of the night and then there was the next morning.

"It is safe to look at me, Ida," he said in an amused tone. As though he knew the quandary she was in and was laughing at her. Again.

She was as unaccustomed to being laughed at as she was sharing a room, and yet both felt so comfortable. As comfortable as she'd been apparently sleeping on him.

Had she drooled? Dear God, she hoped she hadn't drooled.

She found her chemise and flung it over her head, shimmying to let it drop to the floor. Hearing his intake of breath in response.

Oh. Well, that was intriguing.

She found her gown and put that on also, turning back around before she'd properly drawn it up over her body. Smothering a satisfied smile as his eyes widened as he saw her.

So perhaps it wasn't entirely odd that she would want to see more of him the next day, since it seemed he was just as interested in seeing her.

She walked toward him, a strangely power-ful feeling surging through her as she saw him swallow. "Can you do up my buttons, please?" she asked, spinning to present her back to him. She swept her hair over one shoulder and glanced back.

His hands skimmed over her waist, drawing the edges of the gown together, and she took one step back so she was closer to him. So close she could feel his breath on her neck.

But much as she'd love to explore more of what else might happen, Della was out there. Not waiting for her sister, since she had no idea Ida was coming, but out there, nonetheless?

She regretfully decided against more provoca-tion, waiting as she felt his fingers do up the last of her buttons.

She bit her lip as she felt his mouth graze her nape, kissing her so softly she might have thought she'd imagined it if she weren't so at-tuned to every single thing that was happening at the moment.

What were they even doing?

She probably shouldn't spend time answering that, either. Mostly because she didn't think that even she, Ida of the Honest Truth, could face the reality, and the fact that this would all be over as soon as they found her sister.

"Are you ready?" she asked, turning back around as she smoothed her skirts. Trying not to meet his gaze, not wanting to know what she'd see; passion, impatience, frustration? Any of them would remind her who she was and who he was and that they were here for no other purpose than to locate her sister and bring her home. "I hope Della is pleased to see me," she said hesitantly, not at all how she would sound were she with anybody but him. Even her sisters.

She trusted him. Trusted him in a different way than she had ever trusted anyone.

It was terrifying and wonderful, all at the same time.

And it would be ending soon.

"GOOD MORNING, MY lady, my lord."

A fresh-faced boy—remarkably different in both looks and attitude from the otherwise dour staff—greeted them as they descended the stairs, Bennett holding both of their bags, his hand resting on Ida's back. For protection, he assured himself.

Not that she needed protection. He just liked touching her. He could admit that to himself.

"Good morning," Ida said, returning the boy's smile. "Are you serving breakfast this morning?"

"I am," the boy said in a proud voice. He was probably about thirteen years old, with dark, unruly hair that needed to be cut.

"What is your name?" Ida asked as she sat down. "I am Ida."

The boy bobbed his head as Bennett took a seat in the chair opposite. "Sheldon. I help out here since my mother was hurt."

"What happened?" Ida asked in a concerned tone of voice.

Bennett watched her expression—how had he ever thought she was just incredibly intelligent, without regard for her fellow human? Right now, her eyes were warm and interested, and there was a softness about her mouth that indicated she truly cared.

"Mam worked here, in the kitchen, but had a pot explode or something. Right in her face. She hurt her eyes real bad, and the doctor said she can't work until they're healed. It costs money for the doctor, and there's me and my brother and sister."

Ida reached out and touched Sheldon's hand, her eyes moist. "That is terrible. Here," she said, digging into her pocket and withdrawing some change. "Take this. For your Mam and your siblings."

"I couldn't," the boy said, even as his fingers were closing over the money.

"You can," Ida said in a firm tone. "You will." She looked at Bennett. "It isn't right that this family suffers because of an accident, is it?" It was a demand, not a question. "This is the kind of thing your efforts prevent, I hope?" she asked.

Bennett swallowed. Yes. All those people, all those families, depending on his work and the family's support so they could live and even thrive. "Yes," he said. "Yes, it is."

"Can I get you tea? Toast?" Sheldon asked as he wiped his eyes.

Bennett nodded.

"Please, Sheldon. And thank you," she added, offering another warm smile.

Bennett leaned across the table after Sheldon had returned to the kitchen. "You do know that you have drastically reduced our funds," he informed her. "Thankfully it seems we won't need to be on the road for too much longer. Are you always this impet—never mind, I know the answer."

She wrinkled her nose at him.

"Hedgehog," he said.

"It is the right thing to do, and you know it. How can we listen to something like that and not do something?"

Oh. She would do something, wouldn't she? Always.

She must have read his expression accurately, since she lifted her chin, all of her prickly demeanor on display. "Another reason why it is such a good thing we will not, in fact, be married. Can you imagine what would happen when one of your fellow lords—one not as caring as you—makes a comment about the undeserving poor or disparages an effort I've supported?" She shook her head. "You would not want a wife like that." She snorted. "I imagine even Charles Dickens would find me too opinionated on occasion. Your *soft and welcoming female* would never embarrass you in that way."

Nor would she inspire me to greatness, Bennett thought.

"Nor would you want a husband who had to associate with that type of person, I assume."

She lifted her chin even higher. "Of course not."

His prickly, forthright, opinionated hedgehog. She would never compromise on anything. Something he should keep in mind when regretting not being able to spend the rest of his life with her.

"WHAT DO YOU mean the carriage is gone?" Bennett took a step closer to the innkeeper, whose belligerent expression grew more truculent.

"My boy took care of your horses, and then went to bed. When he got up this morning, everything was gone." The man shrugged, as though it was an everyday occurrence. Perhaps it was, and Bennett was an idiot for having stopped here. But they had no choice.

"Are there any conveyances for hire?" Ida interrupted.

Not that they had enough money, Bennett thought. Since Ida had handed most of it over to Sheldon, who was standing by the doorway, his mouth hanging open as he watched the discussion.

The innkeeper shook his head. "Nothing out here. It's not as though this village is overflowing with fancy traveling rigs like yours."

"Probably why ours was taken," Bennett said in a bitter tone.

"You can wait and send for the magistrate if you want. He normally stops by once a week. He was here day before last, so he should be here in five days."

"Five days!" Ida exclaimed. "We cannot wait five days. We have to get to where we're going now."

Bennett turned to look at her, her eyes wide and pleading, her voice shaking with emotion. How could he deny her the chance to see her sister as soon as possible? Besides which, there was the whole "enough funds" thing.

"We'll have to walk."

Ida threw her hands up. "I don't care if I have to crawl. I have to get there."

Bennett looked at her for one more moment, taking in her determination, her fierce commitment, and knew there was nothing he would do to prevent her from seeing Della as soon as they could get there. Even if he had to carry her.

"Fine." He strode over to their bags, which they'd brought out into the courtyard. "We'll need to take only what's absolutely necessary," he said as he crouched down and opened his valise. He took out his torn nightshirt, his mood lightening as he recalled just how it ended up shredded in two.

Although now it meant he had no nightshirt. So there was that.

"I don't need much of anything," Ida said as she knelt beside him, opening her own bag. He appreciated how well she was able to adapt— most young ladies would need no fewer than three trunks to gallivant around the countryside.

Granted, she had left on impulse, bringing only the clothing she was wearing. But still.

"Here," she said, holding up one of her serviceable gowns toward Sheldon. "Your mother can likely use this."

The boy stepped forward and took the garment, his eyes wide in astonishment.

Bennett bit his tongue before suggesting perhaps they could sell the gown for some extra money. It wasn't as though this town appeared to be a place where people would have enough to purchase used clothing from impulsive young ladies.

So in that spirit—"Here," Bennett said, taking one of his shirts out from the bag, "this might fit you in a year or so." Sheldon took the shirt and folded it over his arm.

"Thank you," he said in a wondering voice. "I didn't know that—I wasn't sure that there were people who would—" And then he blinked rapidly, looking down at the ground.

"Get to work, boy!" the innkeeper yelled from across the yard. "And you, if you don't need food or another night's lodging, you two can be on your way."

Bennett put his hand over Ida's mouth as she opened it to reply. "There is no point to it. He'll just end up being meaner to Sheldon here, since we will be long gone."

Her lips were warm on his palm. She glared at him, and he held her gaze until eventually she gave a reluctant nod.

So perhaps his termagant could be tamed. Good to know.

SHE SWUNG HER arms as she walked, glad not to be in that miserable village any longer, even though now they had to walk all the way to Haltwhistle.

He was beside her, taking one stride for two of hers. He did have very long legs. She sighed as she thought about them, and about the night before.

His voice interrupted her sensual recollections, and she felt herself start to blush. *Ridiculous, Ida. You are both agreed as to what this is, and you should not be embarrassed.* Even though she absolutely was.

Because, apparently, she was more of a traditional young lady than she realized. Did that mean she also wanted what traditional young ladies did? Marriage and children and all of that?

But he was speaking, thank goodness, so she couldn't ponder that.

"Have you thought more about your plans if you are able to persuade your sister to return with you?"

"*When* I am able to persuade my sister to return with me," Ida corrected, sounding much more confident than she felt.

"When. Of course." He spoke in the tone he used when he called her a hedgehog, and she wished he were wrong—but no, she was being prickly again. She could admit that, at least to herself.

But she was his hedgehog.

Oh, no. No, she wasn't. She was her own hedge-hog? That sounded entirely odd.

"I expect that our parents will refuse to have anything to do with us," Ida said matter-of-factly. "Unless we are somehow able to pull off some sort of reputation miracle, we will be on our own. But we'll be together, and it will be wonderful." Now she did feel as confident as she sounded. She hadn't valued family as much before, but as soon as Della had left, she and her sisters had begun to support one another, so much so that Ida had made herself a spectacle in society to ensure her sister Eleanor could have time to find her own happiness.

That Ida's happiness was likely to be loving books and her sisters rather than in a marriage was that thing she couldn't consider right now.

He hadn't replied, she realized. "Do you think it's a stupid plan?" she asked. Drat, she had never cared what people thought of her or her ideas before.

"Nothing you could possibly think of would ever be stupid," he said, making her chest relax. "Except for, perhaps, stealing a carriage without a clue about how you plan to accomplish what you want."

She laughed, nudging him in the ribs with her elbow.

"But I want you to do what you think is right."

"Thank you. I haven't figured out how we'll live."

"I am certain you and your remarkable brain will think of something," he replied.

She turned to him and smiled. "That is a lovely thing to say."

DEAR LORD. THAT smile. She'd smiled at him, and it was as though a billion stars shot through the darkness to light up the night. He never wanted to stop seeing that smile.

Damn it.

He'd done it.

He'd gone and fallen in love with his prickly hedgehog, the woman whose future plans most definitely did not include him.

Why did he have to go and fall in love with the one woman in the world who didn't want him? Who wasn't a Carson-hunter? Who couldn't compromise, even if it meant their happiness?

He wished he could just stop in the middle of the road and howl his frustration, but he wouldn't slow her down just because he was anguished and in love.

God damn it. He couldn't even tell her, because he knew her first obligation was to her sister, and he wouldn't muddle her mission up with his admission of love.

And even if he told her, he had no idea if she

reciprocated. *Neither one of us has any expectation that it means any more than it does*, she'd said.

He had no basis for thinking any of that had changed. Yes, the night before, they had found pleasure together—the thought of how she looked and sounded as she climaxed was enough to get him hard, even in the throes of love-soaked agony—but that didn't mean she would welcome his proposal.

She'd likely be stunned to receive it, in fact; hadn't he told her he wanted someone soft and gentle as a wife? He winced as he thought about it.

"Are you all right?" she asked, interrupting his thoughts. Thank god.

"Fine, yes." He glanced up at the sky, grateful there was something to comment on. "It looks as though it might rain."

She lifted an eyebrow as though to call him out on his obvious comment, but refrained, instead peering up and nodding. "It does. How much longer do you suppose we have to go?"

Bennett shifted the bag from one hand to the other as he thought. "Maybe another two hours? Do you need to rest or—or do anything else?"

She chuckled. "I am fine. I can feel a blister forming, but I should be—"

"Let me look at it," he interrupted, dropping the bag. If he couldn't tell her he loved her, he could at least take care of her while they were together. "Sit down there," he ordered, pointing at a log that lay to the side of the road they were on.

"So bossy," she murmured, but she did as he'd said, lowering herself to the log and beginning to remove her shoe.

He knelt down in front of her, swatting her hands away as he undid her shoe. There was the beginning of a blister there, right on her big toe, and he took her foot in his hand and began to rub her instep.

"Mmm," she said. "That feels wonderful. I am not certain it is helping the blister, but it feels fantastic."

He rubbed her foot for a few more minutes, then let go to undo his cravat. "Here, we can put this around that area. It might protect your skin."

He wrapped the fabric around her foot, tucking it in on itself so it would stay in place. He picked up her shoe and slid her foot back into it, making sure the fabric remained tight.

"You are so clever," she said, and the impact of her words were as though she'd smiled at him all over again.

"I cannot believe the redoubtable Lady Ida has just told someone else that they were clever," he replied, getting to his feet and holding his hand out for her to rise as well.

"I have told you many times you are clever," she retorted. "Haven't I?"

"I suppose. I like to hear you say it, though."

"You are so clever, my lord. My leopard," she said with a grin.

She stood, leaning into him as she wrapped her arms around his neck. He slid his arm around her waist and yanked her up against his body, relishing the feel of her soft curves as he lowered his head to hers.

Fine, so he wouldn't offer her protestations of love, but he could kiss her, and that would have to do for now.

Ah, THIS WAS what she'd been missing all day. His kiss. Them together, his body pressed into hers, that part of him making its presence known against her belly.

She raked her nails down his back, as she knew he liked, her mouth tilting up as he groaned.

She bit gently on his lip, then slid her tongue inside his mouth where it found his tongue, and she sucked on it as she slid her nails down, grabbing hold of his firm arse and squeezing.

His hands were at her waist, sliding up her body to find her breasts, and her body went all tingly as he palmed them in his hand. Her breasts felt fuller and so, so sensitive, and she wished she had known all this the night before when they had been in bed together.

Just the thought of him touching her bare

breasts as his fingers worked their magic down there was enough to make her moan, and she pushed up against him, kissing him fiercely, ferociously, until his mouth, his touch, his body were all she could think of.

"God, Ida," he said, breaking the kiss as he lowered his mouth to her neck. She raised her head to give him better access, and he took it, licking and sucking her skin as his hands rubbed her breasts, his fingers dragging across her nipples, which felt achingly responsive.

"Touch me," she whispered, and he slid his fingers down into her gown, finding her nipple and pinching it between his fingers, making her feel a delicious agony.

A past Ida, an Ida who hadn't kissed him, who hadn't touched him or been touched by him, would have said this constant wanting, this need, was irrational. That it didn't make sense for someone to be so consumed with passion.

But it was rational; all of this made her feel better than she'd ever felt in her life, and it was natural, it was *rational*, to want to continue to experience it. To experience him.

He slid his palm to lift her breast up and out of her gown, the air on her skin making her shudder.

And then she shuddered even more as he moved his mouth down, his lips on her nipple, his tongue licking her, making her arch her back.

More. She wanted more.

She could feel him, hard and erect against her body, and she moved her hand so it was between them, rubbing that firmness as he continued to suck her nipple.

"God, Ida," he said again, and she traced the outlines of him with her hand as he rocked his hips forward.

She heard a noise, and didn't know if it was him or her, she just succumbed to the feeling, the emotions swirling through her body, each one of his touches making her shiver, until—

Crack!

They sprang apart at the sound of the lightning, both of them immediately looking up into the storm-darkened sky.

And then the rain started as they heard the thunder, a mild rain that turned into a torrent within moments.

She spared a moment to think ruefully about her previous refusal to discuss the weather. If they had discussed it more in depth, perhaps they wouldn't have just been startled by a storm. Then again, it would have meant they wouldn't have been kissing.

Ida yanked her gown back up as Bennett sprinted toward their bag, picking it up and tucking it under his arm before returning to her.

He held his hand out, rain already streaming down his face, and she took it, shaking her skirts out as she started to run. Feeling an irrepressible urge to laugh, despite it all. Or perhaps because of it all.

"We should find shelter," he shouted as another bolt of lightning sizzled across the sky.

"Why didn't I think of that?" she retorted, and he laughed, shaking his head as rain streamed off his head.

Eventually, Ida had to slow; Bennett looked inquiringly at her, then slowed his own pace down.

He was still holding her hand, and it felt as though that was the only warmth she was experiencing. Her feet hurt, her hair was sopping wet, her whole self felt as though it had been submerged in a rain barrel.

A good reminder never to mock weather discussions again. Or, at the very least, make certain an umbrella was included in the essential items needed when one left London in search of an errant sister.

She'd make a note of that for next time.

"I see a farmhouse up ahead," he said, nodding toward that direction. "Hopefully we can persuade the people there that we're not dangerous. I'm sure we look terrifying," he added with a smile. His hair was plastered against his head, and she could see raindrops on his eyelashes. The rain had lessened, but it was still steady, and Ida was entirely and thoroughly soaked.

At least she wasn't thinking about her blister anymore.

"You do look terrifying. I'm certain I do as well."

His eyes found hers. "You look beautiful, as you always do," he said in a quieter tone, so low she wasn't certain he'd actually said it.

But his expression and how his hand tightened on hers confirmed that he had. And now her hand wasn't the only warm thing; her heart felt all melty inside her chest as her body responded to the compliment.

The only person who had ever commented on her appearance was her mother, who had admonished her to be less . . . *less*, whatever that meant.

But his words were sincere, even though she knew she was drenched and likely looked like a drowned rat. And it didn't matter, she felt beautiful. Even if she also felt soaked through.

"Let's go," he said, walking swiftly as she followed.

Chapter 13

*The mode of transportation is not important—
take a carriage, a train, or walk. The important
thing is to go.*

LADY IDA'S TIPS FOR THE
ADVENTUROUS LADY TRAVELER

$\mathcal{U}$p there," Bennett said, turning back to Ida. She was walking just a few steps behind him, holding her skirts up, rain streaming down her face, her hair undone, entirely wet and sticking to her skin and her body.

She had never looked more gorgeous.

"Up where?" she said in her prickly hedgehog voice, ameliorated by the grin she shot his way.

He would never get tired of her smile.

"There's a building up ahead. We should head that way. At the worst, it will be a roof."

"And at the best there will be a fire." She sounded rapturous, and she quickened her pace to come alongside him.

"And possibly a delicious stew. And tea. With lemon, of course," he added.

He heard her make a startled noise, and turned to her, hoping she hadn't stepped on anything. But her face was delighted, and it was almost as though the sun was breaking through all this rain. Even though it was just her expression.

"You remember how I take my tea," she said in a wondering voice.

"Of course I do. I remember all sorts of things." He took her arm and walked even faster. Now that they were in sight of the building, he was feeling just how sodden he was. And he didn't want her to catch cold or anything, given that she was so close to seeing her sister.

"You like your tea with lemon. You get sore after riding in carriages for too long—you didn't hide ours, by chance, did you?"

She laughed.

"You like cheese. You love your sisters. Your parents do not understand you. You don't like white gowns. You are adventurous, and intelligent, and fierce, and surprisingly funny."

"Funny?"

"Yes, you have a sharp sense of humor. Even if you yourself don't realize it." *But I do*, Bennett thought, *and that's one of the many reasons I love you.*

He continued. "You don't value yourself enough

as a kind human being. I know you're not out here, doing what we're doing, because you are too stubborn to allow your sister to live her own life. You are worried for her, even if you hide it."

"Oh." Her voice sounded small, and he didn't think it was just because she was drenched.

He waited. Nothing else from his hedgehog. And, yes, she was his hedgehog now. At least in his thoughts.

They walked quickly, Bennett thinking he might never feel dry again. And then they were at the door to what appeared to be a small cottage, a few broken windows and a general air of neglect indicating there would be neither fire nor stew.

At least there seemed to be a roof.

Bennett pushed on the door, finding it locked, then leaned into it with his shoulder, pushing against the wood.

It opened, sending him flying into the room, which smelled musty, but at least appeared to be dry.

She came in after, shutting the door behind them.

"I don't think we'll need to ask permission," she said softly.

Bennett glanced around the clearly deserted abode. A few broken chairs lay on their sides next to a large wooden table, while in the corner he could see a pile of what appeared to be old blankets.

"I wonder why the people who lived here left," he said, going to the corner to pick up the topmost blanket.

It actually wasn't a blanket, as it turned out, but a coat that had apparently been feasted on by moths, judging by the holes. Underneath that, however, was a blanket, one that had some hay stuck to it and had clearly been used in a stable. But thankfully was relatively intact, so the moths hadn't gotten to it.

Bennett dragged it out from the pile and laid it on the floor, gesturing to Ida. "We will at least be able to rest a bit. Even if we never are able to dry off," he added, wiping drops of rain away from his face. She stood in the middle of the room, a puddle forming rapidly at her feet.

"You should get out of those wet clothes," Bennett said, trying to sound as neutral as possible. Because of course he wanted to see her naked, but he didn't want her to think he was saying that just because he wanted to see her naked.

He also didn't want her to get ill or melt away.

Although the naked part was the one he was thinking the most about.

"You should too," she replied, raising an eyebrow toward him.

"I should." He took hold of the edge of his sleeve and began to draw it up his arm. "I will."

Her eyes widened. "Right here? Now?"

As though she hadn't seen him unclothed the night before. Reminding him that even though she was the redoubtable Ida, she was still a young lady who was somewhat innocent.

Albeit less innocent than before they'd come on this journey.

"It is your suggestion," Bennett said, taking his jacket off and folding it before placing it on the wooden table. He yanked his shirt from his trousers and drew the bottom of it up so he could remove it over his head.

He already felt much better, even if it was cold in the cabin.

And he was already thinking of ways he could warm up. And of course she would need warming too.

He bent down to remove first one boot, then the other, wiggling his toes on the floor.

And then his hands went to his trousers, and he began to undo them, only to pause as he saw what she was doing.

She'd shaken her hair out, and it hung down around her face, hiding most of her features. Her hands were at the back of her gown, and she was wriggling as though to unbutton herself. She was worrying her mouth with her teeth, and he felt his cock react as he thought about her putting that mouth on him—licking his nipples, taking his cock between his lips.

Dragging her fingernails over him as she sucked.

"Can you help me?" she asked in a huskier voice than usual. His hedgehog also seemed to be getting ideas.

"I can help you with so many things," he replied, smiling in satisfaction to himself at her intake of breath. He strode toward her as she presented her back, and he undid her buttons swiftly, shoving her gown down her arms so it fell in a crumpled sodden heap to the ground.

Leaving her in only a shift that was damp, clinging to her magnificently rounded arse.

She bent over to pick up the gown and shake it out, meaning she was leaning over in front of him.

God. He was speechless.

She stood and placed the gown on the pile of blankets.

He cupped the globes of her arse in his hands, lowering his mouth to her neck. Biting her gently at her nape as he kneaded the soft flesh. "Are you warming up?"

She pushed back against him, tilting her head up to allow him better access to her neck. Placing her hands on his thighs and gripping hard.

His cock throbbed, and he turned her in his

arms, capturing her mouth in a fiercely posses-sive kiss, wrapping his arms around her body and pulling her against him so he could feel the soft push of her breasts on his bare skin.

He broke the kiss and pulled her shift up, his fingertips skating on her skin as he drew the gar-ment up and over her head.

And now she was entirely and gloriously naked.

"I'm not warm enough," she said, putting her palm on his chest. Then she slid her fingers to the waistband of his trousers, hooking her fin-gers between his skin and the fabric, beginning to tug them down, a wicked smile on her lips.

He wanted to see that smile every day for the rest of his life.

But he couldn't think about that now. Not when he knew that wasn't what she wanted, even though she wanted him, and this, right now.

He would take what she wanted to give, and wouldn't press her.

He bent to take his trousers off, tossing them onto the table on top of his jacket. Standing in his smallclothes, his cock jutting out, tenting the fabric.

She arched a brow as she regarded him there. Frankly, directly, as was her glorious Ida way.

"That is quite large," she said, her tone spec-ulative. Her hands went to her breasts, and she rubbed her nipples, licking her lips as she did so.

"You said you wished you could have seen me do this," she added, sliding one hand down her stomach to the thatch of curls below. His breath caught, and he couldn't have stopped looking if several hundred elephants had come stamping into the room.

He saw her fingers slide over her nub, and he advanced forward, placing his hand on top of hers.

"I'd like to help," he said in a low rumble. His voice was almost unrecognizable to himself; he had never sounded this raw and needy. But of course he did with her. She made him raw and needy, made him see that what he wanted, and what he deserved, were so much more than what he had.

Even if what he wanted the most wouldn't be possible.

"We should take care of this too," she replied, tilting her head up as she reached to take his cock in her hand. Sliding her palm up and down as she'd done the previous night.

She was clearly a fast learner. Not that he didn't know that already.

"I'm not sure I can stand if you're going to continue this," he said in a ragged tone.

She smiled, and lowered herself down to lie on the blanket, wriggling as she got comfortable.

And then she raised her outstretched arms to him, beckoning him to her.

He complied, situating himself between her legs. Looking at her, at that warm, soft, wet place which was where he most wanted to be.

He gripped her thighs and kissed the juncture where her leg met her body. She shifted, and he slid his mouth to there, licking her right on that most sensitive nub.

"Oh," she gasped in surprise.

He wrapped his hands around her legs and began to lick and suck her rhythmically, noting how she reacted, learning from her body the way he could pleasure her the best.

Her hands were in his hair, gripping his head tightly, her moans a luscious, passionate accompaniment.

"Oh, God," she cried as she came on his tongue, arching her back.

He licked her softly, then moved up her body, holding her waist and positioning her so they were lying face-to-face.

Her cheeks were flushed, and her eyes were darkened in passion. Had he thought her the most beautiful outside in the rain? No, now was when she was the most beautiful—proudly naked, sexually satisfied, a smile playing about her lips.

"Take me," she said, reaching up to place her finger on his mouth, sliding her fingertip over his lips. He opened and sucked her finger inside, licking her as he had just licked her there.

"Mmm," she said, biting her lip. "I didn't know all these possibilities existed. There's so much more I can learn."

He wanted to laugh at just how typically Ida that statement was—she wasn't scared by the unknown, she wanted to learn and know more. Focused on the educational aspects of it all. She wouldn't be satisfied until she knew everything. Which meant—

He removed her finger from his mouth. "Take me?" he repeated, his hand tightening its grip on her hip. "Do you mean—?"

"Yes," she said before he could finish. "I want to know what it feels like. What all of it feels like. Here and now. I can't think of a more pleasant way to warm up, can you?" And as she said that, she put her hand firmly on his cock and squeezed, making him unable to speak.

"Fuck, Ida," he said, his teeth gritted.

"That is what I want, yes." Her voice was ragged. "I want you to fuck me."

He closed his eyes, almost unable to bear hearing the words—those blunt sexual words—coming from his Ida.

"I want you to be as educated as possible," he

replied as he opened his eyes to look at her, his eyes moving from her face to her neck to her glorious breasts to where her hand was stroking him.

"So educational," she said in a wry tone. "I am so glad you didn't ask if I knew what I was doing," she said, shifting to her back. "Because you know me, you know I know what I am doing."

"I do know you, Ida." *I do love you.* "I would never argue with a woman whose mind is so sharp, whose intelligence is unmatched by anybody I have ever met."

She took a deep breath, and when she spoke, her voice was low and sincere. "Nobody has ever thought of me that way. For that, for everything, I am grateful."

"Don't thank me until I've made you climax again," he said, moving his hand to her breast, cupping it in his palm.

"Oh, I like that," she said as he took her nipple between two fingers, pinching just a bit.

"I thought you would," he said as he moved, placing himself between her legs, his cock brushing her inner thigh.

"I liked when you did that—that," she said, gesturing downward.

"When I licked your sweet cunny? When I made you come on my tongue? You liked that?"

"Oh, yes," she moaned. "Just like I know I will

like it when you fuck me. When you put your manshaft inside."

"Manshaft?" he said, stifling a laugh. "Please don't call it that ever again. It's my penis, or my cock. Try again."

"I want you to fuck me with your cock," she said, meeting his gaze.

He almost couldn't breathe, never mind speak.

But he could do something, and that was to drag his cock over her nub, making her squirm. "Are you certain, Ida?"

"Yes, I am entirely certain. I want to know."

He didn't wait for her to end her sentence before beginning to slide his penis inside her, going slowly even though it was agony not to just thrust inside.

She bit her lip, her face showing discomfort, and he paused, gritting his teeth.

"It's fine, it just hurts a little." She put her hands on his arse and pulled his body closer to hers, making his cock push inside more.

"Oh," she said, her body relaxing as he pushed all the way in, finding her tight and warm and wet.

Perfect.

"That feels good," she said, sounding surprised.

"I can make you feel better. Again," he added with a grin. He began to move inside her, bracing himself on his arms. Her legs were wrapped around his, and her hands were still on his arse, clutching him as he moved in and out, trying to gauge what angle and rhythm would please her the most.

He could tell he was doing something right when she bit her lip, her expression and her grip on him tightening.

"Are you ready to come again, Ida?" he asked.

ARE YOU READY to come again?

She'd barely been ready the first time. She hadn't been prepared for how incredible it would feel, even though she had experienced the same thing the night before under his hand. But his doing it with his mouth felt so intimate, so passionate, so instinctual.

Her whole body felt as though it were lit from inside, and she wanted more, even though she didn't know if she could handle more.

The words they'd spoken ignited her also—frankly, shockingly crude and so, so persuasive.

Fuck me, she'd said, and she meant it. She liked the harsh click of the "k" in "Fuck," the way she commanded him. It felt empowering.

He was pushing his cock in and out of her, his hair falling over his forehead, his expression one of concentration.

It was endearing, how intent he was on her pleasure. As though he knew how little she'd been taken care of in her life. Not just in this way, of course, because obviously he knew this was her first time. But in general.

He knew how she took her tea. He was watching to see what touch she preferred, and he changed his actions to accommodate that.

He was so protective, and charming, and it seemed he liked to argue with her.

But right now, he was fucking her, and that was what was most important. The movement, the pace, the way his body touched that sensitive spot he'd been kissing just moments ago.

Incredibly, she felt the pressure building again. She hadn't thought it would, not with having happened so recently. But there it was, the want, the need to topple over that cliff all over again, this time with him buried inside her.

"Do you like me inside you, Ida?" he murmured, his hand going between them to touch her there, lighting her up even more.

"I love it," she replied, raking her nails over his arse, running them up his back as he continued to move.

I love you.

Dear lord, she did, didn't she? Oh no. She could not consider all that that meant, not with him naked on top of her, not with her pleasure building and growing. Not when she knew that this was likely to be the first and last time she could be with him like this.

She shoved that thought away in a back part of her brain and slammed the door behind it, instead focusing on how she felt. Which was wonderful.

He shifted position, angling his body another way, hitting that spot even more directly, and she heard herself moan, closing her eyes as he continued moving forcefully, relentlessly driving her to her climax.

And then—"Aah," she said, everything converging together, her whole body alive with the shivers running through it.

"God, you're gorgeous when you're coming," he said, slowing his movements. She opened her eyes to see him gazing at her face with a raw hungered expression.

"What about you?" she asked, moving her hips. He groaned, and thrust faster. His face was so concentrated, so intense, and she wanted to see how he would look when he felt the same thing she had. "Don't stop," she said, as though there was the slightest chance he would.

Although he would have if she had told him to. She knew that.

"God, Ida," he said, his movements getting faster, the force of his thrusts pushing her up the floor.

She held onto him, feeling her whole body jiggle as their bodies moved together, the muscles of his arms standing out as he tensed.

And then he froze, pulling out and spilling his seed all over her stomach.

He was splendid.

And damn it, she loved him.

Chapter 14

Sometimes there are no words for the adventure.

LADY IDA'S TIPS FOR THE
ADVENTUROUS LADY TRAVELER

*W*ell." Not an auspicious beginning, but then how did one speak to the gentleman who'd inserted his penis into one the night before?

"Good morning," Ida continued, feeling her face warm. She had slept surprisingly well, given that she was sleeping on the floor on a horse blanket.

But perhaps the good sleep was due to his being there, wrapped around her body, his hand on her belly, his face tucked into her neck.

She'd never slept so intimately with anyone before, and at first she'd thought it would be difficult or uncomfortable.

Like you can be, she admitted to herself. But he didn't seem to find her difficult or uncomfortable. Or when he did, he also seemed to find it amusing. That, more than the penis-insertion or the fact that they were together at all, might be the most surprising thing. That they laughed together so often. That they amused each other.

"Good morning," he murmured, kissing her shoulder, his hand moving from her belly to cup her breast. "A very good morning indeed," he continued, stroking the nipple. She arched into his palm, feeling his erection behind her.

"Mmm, I wish we could, but I want to get walking as soon as possible," she said. "Della is only a few miles away."

She couldn't forget why she was on this madcap journey. To find Della. To make certain she was all right, to bring her and Nora home.

Even though they'd both have to face what "home" meant when they returned to London.

"Of course." He released his hold on her, and she mourned the loss, even though she appreciated he'd done what she'd asked.

That was rare also—a person who respected another's wishes. Who didn't have to be asked twice to do something.

She got dressed quickly, frowning as she put on her still-damp clothing.

"It shouldn't be more than an hour or so walk from here," he said as he—much to Ida's regret—put his shirt on.

"Wonderful." Even though that would mean the end of this, all of this, of discovering what his skin felt like, tasted like. She knew well enough she wasn't his choice for his future. She was something that happened, just as he was something that had happened to her.

She had her own plan, one that didn't and couldn't include him. Find Della, persuade her to return with her, find somewhere to live all together.

They left the cabin, Ida casting one regretful look behind her.

This was it. This was the end of this part of the adventure.

She wished it didn't also feel like the end of her life.

Not to mention wishing she could end her overly dramatic thoughts.

BENNETT GLANCED UP at the sky, noting the dark, ominous clouds. If they were lucky, they wouldn't get caught in another rainstorm. Although if that meant they had to find shelter again, with the same results, he would welcome all the rain.

Damn it. He loved her. But because he loved her, he wouldn't push her into something she didn't want. She deserved to be treated with respect, not told she should do something because someone else felt a certain way. His thoughts were muddled, chasing themselves like squirrels up a tree.

I love her, she has a certain future in mind, doesn't she deserve to know how I feel about her? But that puts her under an obligation, an obligation I know she won't submit to, so all I'd be doing is being selfish by telling her.

God damn it. There was no way out of this. Or if there was, it would take someone with Ida's intelligence to sort it all out. And he couldn't ask her, so here he was back again.

He just wished this journey had been longer. That there had been one more night to taste her, to savor her, to love her as thoroughly and satisfyingly as he possibly could.

Crack.

God damn it again. The rain was coming once more, the skies opening up as quickly as they had yesterday, drenching their still-wet clothing from the day before. If he were more solipsistic, he'd think the weather was reflecting his mood.

"We don't have a choice. We'll just have to walk until we get there," he said as Ida looked back at him questioningly.

She nodded, quickening her pace.

THEY REACHED THE town about forty-five minutes later, both of them sodden.

"It's here," Ida said as they walked up the path

to a small house. They'd stopped at the inn in the town and gotten directions for Della's house, along with a few skeptical glances.

Whether that was because Ida and Bennett were strangers, or because they were currently wetter than most fish in the ocean he didn't know.

She hesitated at the door, then raised her fist and knocked.

The door swung open a few moments later, revealing a woman of Caribbean descent.

"Can I help you?" she asked, glancing from Ida to Bennett, a curious expression on her face. Her voice was smooth and cultured, her gown a ladies' gown, not that of a servant.

Surprising, but he shouldn't be surprised—the Howlett sisters were nothing if not unexpected.

"I am looking for Della," Ida explained. "I don't know what name she is using, but her name is Della. Does she live here? We were told she does." She sounded anxious, and he felt his chest constrict at her obvious emotion.

The woman's face cleared, and she smiled. "Oh. You're one of the sisters." She brought her finger up to her cheek and tapped it as she thought. "Are you Lady Eleanor?" She peered at Bennett. "And this is Alexander?"

"No, I'm Ida."

The woman's eyebrows rose. "Ah, Ida. The smart one."

"Yes, that's me." Ida took a deep breath. "But is she here?" Ida repeated, glancing past the woman's shoulder into the house.

"Of course, my apologies," the woman said, swinging the door wider so as to allow them entry. "She's teaching at the moment, but she will be done shortly."

They went in, Bennett feeling protective of his Ida even though she was neither his Ida nor was there anything to be protective about. The house was cozy and charmingly furnished, a few scattered rugs on the wooden floors, children's toys scattered in what was clearly a well-lived-in area just to the left of where they stood.

"Please come in. Would you like tea?"

"I'm a bit worried about getting everything wet," Ida said as the woman brought them into the room to the right, a small space that held a sofa, a few tables, and some comfortable-looking armchairs.

"Don't fuss about that. I'll just put something on the sofa," the woman replied, grabbing a blanket from the back of a chair. "Tea?" she repeated.

"Yes, thank you. Lemon, if you have it." Ida extended her hand. "You know who I am, but I am not certain who you are?"

"Oh, of course," the woman said, taking Ida's hand in hers. "I am Mrs. Sarah Wattings. Della and I share this house and share the teaching duties. She said she'd written her sisters about that? Her Nora and my Emily are about the same age."

"Oh, you're the lady Della wrote us about. I'd forgotten that part. I was so struck by the inclusion of the town on the paper."

Mrs. Wattings looked confused. "The town?"

Ida gave a vigorous nod. "Yes, Della's most recent letter had the faint outline of the word *Haltwhistle* on it. So when we saw that, I knew I had to come."

Mrs. Wattings laughed, shaking her head. "I believe the children were practicing their writing. One of them must have gotten hold of the letter, and let the clue slip." She smiled at Ida. "But I can't say I'm sorry you've come. Della has missed you." She looked over at Bennett.

"Oh, this is Lord Carson." No explanation of why they were traveling together, nor of their relationship.

Although what would she say? *This is Lord Carson, the gentleman who did not marry two of my sisters and will not be marrying me. This is Lord Carson, who has seen me naked.*

This is Lord Carson, who I will not be marrying.

"It is a pleasure to meet you, my lord." Mrs. Wattings held her hand out, a speculative look on her face.

He took her hand and shook it.

"Sarah, we're done," a voice called from down the hall. Ida stiffened, her whole body practically vibrating with excitement, and Bennett looked to the door, every sense on alert to ensure she would be protected, no matter what occurred.

A woman strode in, accompanied by two children of approximately the same age on either side. One clearly was Mrs. Wattings's daughter, while Bennett presumed the other was Nora.

"Oh!" Della exclaimed, her eyes wide as she stared at Ida. "I—"

And then Ida rushed forward, clasping her sister in a hug, her shoulders shaking.

Bennett felt his throat tighten as he watched. The sisters were holding on to one another, both of them crying, while the two little girls stared up, their eyes wide.

Eventually, the sisters withdrew from one another, teary and smiling.

Della recovered enough to speak, gesturing toward Ida. "This is your aunt, Nora. This is Ida."

The little girl looked up at Ida, her eyes wide. "I didn't know I had an aunt." She looked at her mother. "What is an aunt?"

Both women began to laugh.

Ida knelt down in front of her niece. "An aunt is the sister of a mother. I am your mother's sister. So I am your aunt."

"Oh," Nora said, her eyes wide.

Ida held her hand out for the little girl to shake. "I am so glad to meet you, Nora. And this is—?"

"This is my friend Emily," Nora said, holding the other girl's hand.

"It is a pleasure to meet you, Emily," Ida replied, shaking Emily's hand as well.

"But where did you come from? And why are you here? How long are you here? Who's that?" Nora asked, her questions strung together with no pauses.

"Let's go find a treat," Mrs. Wattings said, her tone making it clear she was accustomed to being obeyed. And that Nora often had many questions. "I'll make tea," she added as she walked out, accompanied by the girls.

"And biscuits? And bread?" Nora asked as they walked out of the room.

Della regarded them with a warm look in her eye, then she turned and gave a questioning look toward him. Ida, he noticed, blushed.

IDA ADDRESSED HIM. "My lord, please allow me to introduce my sister, Lady Della Howlett. Della, this is Lord Carson."

The other woman stepped forward, her hand outstretched. She looked similar to her sister, but wasn't as dramatically black and white in coloring. Instead, she was lushly beautiful, with a generous mouth, a tumble of brown hair, and an equally generous figure.

"It is a pleasure to meet you, my lord." Lady Della's voice was quiet but confident. "Thank you for escorting my sister." She looked at Ida again, her expression softening. "I knew one of you would show up eventually. I shouldn't be surprised it is you. You are the most obdurate of sisters."

"I will take that as a compliment," Ida replied, going to sit on the sofa, leaning down to remove her wet shoes. A puddle began forming at her feet. "We'll need to hire a carriage to return to London. Ours went missing. We can wait a few days while you settle things." She spoke as though it were a certainty. As always, Bennett admired her confidence, but knew that it was misplaced in this moment.

A fact confirmed when Lady Della spoke.

"Return to London?" She sounded startled. "I don't plan on doing that, Ida, no matter how far you've come. I want you to stay for a while, but I won't be returning."

"Not return?" She looked at Bennett, scowling. "For goodness' sake, can you sit down, please? You're all looming over there."

Bennett shared a commiserating look with Lady Della, then sat next to Ida on the sofa, ensuring he was sitting only on the blanket so as not to damage the furniture too much.

Lady Della sat in one of the opposite chairs, folding her hands in her lap. It was easier to see the resemblance between the two sisters when Lady Della was looking stubborn.

Which Bennett would not be pointing out to Ida. Or Della, for that matter.

"I love that you traveled all this way, and I am grateful to see you. But I can't go home." She held her hands out in a broad gesture. "I have a life here. Sarah and I teach the girls, and we're happy."

"But you're not with your family," Ida replied, her mouth set in a firm line, betrayed by the tremor of her chin. "Don't you want Nora to know her aunts?"

Lady Della blinked as though holding back tears. "Family means everything to me, Ida. I have family here. Sarah and her daughter are my family now. The children we teach are family as well. Do you truly want me to return to all that gossip? I highly doubt our parents will welcome me back with open arms."

Ida opened her mouth to argue the point, then snapped it shut again.

Bennett had never seen her concede so quickly.

Ida gestured toward her clothing. "If you could

lend me a gown so I could get out of these wet things? And perhaps we could discuss this in private?"

Della rose. "Of course, how unthinking of me not to ensure you are dry. My apologies." She glanced at Bennett, frowning. "I don't have anything you can wear, my lord. Perhaps you would want to borrow a dressing gown and we can air your clothes out by the fire?"

"Thank you, yes," Bennett said. Wandering around a stranger's home in a dressing gown wasn't the oddest situation he had found himself in during the course of the last few days.

Chapter 15

Adventure hurts.

LADY IDA'S TIPS FOR THE
ADVENTUROUS LADY TRAVELER

I won't go back, Ida."

Della sat on the bed, her hands folded in her lap, her expression firm.

Ida stood by the fire. She'd removed her gown, which was currently being cleaned by the house-maid whom Della had summoned on their way upstairs.

If Della could afford help, perhaps her life here wasn't as desperate as Ida had imagined. Perhaps it wasn't imperative that Della return to London.

But that would mean none of the sisters could get to know Nora, nor would Della have the op-portunity to meet someone who would deserve her. Who would take care of her and Nora as they deserved.

Was she being selfish, to want her sister to return?

There was an element of that, certainly. Ida loved all of her sisters, and she wanted them to be in proximity to one another, even if two of them had gone off and gotten married, the traitors.

But more than that, Ida wanted to get the opportunity to give Nora all the love in Ida's heart, to let Della know that her actions weren't to be deplored but applauded—she'd gone off of her own volition, realized she'd made a mistake, and taken responsibility for what she'd done, refusing to let it define her.

Returning to London would give her the chance to announce that to everyone who still gossiped about the Duke's Disgraceful Daughters, to show them that a good person can persist through adversity, that she isn't knocked down when others think she should be.

"Let's talk for a bit," Ida said, trying to remember everything Bennett had suggested. "You want Nora to know your sisters. Eleanor and Alexander are so happy, and Olivia and Edward are even more revoltingly so," she said, as Della smiled.

"You made a mistake," she continued, with Della nodding agreement. "But that mistake doesn't have to change your life irrevocably."

"Doesn't it?" Della asked in a resigned tone.

"I cannot imagine anybody would welcome me back. Nor do I want to come back, not if it means facing those people and that gossip."

Ida swallowed. It would be hard to argue against that, especially since she knew that her reputation would also be in tatters.

"What if you don't have to face them? What if you can just—just live with me and Pearl and open a home for scandalous women or something?"

The reckless bravery of the idea would likely appeal to Della.

Della tilted her head in thought. Clearly considering it. Ida felt herself relax just a fraction.

Ida had not misread her reckless sister. It was that recklessness that had landed Della in this in the first place. Although it had also brought her Nora, who seemed like the light of Della's life.

"I don't know, Ida. I will have to think about it. And talk to Sarah, of course."

Della rose, clearly finished with the conversation. Ida nodded, wracking her brain for more arguments to present.

Later, when she was more dry and therefore, hopefully, more persuasive.

THE DINNER THAT evening was the most unusual experience Bennett had ever had. Well, besides the event that had happened over the past few days, falling in love with Ida and all.

Lady Della and her friend, along with their two girls, all ate together, a rollicking, noisy event where everyone was encouraged to share their opinion and comments.

He'd never been with family that was so clearly adoring of one another, and also so convivial.

It was charming while also entirely over-whelming.

"Did you read the collection of Elizabeth Barrett Browning poems?" Della asked Ida, a sigh accompanying her question.

Ida rolled her eyes. "You know I have no patience for poetry."

Della shot a mischievous glance toward Bennett. "I wasn't sure if recent events might have persuaded you to try it again."

Ida bristled visibly, although Della did not appear daunted.

"And it talks about those heartfelt emotions with such depth and strength," Della continued.

"I'm glad you haven't given up on love," Ida said in a soft voice. "It's just that I don't want to read those things when—" And then she stopped, looking down at her plate.

When what? Bennett wanted to ask. *When you don't think you'll have those things in your own life? When you are looking forward to a life with books and sisters and nothing else?*

When you know you won't compromise to have the kind of life that poems are written about?

Damn it.

"So how exactly did you come to get here, Ida?" Lady Della asked, wiping her daughter's face with a napkin. "Butter goes on the bread, Nora, not your cheek," she said with a grin.

Nora nodded, then put another piece of buttered bread in her mouth.

"Well," Ida began, shooting a look toward Bennett, who cocked his head at her, "there was a carriage, and I took it."

Bennett smothered a laugh.

Della's eyes went wide. "There was a carriage. And you took it," she repeated.

Ida waved her hand. "There's more to it than that, of course."

"I assume so," Della said dryly as Mrs. Wattings tried not to smile.

"I was in the carriage," Bennett added. Making Ida glare at him.

Della's eyebrows shot up. "You were in the carriage? So you didn't plan on coming here together?"

"Not . . . exactly," Ida replied in a reluctant tone.

Della cradled her chin in her hand. "So how was it, exactly?"

"Uh . . ." Ida said.

Bennett leaned back in his chair, folding his arms over his chest. He couldn't wait to hear what she was going to say.

IDA SHUT THE door to the room Della had shown her, her heart constricting with all sorts of emotions.

Conflicting emotions, ranging from exhilaration at having been reunited with Della again to anxiety that she wouldn't be able to persuade her sister to return with her to a heartsickness that felt as though it were taking over her entire body, knowing that Bennett was down the hall, again, but she couldn't see him in that way ever again.

They were both so set in their respective lives. And she couldn't shake the thought that even if he were to say something, anything, about how he felt about her, she couldn't with any kind of good conscience agree.

She would ruin his life. It was dramatic, but it was also true.

She undid her gown, twisting as she reached some of the buttons. Wishing he were here to help. Wishing he were here.

But if he were there, they'd be doing things. Things that made her heart race, and her breasts get heavy, and her whole mind get filled with thoughts of what could never be.

There were many reasons why. She just had to remember them.

For one: What would happen when somebody he had to use his diplomacy on said something that irked Ida? She was bound to say something opinionated and strident, leaving Bennett to try to explain away his outspoken wife.

Or two: Or when his family responsibilities took him away when she needed him? Was that any kind of way to live a life?

Well, yes. But not a way to live *her* life.

He would ruin her life, too. Because if she had to watch herself she would be less than the Ida she knew she was meant to be—a woman who spoke her mind, who exercised her intelligence to help others, who refused to relent when she knew she was in the right.

That was why she had come on this journey in the first place, wasn't it? Because she refused to accept that this was the way it would be. That Della would be lost forever to them. That they would never know Nora.

It was that stubbornness that served her well now, but that would invariably ruin someone's happiness.

She couldn't. She would not.

She heard a sniffle, and realized it was her. Damn it. She did not want to cry over it all, but it appeared that that was what was happening.

She got onto the bed, letting herself sob with abandon, falling into the heartache as thoroughly as she did anything.

THE NEXT MORNING, her eyes were weary, but at least she was resolute.

She had to return to London as quickly as possible, she knew, because the longer she stayed away the more likely it was that her reputation be ruined. Not that she cared about that, but she didn't want to taint Pearl's chances of finding a husband.

"Della," Ida said, after finishing her tea, "may we speak? In private?"

Della glanced at Mrs. Wattings, who nodded in agreement.

"Fine. But I have to be finished so I can teach my pupils in about half an hour," Della said.

Half an hour. Fine. She could do this. She was Ida the Intelligent, wasn't she? The most argumentative of the Howlett sisters?

Della led her upstairs to her bedroom. It was a lovely room, with a large striped coverlet on her bed, paintings clearly done by a child tacked up on the wall, a few pieces of jewelry on the dressing table.

"You have made a good home for yourself," Ida said, picking up one of the necklaces.

"Mr. Baxter knew those were cheap, so he

didn't bother taking them when he left," Della commented ruefully.

"They're pretty."

Della smiled. "Nora likes to play dress-up with them."

"Nora seems like a wonderful child. One I want to know better," Ida said in a meaningful tone.

Della rolled her eyes, but gestured for Ida to sit down, sitting down beside her on the bed.

"Can I offer you a bargain?" Ida began, hoping this would be the argument that would work. "You know all the reasons I want you to return. Coming back to us, giving Nora more of a family, knowing the two of you are safe. But I have a selfish reason as well."

She took a deep breath. "The thing is, my travel here was somewhat unusual, and I know that if I return by myself, I will be forced to marry Lord Carson, who has no desire to marry me. Nor I him," she added, even though she knew she wasn't being entirely truthful.

"You have no wish to marry him, Ida?" Della sounded skeptical.

Ida took a deep breath and lied to her sister. "No."

"I don't believe you," Della said. "I believe you have fallen in love with him."

"That might be true," Ida admitted. Della was too smart, and Ida too bad at lying, to prevaricate.

"But it doesn't mean I want to marry him. You, more than anyone, know what that is like."

"It's not the same thing at all," Della said in a scornful voice. She bit her lip, looking past Ida in thought. "I did not want to marry Mr. Baxter, not after I discovered who he was. Thank goodness he left before I had to throw him out. And thank goodness Sarah was here, she helped me through the worst of it."

"I'm so sorry I wasn't here."

"Thank you. It was my own foolishness, I know that. But I also know that I am impulsive and impetuous." She smiled. "As it seems you are, since you tore off after me." She frowned. "I know you stole a carriage, of all things, but how did you know where to go?"

Ida grinned. "Well, it appears one of your students was practicing penmanship or something. I saw 'Haltwhistle' written on your latest letter. And since our mother was being our mother . . ."

Della's eyes widened. "You mean she wanted to marry you off?"

Ida nodded.

"Not to Lord Carson, though?"

Would she have agreed if it were Bennett her mother had presented?

Likely not; her initial impression of Bennett was so different than what she thought now. She would have refused him with as much alacrity as she would have refused Lord Bradford, if he'd been offered the opportunity to propose.

"No. Even worse. It was to Lord Bradford. Do you remember him?"

Della wrinkled her brow in thought, then her expression cleared. "No. Him? He once explained that breakfast is first thing in the morning because it is when you break your fast. Only, he said in painstaking explanation, you don't actually break anything."

Ida gawked at Della for a moment before bursting into laughter. Della let out a peal of laughter as well, and the two sisters both collapsed onto the bed, holding their sides.

Eventually their laughter subsided, and Della's expression turned serious again. "So you're saying that unless I return with you you'll be forced into marriage? How would that work? We'll both be disgraced."

"But we'll be together," Ida pleaded. "And all of those other arguments I presented, don't forget about them. Aren't we stronger together?"

"We are."

Ida felt her heart lift at hearing Della's confirmation.

Della continued. "You are as clever as always, Ida, presenting me with a request I can't possibly refuse." She reached over and took Ida's hand in hers. "I will return with you, then, if only to ensure you won't have to marry where you don't want to. Not that I think for one moment that you would actually be forced into it, since I do know you, and your stubbornness. But I want Nora to know her aunts. All of her aunts."

She looked up at the ceiling as she thought. "I expect we can stay with Eleanor. I do not wish to return to our father's house, not until they've had a chance to decide how they feel about my return."

She returned her gaze to Ida. "And I'll speak to Sarah. I will invite her and Emily to join us, since they are my family."

"Of course." Ida hadn't anticipated being joined by the other woman and her daughter, but if it meant Della wasn't going to argue anymore about it, she would accept it.

She knew Eleanor would be thrilled to have Della and her friend and their children stay with her; Eleanor's own baby was just a few months old.

"We can spend a few days here while Lord Carson obtains the funds and the carriage to bring us back. I might dry out by then," Ida said in a wry tone.

"It is good to see you," Della replied, squeezing Ida's hand. "You don't know what it means to me that you came all this way with your friend to find me. You must promise me, however, that once you are seen to be not at all compromised that you will allow me to make my own decision about my future. As I am helping you do with yours by my return."

"Yes," Ida responded immediately. "Of course. And if that means that you and Nora and Sarah and Emily come back here to your life, that is fine. I cannot promise I won't join you, however." Especially if it meant she would escape seeing Bennett being eventually married to the woman his life deserved—someone safe, and warm, and comforting. Someone who was everything that Ida was not.

"I'll speak with Sarah and then I'll start preparing for the journey." Her lips twisted into a wry smile. "Nora will be thrilled."

As was Ida. She and her niece had that in common then. Hopefully she would be able to get to know her niece. In London, with all of them together.

And if Della refused? Well. She should make certain to spend time with Nora now, since she might not get to see her again for a long time.

"My pa is a sailor," Emily said.

She, Nora, and Ida had walked to the little pond at the edge of the property. Normally, the girls said, they weren't allowed to come down there, not without one or the other of their mothers, but since it was their aunt—Emily had adopted Ida as her aunt as well—Della had said it was all right.

It gave Della a chance to speak with Sarah about London, and it gave Ida the opportunity to know her new nieces.

She hadn't seen Bennett—Lord Carson, that is—yet that day, and she reminded herself that that was how it would be when they returned. She wouldn't see him, he wouldn't see her, they wouldn't see each other.

Conjugating again? his voice said in her brain.

"Aunt Ida?" Nora asked.

Ida blinked as she focused on the girls. Both were staring at her wide-eyed, so apparently she'd made a noise or a face or something to indicate her scattered state of mind.

Wonderful. Now she was making small children question her sanity.

As she was questioning her choices.

The girls had brought paper boats to the pond, and were holding them over the water set to launch them. Ida didn't have a lot of faith that the boats would do anything more than absorb water and sink, but she would not be explaining any of that to the children, whose expressions previously were those of excitement. Before Ida got odd and made them anxious.

"Nothing, girls. Sorry. Just remembering a story I heard."

"You're going to tell us your story." Nora spoke in a commanding tone. Yes, she was rather like her aunt, wasn't she?

Also, Ida didn't have a story in mind. She wasn't good at this whole prevaricating thing, was she?

"Emily, you said your father was a sailor?"

The little girl nodded.

"And you are here launching ships!" Ida could feel herself clutching at straws.

But she had done this before, hadn't she? Talked at length about a topic just because someone mentioned something tangential to it?

"Do you know that in the Americas they call our sailors 'lime-juicers'?"

Both girls shook their heads. Of course they didn't know that. Ida had only stumbled upon it in a periodical she'd read at Mr. Beechcroft's, one from New York that mostly contained shipping news. No wonder they'd never heard it.

"What is a lime-juicer?" Nora the Inquisitive asked.

She really was an excellent child.

"Well, you know what limes are, don't you?"

Emily frowned and shook her head again. Nora beamed and folded her arms over her chest. "I do."

"Do you want to tell us?" Ida asked.

Nora looked hesitant. "I think it's green. And it's food."

"It is," Ida replied, suppressing an urge to list all of the green food items in her mental inventory. That could take several hours, and it wouldn't be useful toward helping the children understand now.

That she had to suppress the thought at all meant she hadn't entirely lost her urge for pedantry. She'd have to be mindful of that. There was no reason to dissuade learning in the young just because the older teacher was determined to show just how much she happened to know.

"A lime is a member of the citrus genus." Not that they would know Linnaeus either. "In order to organize things, we put them into categories. Like your hair ribbon, Emily, is like Nora's hair ribbon. Only they are not the same hair ribbon, or it would be very difficult for both of you to wear them."

The girls looked at each other and giggled.

"A lime is similar, but not the same, to lemons and oranges and other members of the citrus genus. It's got a green outside and a lighter green inside."

"What do limes have to do with sailors?"

Ida beamed at Nora. "That is a very good question. Americans noticed that our sailors, sailing in the British Navy, ate a lot of limes. Well," she amended, knowing the girls wouldn't care about absolute accuracy but not being able to leave a misapprehension alone, "they actually put lime juice into their grog."

By this time, the girls had abandoned their boats and were seated on the grass, one on each side of Ida. Nora was leaning her head against Ida's arm, while Emily had hold of Ida's hand.

It felt so different from anything she'd ever experienced before.

It felt strange and wonderful, and her heart constricted. This was what it would be like if she had children of her own. Not that she was planning on having children; if she wasn't planning on getting married at any point in her life she wouldn't be considering children.

She was not Della, after all.

But the thought of it, of having a young mind or minds to nourish and grow . . .

"What is grog?" Nora said, interrupting Ida just as she thought she might burst into tears.

"Grog?" Ida blinked, her brain recalling what she knew so she could report it accurately. "Grog is a drink that sailors drink. Perhaps your father has had it, Emily."

Emily gave a shy smile.

"It's rum mixed with water. I heard that it is

named after some admiral because he wore a coat made of grogram. What the French call *gros grain*."

The girls' expressions were puzzled. No wonder, since she had just given the worst possible explanation of the word *grog*.

"We should get back," Ida said, getting up to her feet.

If she was going to confuse the children, she could do that just as well at Della's house, where he might be.

Not that she wanted to see him.

You can't even lie to yourself properly, a voice chided in her head. A voice that sounded a lot like Pearl's.

She wished, suddenly, that she had some grog. She would drink it until she could not think anymore, and then she wouldn't have to be bothered with thoughts of him and children and what could never be.

But she didn't have grog. What she had was an undecided sister and a gentleman with whom she didn't want to do the honorable thing, no matter how much she truly did want that.

She took the girls' hands and began to walk back toward the house, feeling the alternating tug of her heart as it cycled through what could and would not happen.

Lecturing about life and the natural order of things was far less complicated than living life.

Contradictorium Idatum, indeed.

BENNETT HAD LEFT the house early that morning, not wanting to torture himself by seeing her. Even though it was torture not seeing her, but that was a different type of torture.

No doubt she could have explained the cognitive differences.

He smiled even as it hurt to think about her.

Never mind that it was already torture to be wearing his clothing from the day before, which was still damp from the rain. The alternative to that, however, was venturing into town in Lady Della's dressing gown, which he didn't think the town was ready for.

Already that day, he'd sent a letter to his bank, asking for funds, and then found a stable where he could rent a carriage and horses. The proprietor had been suspicious, at first, but had warmed to him as soon as Bennett gave his title and the amount he was willing to pay.

Then he found a place to sell him a suit—not one as good as the one he was wearing, from Mr. Holding. But it was dry.

His business finished, he walked back to Lady Della's house, moving swiftly when he thought about seeing Ida, and then slowing his pace as he thought about her.

About them, and this magical journey they'd been on. That was about to end.

"You've returned," Mrs. Wattings said as he

stepped into the house. "Lady Ida is waiting for you in the sitting room. Just there," she said, gesturing to the room they'd first gone into the day before.

Lady Ida. Had she spent all morning thinking about him as well?

He nodded, stepping quickly into the room.

It was surprisingly cozy, with rugs scattered on the floor in front of the fireplace and the sofa. A well-worn desk was at one end, while a bookcase that appeared to house both adult and children's books was in the other corner.

She stood in the middle of the room, clasping her hands in front of her, her expression nearly blinding in its joy. So it was unlikely she'd been thinking about him after all. He shouldn't be disappointed, and yet he had to admit wishing she were slightly less happy.

"You're back." He saw her swallow, and he braced himself for whatever she was about to say. "She and Nora will come with us. And Mrs. Wattings and Emily."

"Everyone is coming to London?" So her mission would be fulfilled. And his adventure would be over. He sat down heavily. "I shouldn't be surprised that you were able to convince her, I know how insistent you can be, but I have to admit to being surprised in this case."

Ida's expression was almost bashful. As though

she was pleased by the compliment, but not quite sure how to react. "I told her that if she didn't return that I would be entirely compromised." She lifted her chin as she took a deep breath. "That if we returned alone there was no way for us to avoid marriage. I know neither of us wants that." She lifted her chin again as though to dare him to challenge her statement. Did she want him to?

"You are certain about that?" he asked, getting up but not allowing himself to go to her, to take her in his arms as he wished to. This had to be entirely her choice. He wouldn't do her the disservice of arguing with her. She deserved that respect.

She nodded. "I am." She walked to him, slid her hands under his coat to draw him close. He breathed in the scent of her hair, felt the warmth of her body.

He was going to have to give all of this up? It hurt already.

She spoke in a voice that resonated with emotion. "I have enjoyed spending time with you, far more than I anticipated. But I am not for you, and you are not for me. We both know you require a certain type of lady, and I will not, nor would I ever be, that person."

His chest tightened, and he swallowed hard against the words that clogged his throat—*what if you could change, what if I could change, can't you at least try?*—because he knew what his family and his situation demanded, and he knew she was right.

Damn it, she was always right. And was right for herself, as well.

She would be miserable if she tried to change for him, and he couldn't allow her to do that. Never mind she'd likely refuse anyway.

So instead of speaking he lowered his head and kissed her. Softly, tenderly, as though this was the last time their lips would meet.

Likely it was.

Dear god, this hurt. But not as much as it would hurt if he had to watch as she shrank into someone she was not, merely to fit in. The Ida he loved would become diminished, day by day, until she was just a shell of her previous self.

He heard her make a small noise, and he held her, breaking the kiss as he rested his chin on her head. She held him tightly, pressing her face into his chest. "I wish it could be any other way, I do. But I have obligations to my family, and so do you."

She exhaled. "Besides which, I cannot be the soft and gentle wife you want. The soft and gentle wife you need in your life."

He couldn't speak. The woman he loved, whom he was fairly certain loved him, was being sensible about their future, was refusing to compromise. He wouldn't want an Ida who was willing to compromise—that wasn't her, that wouldn't be the woman he loved.

So this was it.

This was their good-bye.

"Thank you," he said in a soft voice.

"For what?" she asked, raising her head to look him in the eye. She arched a brow, clearly trying to lighten the moment. "There are so many things you could be thanking me for."

"And you me," he retorted smugly, liking how her cheeks colored at the recollection—of his bringing her pleasure, of their shared intimacy.

"But I am thanking you for ensuring both of us are free to choose," he said in a serious tone of voice, "and for reminding me that you are the strongest, bravest, most intelligent woman I know."

"Oh," she replied in a low voice. "Thank you."

IDA HADN'T EXPECTED a broken heart to feel so . . . *broken*. She walked upstairs, her pace slow, her thoughts churning. He respected her too much to argue with her, that was obvious.

Although she had to admit to wishing that he *had* argued, that he had told her how he felt about her.

Would she have changed her mind?

She knew she'd be tempted. To spend the rest of her life with him, in his bed, having their children. Especially after seeing firsthand what it would be like to converse with a curious child.

But she knew it wasn't possible, not the way they both saw their futures. He would return to being the responsible member of his family, and she would forge her own path, refusing to submit to anyone else's plans.

Besides which, even if she had agreed, she knew herself too well to think she would have been able to be the wife he needed. Eventually she would make her opinion of someone or something known, ruining his chance of success in one area or another. Perhaps all the areas, given how forthright she was.

And then she would destroy what he was trying to do. The good he was trying to create.

She couldn't live with that possibility, no matter how much she loved him. She understood duty and honor and responsibility so much more now, thanks to him. She knew it was her duty to keep his future clear and direct.

She wouldn't want him to have to monitor her words to make certain she wasn't going to offend anyone. He'd be kind, and diplomatic as he told her why she couldn't or shouldn't say something. But it would fray their relationship, and she wanted an equal partner, not a manager.

It didn't mean it didn't hurt, though.

She began to turn the handle on the door to her bedroom when she heard a voice in the hallway.

"Lady Ida?"

Ida shifted to see who it was. She knew it wasn't him, and that was all her brain could process.

"Della asked me about returning to London."

It was Mrs. Wattings, who stood halfway down the hall, wearing a gown in a serviceable color that nonetheless managed to make her look elegant.

The woman was beautiful; only perhaps as old as Della, with wide dark eyes that looked almost haunted. But she had a tentative smile on her face, and Ida couldn't help but warm to her. Not to mention how she'd come to live in Haltwhistle, of all out-of-the-way places. And found, apparently, a best friend in her sister.

Ida was struck by Mrs. Wattings's words. "I didn't realize you had lived there before. Della didn't mention that. Or perhaps she had, but I hadn't expected someone like you."

The woman nodded as she spoke. "I can imagine someone like me is not who you'd expect to find with your sister."

Ida opened the door to the bedroom and gestured for Mrs. Wattings to step inside.

"But we got to talking," Mrs. Wattings continued, "and found we had so much in common. It wasn't possible to stay in my current lodgings, so when Della asked if we could share this house, I jumped at the chance." She smiled at the memory.

Ida sat on the edge of the bed as Mrs. Wattings lowered herself into a chair to the right of the door.

"Oh, but you were asking about London." Mrs. Wattings got a faraway look in her eyes. "Yes, I was there before Emily was born. I met my husband there." A sad look crossed her face, perhaps explaining Mrs. Wattings's haunted expression. "He brought me here before going out to sea again."

"Ah," Ida replied. She wouldn't pry, but she was desperate—as she always was—to know what had happened.

Was her husband lost? Had he left? How long had he been gone? Was Mrs. Wattings still holding out hope for his return, or had she accepted what might have happened?

Yes, she was distracting herself with someone else's story. But it was better than sobbing on the bed again.

"I have family there, but it's not family I particularly wish to see." Which only made Ida more desperate to know more. *Curiousulus nasus*, indeed. "But Della spoke to me about going back, and giving your family the chance to know

Nora. And I thought my family should at least meet Emily. Even if they don't wish to have us in their lives."

"Won't that be painful for you?"

Ida heard the woman swallow before she answered. "Yes. But Della and I have become a family here, so Emily will never be without love. And my younger brother—he was too young when I left to understand the choice I had to make. I want to give him the chance to make the choice again, to let us in his life. Della says she will work on finding Sam. My husband."

Ida bit her tongue to keep from asking more questions. It was enough, sometimes, for people to talk to her. She didn't always have to be demanding information. That was another thing the past week or so had taught her—she should listen as well as speak.

No matter how many questions she wanted to ask, or how much advice she wanted to give.

Mrs. Wattings shook her head. "I don't know why I am telling you all this, except to say I understand how important family is, and that is why I know it is important for Della to go back. And for us to return as well. That you and your friend can provide the means for us to do it makes it impossible to refuse. So thank you."

"You're welcome." That was the second time in

less than an hour that Ida had been thanked, and she didn't think she had ever had that happen before.

Even if one of the thankers was thanking her for not marrying him. She would perhaps not dwell on that too much.

"Well, we should be able to depart in a few days, provided Lord Carson can make the necessary arrangements."

And then the adventure would be over.

Chapter 16

Sometimes the adventure begins at home.

LADY IDA'S TIPS FOR THE

ADVENTUROUS LADY TRAVELER

Of course Bennett—or Lord Carson, she should be calling him now—had been able to find money, a carriage, a coachman, reasonable horses, and all the supplies they'd need for the journey back to London within only a few days.

Ida had dried off by then, and had borrowed some of Mrs. Wattings's clothing, since she and Ida were closer in size. She wore one of the gowns in the carriage, a simply elegant garment in a soft green color. Bennett had bought a suit from the small clothier that stopped in Haltwhistle once a week, so he had something besides his sodden travel garb to wear.

The suit wasn't what she was accustomed to seeing him in; it was very plain, a dark brown that was simply cut and fit more loosely than his London clothing.

But he looked more dangerous in it, somehow. As though the suit's practicality meant he would be ready at an instant to go do something terribly masculine and important, hopefully working up a sweat in the process.

Or perhaps that was her own wish.

Nora and Emily were beyond thrilled to be going to London, so most of the first part of the journey was the adults answering all the questions about what the girls would see.

No, there were not elephants roaming the streets, but there might be a zoo; yes, it was usual to see people walking about at all times of the day, but the girls would be safely abed in the nighttime; and, yes, there were shops where anybody could purchase ices, a treat that was promised as soon as they were settled into Eleanor's household.

Ida was grateful for their nonstop talk, not just because the children were so refreshing in their curiosity and the interesting perspective they brought. Their talk also meant she wasn't sitting in the carriage seat constantly thinking about Bennett, and about how miserable and lonely the life she'd chosen for herself was going to be.

"I know your sister Olivia works with a school that helps poor children," she heard Bennett say, speaking to Della. The children's chatter had subsided long enough for Ida to hear the conversation. "They just got a sizeable donation from my friend Edward, Olivia's husband, so they might be looking for new teachers, if either of you two wishes to find work in London."

He was suggesting a duke's daughter go to work. He had truly changed, if he were suggesting anything so revolutionary.

Dear lord, but she loved him.

Della's face lit up, and she glanced at Mrs. Wattings. "That could be something we would be very good at, and it would mean we could set up our own establishment. We would be free to make our own decisions."

Just as she and Bennett were. It was unfortunate that their decision hurt so much.

"You're getting ahead of yourself," her friend replied dryly. "As always. You know you have a tendency to just forge ahead without thinking about the particulars of the thing too much."

"Oh, like when I ran off with Mr. Baxter?" Ida's eyes widened at Della's blithe tone, and she caught herself before she glanced at Bennett to gauge his reaction.

She had to get accustomed to relying only on herself again. It had been a delightful interlude when she could share a joke or swap some teasing moments, but it was just that. An interlude.

She had her obligations, and he had his. She knew that, and yet she longed for so much more.

And even if she could somehow figure out how to navigate her obligations and be with him—would he even want to? Would he be able to spare the time for her? Would he be constantly worried that she would embarrass him somehow? Or that he'd long for someone soft and welcoming after all?

It wasn't tenable. *It wasn't.*

And he knew that as well, which was why they had said good-bye long before they'd all clambered into this carriage.

But it didn't hurt any less.

IT WAS AGONY sitting in a carriage with her. Agony and delight, intermingled. Agony that he couldn't spar with her, note her prickly ways, look at her lovely face. Be the recipient of that breathtaking smile.

Delight that he could spend any time at all with her, given that soon their only meetings would be formal ones. In public, likely with all of Society watching them.

If she survived the scandal, that is.

He watched her out of the corner of his eye, noting how attentive she was to her sister, Mrs. Wattings, and the girls. How she asked questions, and probed further to find out information that would be useful when they arrived in London. How she listened thoughtfully when they replied.

She didn't want to reveal it, but she loved her sisters deeply. Of course, that was why she had embarked on this improbable journey in the first place. But he guessed she would be mortified to know someone else had observed just how deeply she felt.

But he had. And he knew, if it were at all possible, that she would love him with an equal depth.

That tore him apart in its delicious agony, knowing he would never find anyone who sparked his imagination and inspired his passion as much as she.

They'd both been clear, however, that their respective obligations meant that they had no future.

He darted a quick, sidelong glance toward her. She was looking out the window, but her gaze was unfocused, and he imagined that, like him, she was thinking about what had happened, and what could never be possible.

If only—if only.

But then he wouldn't be Lord Carson, Champion of the Needy, Provider for the Family.

If that weight were even lifted a tiny bit, just imagine what he could do. What they could do together.

It didn't bear thinking about, and yet he couldn't stop thinking about it all. About her, about their time together, about how she made him feel.

Was this what love felt like?

He wouldn't wish this feeling on his worst enemy.

And yet he couldn't begrudge the feeling, because it meant he had gotten to know and to love her.

Delicious agony. Agonized delight.

No matter how he phrased it, it hurt, and he never wanted to stop feeling it. All of it.

Chapter 17

Adventure isn't always wonderful.

LADY IDA'S TIPS FOR THE
ADVENTUROUS LADY TRAVELER

*T*he return trip to London was a lot less exciting than the original trip.

Which is to say it was not filled with kisses, banter, and, yes, buckets of rain.

Although there were a lot more questions—about the future, about the town, about everything the children could think of.

It must be exhausting to be a parent, Ida thought, even though she knew the benefits outweighed the fatigue.

Still, though, it was with profound relief, therefore, when the carriage finally rolled to a stop in front of Ida's parents' house. Even though her parents' house would, inevitably, contain her parents.

"You're certain you can just return and it will be fine?" Della asked in a skeptical tone.

"Mother will be too delighted at the prospect of—well, you know," Ida said, not wanting to say the words *marriage* and *Lord Carson* in proximity to one another for fear she'd burst into tears. "I'll have at least a few days before she realizes the truth."

"And you'll come find me when it happens?" Della said doggedly.

They'd been over and over it on the journey home. Della, Mrs. Wattings, and their children would stay at Eleanor's house until the ladies had found suitable lodgings for themselves. Lord Carson, meanwhile, would speak to the Society for Poor and Orphaned Children, of which he was a trustee. He was confident he could persuade them to take on two additional instructors, and he had told Della and Mrs. Wattings quite firmly that he would be paying their salary if the Society were not able to.

If it came to the point where the duchess refused to allow Ida to continue living in the house—not that Ida cared much one way or the other—she would go live with the ladies until she could figure out where she and her books could go live permanently. Perhaps she'd stay with Della; maybe she would set off on her own to find a library home of her own.

It was likely to be a lonely existence, but at least she'd be the one deciding it. She still hadn't figured out a way to reconcile Della to her parents, but that didn't seem to matter to Della that much anyway. Nor to Ida, truth be told.

"Yes, Della," Ida replied in a placating tone, "if Mother becomes too ridiculous for me to bear, I will come live with you."

"I'll see you in a few days then," Della replied, patting Ida on the cheek, a wide grin on her face.

"A few days, Aunt Ida," Nora echoed.

Ida gave a rueful chuckle at the joke, then started up the stairs to the front door.

"You're back!" Pearl said as Ida handed her cloak to the startled butler.

"It is good to see you again, my lady," he said.

"It is good to be back," Ida replied.

Pearl rushed over to hug her, her cheeks bright and her hem muddied, indicating she had likely been outside doing things of which the duchess would not approve.

To be fair, anytime the daughters were not actively engaged in trying to get married was doing something the duchess didn't approve of.

"I brought Della back, too," Ida said in a muffled voice.

Pearl peered around Ida's shoulder, her expression puzzled.

"Not back here," Ida said, rolling her eyes. "I wouldn't have brought her here, not without preparation. Lord Carson is taking her and her friend Mrs. Wattings to Eleanor's house. We'll go there in a few hours, once everyone has been settled."

"Mrs. Wattings? Come, tell me everything," Pearl said, taking Ida's hand in hers and leading her upstairs. "Quickly, before Mother realizes you're home."

Ida increased her pace and the two scurried down the hall to Pearl's room, shutting the door firmly behind them.

Pearl launched herself on the bed, kicking her shoes off as she did, an excited expression on her face. "I knew you could do it, Ida. Bringing Della home. And Nora? Is she wonderful? And what is Mrs. Wattings like? Is Della nervous?"

Ida held her hands up in capitulation. "Slow down, you are worse than Mother."

Pearl's eyes widened. "Don't say that," she replied in a horrified tone. She leaned down to brush ineffectually at her hem. "With all of you gone she's been focusing on me, and I have to say, it is dreadful."

Ida sat down in a chair, glancing around at the familiar surrounding.

It felt odd to be here, back in her house, having experienced everything she'd experienced over the course of the past few weeks. Going from thinking Lord Carson was merely someone her sisters hadn't married to thinking about him all of the time.

Fine. She was in love with him, and she should just keep that in mind and try to move on with her life.

"Tell me about Della," Pearl urged, jarring Ida from her thoughts, thank goodness.

"AND SO SHE's here, and Mrs. Wattings, and the two girls," Ida finished as Pearl listened, her eyes wide.

Pearl leaned back on her elbows, an admiring look on her face. "I am so impressed you were able to achieve it all. And Lord Carson ended up going with you? How did that happen?"

"Well," Ida said, anticipating Pearl's inevitable laughter, "he was in the carriage I stole."

Pearl's expression was shocked. *Imagine how I felt when I heard that thumping*, Ida thought.

"And he didn't force you to turn around?"

He'd never force me to do anything I didn't want to. "No, he insisted on accompanying me. To keep me safe."

Pearl frowned in confusion. "So—then what happened while you were traveling? Was it awkward?"

Ida's expression must have slipped, since Pearl sat up and clapped her hands together. "You did not," she exclaimed. "Did you?"

She got up from the bed and skipped toward Ida. "I knew it! You fell in love, didn't you?"

"Uh—" Ida began.

"Does he know? Does he love you? When are you getting married?" Pearl's words came out in one long string of questions, battering Ida with their intensity. Like their mother, only with thoughtful questions.

Her heart constricted. "We're not."

"You're not?" Pearl said, looking suddenly deflated as her skipping stopped.

"He has things he has to do"—at which point Pearl rolled her eyes—"and he doesn't need me as a wife to interrupt any of that."

"Did he say that?" Pearl asked.

"No," Ida admitted. "I did."

"That is the weakest argument I have ever heard you make," Pearl said with a sniff as she leapt back onto the bed again. "He might not think he needs you, but does he want you?"

Ida couldn't help but blush.

"He does! Have you told him how you felt?" Pearl waved her hand in dismissal. "Of course you did. You tell people everything."

Ida bit her lip. "Actually, no. I didn't. I didn't tell him."

A moment as Pearl absorbed Ida's answer, and then Pearl got up again to punch her sister on the arm. "Why ever not? Doesn't he deserve the truth?

The ability to make up his own mind? Shouldn't he be given just the same courtesy he would give you?"

Oh.

She hadn't thought of it that way. She'd been too concerned with not ruining his life, she hadn't thought if he would want her to ruin it.

"I hadn't thought of that," Ida said slowly.

"I never thought I would say this, but Ida—you are an idiot," Pearl declared.

Ida's mouth opened to utter a blistering reply, but then realized her sister might very well be right. Was she an idiot?

Did he want her to ruin his life?

How could she be asking that of herself? Would he ask the same thing of her?

Why were there so many questions?

She and Nora had a lot in common.

Instead of answering, however, she leaned over in her chair and put her hands over her face. What a muddle.

And she, who she knew was the most intelligent woman of her own acquaintance, couldn't figure any of it out.

"YOU'VE RETURNED," ALEX said, a wide grin on his face. He gestured toward his study. "And I hear you've brought visitors."

Bennett followed Alex into the study, shutting

the door behind them. Eleanor had been both startled and delighted to see Della and Mrs. Wattings, taking them upstairs nearly as soon as they walked in the door. A young housemaid was drafted to play with the girls while the women took tea.

When he'd excused himself, the three were strategizing future plans.

"Yes, Lady Della and her friend Mrs. Wattings are taking advantage of your hospitality. Eleanor is with them now. Thank you for inviting them."

"Even though you did," Alex said with a grin. "But this is the first time you've done anything unexpected—you do have to admit to being somewhat predictable, brother—so of course I support whatever it is you're doing." Bennett's throat grew thick at hearing his brother's confident tone.

Bennett sat down on the sofa in front of the fire, Alex sitting down beside him, both of them stretching their legs out in front.

The fire felt warm, and Bennett realized he hadn't relished the warmth, not truly, since he and Ida had agreed to part.

Damn it. Two words that had run through his mind at least once an hour since they'd spoken in Lady Della's sitting room.

"I don't know what I'm doing," Bennett admitted. It felt so freeing to be able to express his emotions. He usually held everything in, even with Alex, who wouldn't judge him no matter what he'd gotten into.

Truth be told, Alex would probably appreciate him even more if he had gotten into trouble. His younger brother was always concerned Bennett was too serious.

"That is a surprise," Alex said. He narrowed his gaze. "Lady Della doesn't have anything to do with that, does she?"

Bennett straightened up on the sofa. "No! No, of course not. She is a kind and interesting person, but she is not—"

"Not Lady Ida?" Alex finished, a sly smile on his face.

Damn it again. So Alex knew, and was just teasing him.

"How did you know? I've just arrived!" Bennett said.

Alex laughed at him. The most annoying of brothers, to be sure.

"Eleanor said you two would do well together. I never mentioned it, though, because I knew you would bristle." He shrugged. "So we agreed to let nature take its course."

Bennett exhaled. "No, she is not Lady Ida." *Nobody is.* Well, except for her herself, he could hear Ida point out, somewhat pedantically. He smiled at the thought.

"So what are you going to do about that problem?" Alex asked, folding his arms over his chest. "It's not as though there isn't precedent for a member of our family marrying one of their family." He paused. "And our father would be happy about it. Is that—?" he began.

Bennett groaned. "I promise, that is not why I am not immediately rushing over to propose, just to annoy our father."

"Then why aren't you?" Alex asked in a much more serious tone.

Bennett hesitated. There was so much to that answer, and he didn't want Alex to get the impression that Ida was difficult—even though of course she was. Or that she was stubborn. Even though she was. Or unlikely to compromise.

"Damn it." Well, now he was changing it up by saying it aloud, at least. "I don't know if I can explain it. Except that I could never ask her to change."

Alex held his gaze as he thought. It was odd to see Alex so contemplative; normally he was making light of every situation, deflecting anything that might make him personally responsible.

Except he'd offered to step in if—when—Bennett needed to escape.

Except he was here, asking the difficult questions that Bennett did not want to answer. But knew he should.

Except Alex was different than he'd ever been before.

"It's not always a bad thing when people change," Alex said, confirming Bennett's thoughts. "And it's not so much asking as loving someone enough to grow together in compromise."

Bennett couldn't speak for a moment. "That is—that is a very deep statement."

Alex cocked a brow. "Never thought I'd have one of those, did you?" He leaned forward toward Bennett. "That is because I've changed. Love changes you."

Bennett stuck his hand out to push Alex back. "Cut it out. But what if she doesn't want to change?"

"What if she wants you to change?" Alex said in a challenging tone. "What would you say to that?"

"Well, of course I would, because I love her," Bennett answered automatically. Inhaling as he realized what he'd said. He hadn't said it aloud yet—had he?

"You love her," Alex repeated.

"Yes," he admitted. "I love her."

"Do you think she loves you?"

He took a deep breath. Recalling every time she had looked at him, during arguments, conversation, and passion. Knowing the answer to the question even though she'd never said it.

"I think so."

"But you never told her?" Alex continued. "Sometimes it is useful to speak directly. Just look at me, I have the lady I love. Because I told her I loved her."

"I'm not you."

Alex rolled his eyes. "Now that you have confirmed that, and that you never did tell her how you feel, what are you going to do about it?"

Bennett shook his head. For once not having the answer. "What can I do about it? She and I talked, we agreed that it was impossible for us to marry."

"Why not?" Alex sounded genuinely baffled, and as always, Bennett admired his brother's directness. "Because if you love her—which you say you do—and she loves you, which I believe might be possible, even though you are a dull stick in the mud, and I can't see the appeal, that should mean there is no impediment to marriage."

"Thank you for your honesty," Bennett said in a dry tone.

"You're welcome," Alex said, dipping his chin toward his brother. "Now you just have to stop being an idiot and ask her. You want her in your life more than anything, don't you?"

Bennett swallowed. Hearing the truth of it stated so bluntly, in Alex's usual manner, made it so much more forceful.

"I do."

"Then go do something about it," Alex said.

"I will," Bennett said as he rose from the sofa. Alex rose as well, patting Bennett on the arm, as though for encouragement.

"Go," Alex urged.

"On my way," Bennett promised. But first, he'd have to confront his responsibilities.

"Is MY FATHER here?" Bennett asked as he entered the house.

"No, my lord," the butler replied.

"Of course not."

He was both relieved and disappointed he wouldn't be able to speak with the marquis at this moment. But at least, perhaps, he could see his mother. He'd missed her. She was the primary reason he did everything he did, and it was worth it when he saw her smile.

Bennett bounded up the stairs toward her room, hoping she would be awake.

He tapped on the door, opening it when he heard his mother's nurse call for him to come in.

The room was dark, the curtains pulled over the windows, allowing just the barest hint of light in. There were a few candles lit around the room, giving a warm glow to the otherwise gloomy setting. His eyes had to adjust before he saw who was in the room.

"Bennett!" his mother exclaimed as he walked toward her.

His mother was sitting up in bed, a cup of tea in her hand, her nurse at her side. Nurse Cooper sprang up as he walked in, quickly taking a different chair at the foot of the bed.

"Good afternoon, my lord," the nurse said in a quiet tone.

Bennett went to sit down beside his mother, pleased to see she looked relatively alert. She spent more and more time, it seemed, in a kind of twilight fog, exacerbated by her medications and her husband's neglect.

"You're back," she said, putting her tea to one side. "I've missed you, but I am certain you had good reason to be gone."

I had the best reason, he wanted to say. But it felt too new, too fragile, to share with his mother just yet. Plus, he had no idea how to begin—*I longed for escape so I got into a carriage that wasn't mine, only to be taken on a journey to the north of England with the smartest lady of my acquaintance?*

It sounded ridiculous, even in his own mind.

"Yes, I've returned." Unnecessary to say, since he was right here, but he had grown accustomed to reassuring his mother whenever possible. No matter if it was redundant.

"Alexander told me you were on a trip. I didn't

know you were planning one," she said, and Bennett felt guilty. Not that he should; he often went on trips, sometimes for longer than this one, but he usually warned his mother ahead of time.

Since he'd had no warning himself, he hadn't been able to tell her. "Alexander and Eleanor came by several times with the baby." She glanced over at Nurse Cooper. "What an adorable child, don't you think?"

"Yes, my lady," Nurse Cooper said.

"She played on my bed and cooed and gurgled and I was reminded of when you and Alexander were young."

Bennett smiled at his mother's obvious happiness.

"Nurse, would you excuse us for a moment?" his mother asked after a few moments.

"Of course, my lady." Nurse Cooper left the room in her usual quiet fashion as Bennett waited for what his mother might say. It wasn't usual for her to ask for time alone with him.

"What is it, Mother?"

She clasped his fingers. "You know I want you to be happy."

"Of course."

She shook her head impatiently, as though wanting him to dive deeper into the conversation. "I know you haven't been happy. It wouldn't be possible, not living the way you do, being busy all the time. That was why I was so glad to hear you'd left so unexpectedly. I was hoping it was something you wanted to do for you."

Oh. First Alex, now his mother. Both of them concerned for his well-being. Both of them urging him to do something for himself.

When had he become so obviously self-sacrificing?

"Actually," Bennett said, clearing his throat, "I've brought Lady Della Howlett home with her daughter. And their friend and her daughter. It was a bit of a rescue mission." Undertaken all because of Ida.

His mother smiled. "Of course it was doing something good. That is so you." She spoke in a heartfelt tone as she continued. "But the thing is"—and she sounded much more serious now, leaning forward as she spoke—"I will not have you put your own wants and desires aside for this family anymore. You think I don't know what you do for us, what you've done for me, but I do." She nodded. "I do. And I may not be here for much longer, and then what will become of you? Lost to work, the way your father is lost to—" And she stopped speaking, her mouth tightening at the hurt.

Of losing her husband, his father, to another woman. Another family. Another life.

"But never mind that." She waved her own

misery aside as she focused on him. "You have to promise me," she said in a low, fierce tone, "that you will do whatever you need to do to make yourself happy. Alexander has found Eleanor, and he is as happy as I have ever seen him. It is your turn. It is past your turn. Do not deny yourself simply because you think others expect it. They will take it, if they think you are going to give it. Don't let them. *Don't*."

He saw her eyes sparkling with tears, and his heart hurt at her loss. She had given for years, first to her husband and then to him and Alexander. She was clearly speaking from her own experience, but that didn't mean it wasn't just as relevant to him.

His throat closed, thick with emotion. His mother was the biggest reason he had made the sacrifices he had, and he knew—because he knew how much she loved him—how earnestly she wanted his happiness.

And happiness wasn't possible if he didn't do something to change his life. To dare to compromise.

To dare *her* to compromise.

"I will, Mother," he said, getting up to place a kiss on her forehead. "I promise you, I will do whatever it takes to find my happiness."

Her eyes were moist. "Is there—is there someone you have in mind?"

He winced internally at how obvious he must be. Did he have "I have fallen in love" painted on his forehead?

"As a matter of fact, there is," he said.

"Oh!" she exclaimed, a few tears spilling down her cheeks, "that is wonderful. Tell me about her."

Bennett took a moment before replying. "She's intelligent, courageous, good-hearted, and fiercely argumentative."

His mother's smile faltered at the last part, but then she chuckled. "You wouldn't be satisfied with a woman who was any less than that. Imagine how dull it would be to come home to a person who agreed with you all the time."

"Like being married to a fuzzy blanket?" Bennett asked in a wry tone. Reminded of Ida's disdainful words when they'd first met.

"Precisely!" his mother exclaimed. "Very clever. Have you asked her to marry you yet?"

Bennett shook his head slowly. "Not yet, no."

She frowned. "And why not?"

Just like Alex had said.

"I will. I promise."

"Good." She gripped his hand tightly once more, then released it with a sigh. "And those ladies and their daughters will come visit, won't they?"

"Yes, and perhaps if you are strong enough, you can go out with them to the park."

She smiled. "That would be nice. I will scold Nurse Cooper into making me better. I've been lying here for far too long. It seems I have a wedding to attend."

It wasn't a guarantee that she would recover, but at least she had intimated she would try.

"Thank you." Bennett raised her hand to his mouth and kissed it. "And now I should let you rest. I've got some happiness to gain."

"That you do," she said in a pleased tone of voice.

Chapter 18

Stand up for your own adventure.

LADY IDA'S TIPS FOR THE
ADVENTUROUS LADY TRAVELER

"*Ida!*"

Ida froze in mid-step on the stairs as her mother walked inside the house. It turned out she and Pearl hadn't had to rush off to Pearl's bedroom because the duchess had been out paying calls.

But now Ida had to brace herself for a talk with her mother.

"You are back!" The duchess strode forward, holding her arms wide. She folded Ida in an unwilling hug, patting her back as though approving of her.

How long would it be before her mother returned to strong disapproval of her youngest daughter?

"I was expecting to see Lord Carson here with you, but I suppose he has to go see his family."

The duchess spoke as though it were an inconvenience for Bennett to have his own family to care about.

"It was so exciting to hear that you and he had gone off together!" the duchess continued. "I wish you had written to me, and not your sister."

"Pearl," Ida supplied, in case her mother had forgotten.

"But to hear that you and Lord Carson! Of course I had to break the news to Lord Bradford. He was terribly disappointed."

"About that," Ida began, taking her mother's arm. "Could we speak in your sitting room? I want to share some news."

Her mother nodded, clasping Ida's hand in hers. "I think I can guess what the news is! And may I say I am so happy for you."

The unsettled feeling in Ida's stomach grew. She wasn't dreading telling her mother not to expect her to marry Lord Carson after all; she had spoken enough truths, no matter how unwelcome, in her lifetime to have gotten over the potential awkwardness.

It was just that now that she knew how she felt, truly felt, it was agony to even speculate that it might not happen. Even though that was just what she had planned back in Della's sitting room.

But Pearl was right. She should give him the chance to know how she felt, to allow for the possibility of their being together, no matter how much Ida feared she would do or say something that would harm his business or his family.

"So Lord Carson and I," Ida began as she followed her mother into her sitting room.

AN HOUR LATER, Ida's ears were still ringing with the force of her mother's shrieking.

It had not gone well.

The duchess had thought at first that Ida was joking, and then, when she understood she was not, had begun to shout. *She would not acknowledge Della, despite her return to London, she never wanted to meet Nora, and she was looking forward to what the duke would say when he found out.*

And then she started repeating all of it, only louder, at which point Ida excused herself and returned to her room, where she found a concerned Pearl.

And a note.

Lady Ida,

Please do me the favor of appearing at Lady Linden's party this evening.

Lord Carson

"You'll go, won't you?" Pearl said, looking over her shoulder at the note. "I wasn't planning on it, but I will now, if you will be there. Is he bringing Della, do you think?"

"I wouldn't think so," Ida said, shaking her head. "I don't think Della wants anything to do with Society now. I think she just wants to be with her family. With us. And perhaps to help Mrs. Wattings reunite with her own family."

Ida looked at the letter again, her heart fluttering. "I might as well get the ostracism over with. I'll go tonight, if just to see how many backs are turned on me."

Pearl stroked her shoulder. "You're my bravest sister."

Ida lifted an eyebrow. "Because I am willing to go to a delightful party? You have an odd notion of bravery, Pearl."

Pearl poked her gently. "You know that's not what I meant. To see the gentleman you love, you idiot."

Ida laughed.

It reminded her of what it was like when he teased her, all prickly hedgehog-ness of her.

That made her throat get tight, and she tried to shove the thoughts out of her head. Yes. She would see him, and she would tell him the truth. All of it.

THIS TIME, BENNETT was seated at his desk when his father strode in. The viscount frowned, and looked as though he were going to say something, but Bennett raised an eyebrow—Ida style—at him, and he shut his mouth.

His father took the seat on the other side of the desk.

"I've heard a rumor about you and that lady," his father said in a disapproving tone.

"Lady Ida," Bennett said, his voice tight.

"There is no guarantee the duke will dower this Howlett sister well, given the way she has behaved." He looked disgusted. "Running away with you, without thinking of how it would be perceived. The duke might demand we give him money to take her."

The evident scorn made Bennett want to punch his father. But that wouldn't solve anything.

Though it would make him feel better.

"None of that matters." Bennett spoke with a firm resolve. He planted his fists on the desk and rose, standing over his father, who appeared to flinch.

Good.

"I am going to ask Lady Ida to marry me. I am done with compensating for your failures."

The marquis blinked, as though he couldn't believe what he was hearing. And then his face got red, as though his emotions were choking him. "If you do this, you'll be sacrificing everything just because you've compromised some woman."

Bennett spoke in a slow, measured tone. "I have already sacrificed enough for the very same reason. Because you compromised some woman, and all of us suffer for it. I will not give up my own happiness because of familial obligation. The family is going to have to learn that I require a life, too."

"And this female is going to be enough for you? Be enough when your mother suffers because of you?"

"How will she suffer?" Bennett asked, his throat tightening. "Any more than she has already, seeing your perfidy daily. Do you think she doesn't know already? Do you think that if I spend only six hours a day on various business pursuits that she will suffer? I will always ensure she is comfortable. I just refuse to dedicate my life to ensuring your comfort."

The marquis's face twisted, and Bennett wondered if his father was going to strike him. Instead, he stood and pointed toward Bennett, his expression furious.

But no angrier than Bennett was.

"You are no longer welcome in this house," his father declared. "You will not be able to see your mother and you will no longer be privy to the family business."

Bennett snorted. "I wish it were that easy. No, Father, your complete disinterest in what has happened in this family has meant that I am the signatory on all matters of business. All this means is that you and I no longer have a relationship. I will set up my own house once Ida and I are married, and then we will invite my mother to live with us."

"You'll be married to a lady of uncertain virtue and living with the dullest woman that has ever been born." The marquis spoke in a vicious tone, and Bennett wondered when his father had gotten so cruel.

"You will not speak of anybody I care about ever again," Bennett said, his voice shaking. "I have told you what I am going to do, and that I will take care of things as I have. Just not to the extent you wish. I will be living my own life from now on."

"And I hope it is a damned one."

Bennett set his jaw, refusing to respond to his father's childish taunts.

He strode out of the office without a backward look. He should have had it out with his father long before this, but he was constrained by what he thought his mother deserved. But now that she'd told him how she felt, and what she wanted for him, he no longer had to worry.

Unless Ida said no.

"He's over there," Pearl said, pointing.

Ida stood at the entrance to the ballroom, anxiety

knotting her stomach. Not because she was unwilling to face her own disgrace, but because for once she couldn't analyze what was happening.

"You look lovely," Pearl said, touching Ida's waist.

Ida smiled at her sister, knowing that that was the truth. She'd figured she was already ruined, she might as well be ruined in clothing that pleased her. So she'd borrowed a red gown from her sister Eleanor, the red of a literal scarlet woman. The irony of it made Ida smile.

Pearl's skill with a needle—often taken advantage of by their sister Eleanor—helped in adjusting the gown to Ida's figure.

The gown dipped lower than most debutantes' gowns were normally cut, and Ida would have been more conscious of more of her bosom showing, but that concern ranked far behind having her mother scream at her in public, her father turning his back on her, and the man she loved being on the other side of the room.

If she were to make a list in order of crisis, it would be:

1. Man she loved on the other side of the room.
2. Her mother screaming at her. Not because of the words, but because it made Ida's ears hurt.

3. Her father turning his back on her.
4. Her gown. At least she looked good in
   the gown.

"I wondered you were here this evening." Ida turned at the voice, which belonged to a young lady, whose bitter expression made it clear she was a Carson-hunter.

"I am not sure we have been introduced," Ida said, lifting her chin.

"I am not certain we should be," the lady replied, looking Ida up and down.

Pearl looked from one to the other, her mouth open.

Ida shrugged. "Then we are at an impasse," she said, taking Pearl's arm as she began to walk away.

"No, wait," the lady said. "I am Lady Frances Mayweather. I am acquainted with Lord Carson."

"I presumed you were," Ida replied. "So now we know who we both are, perhaps we should agree never to meet again."

She heard Pearl's sharp inhale.

Lady Frances's eyes narrowed. "You do know that if he marries you, it is only because he is an honorable, responsible gentleman."

Ida snorted. "If your argument to persuade me

not to marry him is to tell me he is both honorable and responsible, then I think you should reread Sophocles."

Lady Frances's expression got puzzled.

"You don't deserve him," Lady Frances said.

Pearl tugged on Ida's sleeve. "We should go get some punch. I am very thirsty."

Ida shook Pearl's hand off, stepping close to Lady Frances. "Again, if you are trying to persuade me not to marry him because I do not deserve him, you do not make a compelling argument. I know I do not deserve him. But that doesn't mean I don't love him."

Lady Frances inhaled, her mouth pinched.

Ida hadn't planned on saying that, but of course she never planned on saying anything. *Good work, Ida. You've just told this loathsome debutante you love him before you told him.*

"Now I'm not just wondering why you are here, but why anybody allows you to appear in public," Lady Frances said, glancing over Ida's head to where, presumably, other members of Society were wondering the same thing.

Ida took a deep breath. She had a few choices. One was to nod and smile—albeit a pained smile—at Lady Frances.

Well, she knew she wasn't going to take that option.

She could glare at Lady Frances and stalk somewhere else.

Only, of course, other people would likely give her the cut direct, and she'd end up behind the pillar again.

She was damned tired of hiding behind the pillar.

The third option, the option she knew she was going to take, was a risk. But it was a risk she needed to take.

"Pardon me, ladies and gentlemen," she began in a carrying tone.

She felt the whirl of skirts and the pointed glances as the people in the room either looked at her or tried to ignore her.

"I have returned after a trip." A scandalous intake of breath. "A mission, more accurately."

Whispered bits of conversation washed over her, all of which seemed to be saying, "She is entirely and openly scandalous."

Well, she couldn't argue with them. But she was tired of having to feel guilty for it.

She continued. Recognizing that she might be permanently shunned for what she'd done— what she might say—but not able to care. Not as long as she had her sisters' good approval. "I have been gracing these ballrooms for close to a year now. Since my older sister Eleanor got married."

More whispers. Since Eleanor and Alexander's marriage was nearly as scandalous.

"And in that time," she said, turning to look at a few people in the room, most of whom averted their gaze, "I have learned a few things. Things I would like to share with you."

She suppressed a grin as she heard some people in the crowd utter audible groans. Because of course they recalled other times she'd launched into lectures that had gone on for an interminable time, containing information only she found fascinating.

They should go hide behind pillars and see what their conversational skills were like after that experience. And then come speak to her.

"Knowledge and learning are not always highly valued for ladies. It is better that we spend our time doing embroidery, or doing good works, or learning how to dance."

A rustle in the crowd as some of them recalled that the duke's daughters' dancing master ran away with Della.

Perhaps she should not have brought up that last point.

"But what I want to share with you, what I learned on my recent journey, is that all knowledge is useful."

An obvious point, but one she was fairly certain young ladies generally did not acknowledge.

"For example, on this trip I learned how to listen." She paused so they could all absorb what she'd said. "I learned how to share my thoughts and feelings. I learned"—and then she hesitated, because she wasn't certain how to put it into words—"I learned that there is always more to learn."

Redundant, yes, but true nonetheless. Truly true, if she were being particularly redundant.

"So while some of you might not want to know me after what I've done, and been through, you don't know all the facts. I think learning and asking questions and finding things out is far better than judging someone for who they appear to be, and what you think they might have done."

Silence in the ballroom. Even the duchess was struck dumb—a minor miracle Ida would have to remember for the future.

"I have learned not to judge for myself. Not to foreclose on someone who might appear only to be the sum of his responsibilities. People, all people, have myriad depths and nuances to them." Except for, perhaps, Lady Frances. Ida would have to learn a lot more about that lady before she judged her favorably. "A responsibility might feel like a burden, but it is a burden some people gladly take on. If it's done for the greater good."

She felt something at her side, and realized it

was Pearl, who was taking her fingers in a firm grasp. Giving her encouragement, as she and her other sisters always had.

Even though Ida hadn't always recognized it.

"Thank you for listening."

She stopped speaking, and waited for the response. Pearl withdrew her hand and began to clap; a few other young ladies did as well, despite their parents' scandalized looks.

It was enough. It was, perhaps, her final public speech, and there was no better way to cement her reputation as someone with a firm opinion than tell people precisely what she thought.

"That was very good," Pearl said in a whisper. "Much better than some of your other talks."

"That is faint praise, sister," Ida said in a wry voice, "but I'll take it."

"Ida?" Pearl said. "Over there?" And she pointed to where Bennett stood staring at her. She had lost him in the crowd; perhaps he had been hiding behind a pillar himself.

Even though he was Charming Lord Carson, the most persuasive man in the House of Lords. The one who could likely convince her mother to stop talking.

Ida felt as though her heart stopped, even though she knew that it wasn't scientifically possible for a heart to stop.

And then he started to walk toward her as Pearl

firmly removed Lady Frances from the scene and stepped away herself.

"Good evening, Lady Ida."

The man she loved was directly in front of her.

"Good evening, my lord," she replied.

His eyes traveled down and then up again, an appreciative gleam in his eye. "You look gorgeous. You chose this for yourself, hedgehog?"

His using the nickname in that tone made her heat from the inside.

"I enjoyed your speech. It was remarkable."

Her breath caught.

"If I may?" he said, gesturing toward the dance floor.

He wanted her to come this evening—so they could partner in a dance?

She placed her hand in his and he leaned in close to speak into her ear. His breath tickled her skin. "You told me you do not dance, and I told you that you would enjoy dancing with me. Do you remember?"

When she'd explained about Della's Mr. Baxter.

The words were right there on the tip of her tongue—*but I do not dance*—but that was the Ida who didn't compromise. Who was Ida the Implacable.

Not that she was now Ida the Malleable, but she was more . . . accommodating. And it was him, and she trusted him. So she would dance after all.

Especially if it meant she'd be in the arms of the man she loved. Even though—but she wouldn't ruin this present moment with thinking what may or may not happen in the future.

"Of course," she said, taking the hand he offered.

The crowd hushed as they took the floor, either because they thought they were watching a scandal in the making or watching a respectably betrothed couple share a dance.

She herself couldn't wait to find out which one it would be.

He took her in his arms, and she closed her eyes, swallowing against the joy and agony she felt at being in his arms again.

"You don't have to," she began.

"I want to," he said at the same time.

They smiled at one another, and Ida's cheeks heated at how he was looking at her. As though he—

"I don't understand," she blurted out.

"No, you don't," he said, then whirled her close to where the musicians played, holding his hand up.

The music ceased, and the other dancing couples came to confused stops all around them.

"What—?" she began.

He released her, stepping to the center of the floor.

"If you will pardon the interruption, ladies and gentlemen," he began, and Ida bit her lip, hope winning the war against disappointment in her heart. *Please, please, please.*

"Listening to Lady Ida's speech earlier this evening, I was struck by how seldom we actually ask for things we want. We ask for things we want or need to help others, we ask each other how we are, and if we think it will rain. But we don't ask for us. That bravery, that honesty, is so rare to find, and I am not surprised to find it in Lady Ida. I wish to follow her lead, and ask for something for myself this evening."

He looked so beautiful standing there, lit golden by the candlelight. So confident and proud.

"Most of you know that I am a responsible person. So responsible, in fact, that I wasn't able to court a lady myself, but asked my brother to do it because my responsibilities were so vast."

A few people in the crowd chuckled, since they knew that his brother had ended up married to the lady in question—Ida's sister Eleanor.

"Doing something unexpected is not anything anybody would expect of me," he said, smiling as though to acknowledge the redundancy. "But I have done not one, but several unexpected things."

He turned to face Ida.

"The most important of those things, however, is that I fell in love. Unexpectedly. With a woman who is fierce, brave, intelligent, and stubborn. A woman who is neither soft nor gentle, but is so much more than that. Loyal, independent, and unwilling to compromise."

Oh. That was her.

"The thing is," he said as he approached her, his expression focused entirely on her, "is that she shouldn't have to compromise. Not now. Not ever. Except in one instance." He smiled, and it felt as though her heart were going to burst through her chest.

Even though, again, that was a scientific impossibility.

He turned back to face the crowd again. "I have spent so much of my life doing things for other people. I was reminded recently that it is time I do something for myself. And so I am not going to deny what I want. What I need.

"Who I love."

He turned toward her, his expression softer. And then just before he reached her, he got down on one knee and looked up at her.

"Ida, I won't ask you to marry me."

"You won't?" Ida heard Pearl squawk, and she heard herself snort.

Of course she did.

Bennett shook his head. "Not until I tell her everything I am going to do for her. For us." He took her hand in his. "I promise I will always listen to you and argue, if necessary. I promise I will always love you, no matter how prickly you might get." She felt the beginnings of a smile curl her lips. "I promise to challenge you every day, even though I understand I might be wrong. I promise to put us first and not let anything or anyone distract me from my one goal."

"Which is?" she whispered.

"To love you for the rest of my life, hedgehog," he replied. "Ida, I will ask you now. I want you to partner with me. To dare you to speak your mind and follow your heart. Will you marry me?" As he asked that final question, he put his hand in his pocket and withdrew a box, opening it to reveal a single, brilliant diamond set boldly on a simple silver band.

She nodded, unable to speak for perhaps only the fifth or so time in her life. Likely not even able to make a speech about how diamonds came into existence, or the process by which they were removed from the ground.

He stood, slipping the ring on her finger and dropping the box in his pocket before gesturing to the musicians.

The music began again, and he took her in his arms and started to dance, his eyes smiling down at her. Her knowing she likely looked like an idiot grinning back at him, but unable to stop.

"I dare, Ida. Do you?"

"I do."

DO YOU DARE, *Ida?*

She'd come home with him, his prickly hedgehog, because of course she had. Her reputation was shredded anyway.

He'd brought her up to his bedroom after dismissing the servants, choosing to remove her cloak himself.

They nearly didn't make it upstairs, he was kissing her so ferociously. Not that she seemed to mind.

He opened the door to his room, and she stepped inside, her quick gaze taking in the surroundings—the enormous bed, the books scattered on the desk and on the carpet, the pictures of him and Alex done when they were young.

Only Alex and his valet had ever seen his room before. It was his place to be just him, just Bennett, and he wanted to share all of it with her.

He drew her into his arms and looked down at her. "I'll ask again, only more quietly, since it's just the two of us. Do you dare, Ida?"

She slid her hands up under his coat and began to scratch his back, as she knew he liked. "I dare. As do you. You know who I am, Bennett.

You see me as I am, much better than even my own relatives." She leaned up into him, pressing her mouth softly on his. "I dare."

Bennett slid his arms around her waist, drawing her tight against him. "Show me," he said in a voice ragged with longing. With love. "Show me how you dare."

She gave a sly smile, then tightened her hold about his neck. "Only if you dare to show me as well. Things like what you truly want and need."

You, only you.

"I will," he promised.

"Good. Then let me dare," she replied, unclasping her hands and bringing them to the back of her gown, arching her breasts forward into his body as she did.

She wasn't thinking anymore. She was *feeling*.

And it felt wonderful.

She twisted her fingers at the back of her gown, beginning to undo the buttons, then uttered a snort of frustration as she reached the limit of what she could do for herself.

"Do you need some assistance, hedgehog?" he asked. "Turn around." The last bit was said as though he were ordering her to obey, not something she was accustomed to hearing.

But coming from him, there was something

thrilling about being told what to do. What else might he demand?

She did as he'd demanded, turning so her back was to him. She drew one foot up and slipped it onto the back of her shoe so she could slide one shoe off, then the other, wobbling on her feet as she did so.

He was busily undoing her buttons, and she leaned over to slide her stockings off, which resulted in her pushing her arse into his front.

She heard an indrawn breath, and smiled down at the floor at his response.

"God, Ida, you don't know what you're making me think of."

She straightened, but kept her back to him, beginning to slide her gown off her shoulders. "I dare you to tell me later." She wiggled against him as she slid her gown down her body to pool on the floor.

She didn't like what she wore most of the time, but this time she could say was the absolute happiest she had ever been to remove her clothing. Even though the red gown was the prettiest thing she had ever worn.

She was in her shift, and the freedom from all the constrictive clothing made her feel glorious. Also because she was anticipating how he would react at seeing her less clothed.

"Ida," he said in a warning tone as she pushed

back against him. She felt him, thick and hard against her, and her breathing got faster at the thought. Of him thrusting into her, of him bringing her to that edge of excitement.

Of her doing the same to him.

She turned then as she placed her hand just there, right on his cock. He leaned his head back, his gorgeous muscular neck showing the strain of what he was feeling.

She clasped him through the fabric of his trousers and got on tiptoes to lick his neck on the side where the pulse throbbed.

He groaned, and she smiled, lifting her right hand to the placket of his trousers, beginning to undo the fall.

He brought his fingers to his shirt and she shook her head, moving her lips down to the top of his cravat. "I want to do that. Let me do it for you, Bennett. Let me."

She knew, because he'd shared it with her, that people seldom did things for Bennett. Did they ever do things for him?

He did things for other people, asking for nothing in return. So this moment, where she could do something for him, meant she could show him best how she felt—that he was worth doing things for, that she wanted to do things for him. And to him.

With that in mind, she shoved his trousers over

his hips, pulling them down as she lowered herself onto the floor.

His cock was right there by her face, thrusting out from his smallclothes, and she pushed his smallclothes down too so he was naked from the knees up.

An awkward vision if she weren't so enthralled by the sight of his cock, pulsing and hard. She wrapped her fingers around it and brought it to her lips, giving the top a tentative lick.

"God, Ida," he said in a strangled tone. He clutched the edge of his desk in either hand.

She moved her hand up and down and placed her mouth more firmly around him, licking the top as though it were an ice.

But he was hot and hard in her mouth, and this was far more delicious than even the most delicious of ices.

She slid her fingers down his shaft as she took more of him in her mouth, almost choking from it. But even that felt good; the feeling that she was filled with him, that she was focusing entirely on him, on Bennett, on the man she loved.

"Ida," he groaned, cupping the side of her face, sliding his fingers into her hair. It began to spill out of her coiffure, and it felt as though every part of her was spilling over—filled to the maximum with the emotion of it, of this moment when she was showing him, not telling him, how she felt.

Mere words, even though they were words, things she'd heretofore thought were the most powerful weapon, wouldn't suffice now.

And then he yanked her up and claimed her mouth savagely, ruthlessly, making her knees buckle and her whole body tingle, aware of where every single part of him touched every single part of her.

But those parts weren't enough.

"I want you inside me, Bennett," she demanded as she broke their kiss. His eyes were wild, burning with what she knew was desire. She must look equally disheveled; her hair undone, her mouth bruised from his kiss, dressed only in her shift.

"How do you want me? Tell me. There's this way"—and he picked up one leg and drew it around his waist, his cock bobbing into her stomach—"although that might be awkward after a bit. There's this way"—and he twisted nimbly, shoving everything on the desk to the ground and laying her across its surface—"or there's this"—and he brought her back so she stood again, but facing the desk, placing his hand on her neck and pushing her down so she lay flat on the table, her feet on the ground. "How do you want it, Ida?"

The desk was hard against her cheek, her breasts were flattened on the surface, her hands pressed on either side of her head.

She felt at his mercy. She felt in total control.

"This way, please," she said, wiggling her hips.

"Fuck, Ida," he said, and he caressed her arse with his hand, sliding lower to cup her there between her legs, right where she throbbed and pulsed.

"You're so ready," he said, and she felt his cock nudge at her entrance, his hands spreading her wide, and she raised up on her tiptoes to make it easier for him to thrust into her.

"Aaaahh," he said as she felt him push inside, filling her with a pleasant ache. He ran his palm over her arse again, then put his fingers on her hip and held on as he withdrew and slammed back into her again, so hard she skidded up the desk.

"Too much?" he asked, his tone concerned through the ragged lust. So caring, even when he was inside her and wild with passion.

"No," she said, shaking her head. "More."

He grunted, and withdrew and thrust in again, one hand on her hip, the other holding her neck so she didn't move too far away.

She pushed back to meet him, and it seemed that was something he liked, since he made some more inarticulate noises and pushed harder, and faster, until he stayed inside and she could feel him pulse, and a spreading warmth was inside her.

He pushed in and out a few more times, his hold on her lessening, and she smiled into the surface of the desk.

> *Sometimes you will get bruises, but they will be worth it.*
>
> LADY IDA'S TIPS FOR THE
> ADVENTUROUS LADY TRAVELER

SHE WAS SPRAWLED flat on the desk, his desk, her hair a tangle, her shift hiked up above her waist, her face turned so he could see her expression.

She had a satisfied smile on her face, as though she knew how she'd wrecked him, destroyed his emotions just by submitting to him.

The first time, they'd started out making love, him conscious of her inexperience and that he needed to be gentle.

Now, however, they were fucking, and he didn't feel as though he needed to take care of her—she could take care of herself, thank you very much, and have a good time doing it.

Although—"You didn't come," he said as he withdrew from her.

"No," she said, pushing herself up on her hands so she could stand.

She turned to face him as her shift fell down her body.

"Well, since you have shown me how you feel,

how about I show you? After all, you are a strong proponent of equality, are you not?"

She smiled, one of those heartbreakingly pure and honest smiles he'd longed for as long as he'd known her, and his heart melted all over again.

Dear god, but he loved her. And desired her, and admired her, and wanted to spend the rest of his life with her.

He was beyond besotted. *Obsessi Bennettum.*

"Yes, that would be educational. Possibly even pleasant," she said with a wicked look on her face.

"Pleasant is what you call it?" he said, placing his hands on her shoulders and seating her on the desk. Her legs dangled, and he stepped between them, putting his hands on her knees. "Keep these open for me, and then you can tell me how pleasant you find it." He used his shirt to wipe her clean.

He lowered himself to the floor, positioning himself so his face was right there, right at her entrance.

"Dear God, you're lovely," he said, before leaning in to lick her, the warmth and smell of her making him never want to move away.

"Ohh," she exclaimed, her legs closing instinctively. He put his palms on either thigh and held her open, settling himself in to feast on her.

"Is this pleasant, Ida?" he murmured between

licks, loving how she was quivering under his touch.

"You know it is," she replied in her most condescending Ida tone.

He chuckled before blowing on her, then licking her more intently, paying attention to how she reacted, changing his approach to best bring her pleasure. He curled one finger inside her and felt her jump as he touched that spot that would bring her even more pleasure.

She moaned above him, and he felt her start to shake.

Good. *Pleasant.*

And then he closed his mouth over her nub, licking in the same rhythm, feeling her shudder and pulse on his tongue.

"Ahhh," she cried as she climaxed, and he slowed his movements, breathing in her scent, stroking her skin as she continued to pulse.

At last, she was done, and he rose, stepping between her legs again as he had before.

"Was that pleasant?" he asked in a conversational tone.

She swatted him on the shoulder. "You're ridiculous."

He nodded. "Yes, but only with you. Only for you."

Chapter 19

Dare. Just dare.

LADY IDA'S TIPS FOR THE
ADVENTUROUS LADY TRAVELER

*T*he sky, Ida was pleased to see, was relatively bare of clouds. No chance of precipitation on this most auspicious of days.

Although it was a rainstorm that had precipitated so many things, so she couldn't complain about the weather no matter what happened.

"Are you ready?" Della asked, touching Ida's cheek. Pearl stood behind, fussing with the ribbons at the back of Ida's gown.

"I am."

"Come look," Pearl said, taking Ida by the hand and leading her to where the mirror stood.

"You look beautiful," Eleanor said in a quiet voice.

They were at Eleanor's house, upstairs in one of the guest bedrooms. Olivia was still in the

country with Mr. Beechcroft, but she had hopes
that her father-in-law would feel well enough to
travel soon.

Della and Mrs. Wattings were making plans to
set up their own household, even though Eleanor
begged them to consider staying for longer.

The duchess had refused to acknowledge Della's
return, although Ida knew it must be tearing her
apart, since she was equally desperate to see her
daughters married, and the least marriageable
one was about to fulfill her mother's most fervent
wish, and the duchess would want to be there to
boast her triumph at finally having a Howlett
marry the elusive Lord Carson.

Ida stared back at her reflection, startled to see
how she looked. Not because she didn't know
how she appeared, obviously, but because—

"Is that a happy expression on my face?" she
asked in an incredulous voice.

Della and Pearl both burst out laughing, although Pearl, at least, had the grace to look embarrassed at the outburst. Eleanor just rolled her
eyes.

Ida was all set to glare at her sisters, but then
Della made a funny noise as she laughed so it
was impossible for Ida not to join her. And then
they were all laughing, holding their stomachs as
they shared glances brimming with amusement.

"I am happy," Ida said after the laughter had

died down. "I never would have thought it, that I would be the Howlett sister to finally snare the elusive Lord Carson."

"The way he looks at you, sister, it would be a scandal if you weren't to be married," Della replied in a sly tone.

Ida felt herself blush. Something else she'd rarely done before.

Apparently being happy and blushing were things she could look forward to from now on.

"And you didn't have to wear white," Pearl said, nodding toward Ida's gown.

It was not white. Not in the slightest. It was a rich, glorious purple, the purple of grapes and crocuses and amethysts. Except for the ribbons that wrapped around Ida's waist and tied at the back, it was bare of ornament, and cut low enough that Ida had to resist the urge to tug the gown up.

Pearl had pulled Ida's hair into an equally simple chignon, wrapping a length of the matching ribbon around her head. She'd also found purple gloves that were a lighter hue.

"Lord Carson likes me in rich colors," Ida said in satisfaction. Actually, she knew he liked her best in no clothing at all, but she couldn't very well get married naked.

"Let's go. We don't want to be late," Della said, glancing at the clock in the corner.

"Thank you for bringing Della back to us," Eleanor said. "Thank you for standing up for all of us, for sharing your knowledge and wisdom." She sounded sincere, and Ida felt her heart swell.

They did appreciate her. They did understand her, to a point, but what was most important was that they loved her.

"THERE SHE IS," Alexander murmured, even though his words were unnecessary—Bennett hadn't stopped looking for her since he'd arrived at the church half an hour ago.

He and his brother were standing at the front, watching as she walked down the aisle accompanied by all of her sisters.

There weren't many people in attendance. Not because so many refused to come, but because neither Ida nor Bennett particularly wanted a large crowd for their wedding. When Bennett had asked Ida if she was certain, she'd given him that "are you actually questioning me" look, and he'd laughed.

The only person besides Alexander that Bennett wanted there had managed to make it, and he glanced over to where his mother sat, frail but smiling, under Nurse Cooper's watchful eye.

He had told his father, but he hadn't expected the marquis to make an appearance, and he hadn't. He was still sulking from Bennett's refusal to sacrifice himself, and had taken off to the country, apparently bringing his second family with him.

Bennett had made certain that his father had enough to live on, but not so much it would threaten the family's livelihood.

Ida walked toward him, her head held as proudly as when he had first met her, when she'd shared her dreams of escape and what it meant to be a female in their world. She was so beautiful it made him hurt, but that hurt was assuaged because she was going to be his. She was his.

And he was hers, because he knew she would insist in theirs being an equal partnership.

"My hedgehog," he said in a low voice as she stepped beside him.

She opened her mouth as though to protest—in her very hedgehog-like way—then must have changed her mind, because instead she smiled, that true, wonderful, glorious smile that had knocked him flat when he'd first seen it.

"Stop trying to distract me," she said in a mock outraged tone. "We're here to get married, not have you bestow epithets."

Bennett bowed. "Of course. I do not want to delay a moment more than I have to for you to be my bride."

"And you my husband," she retorted.

"Do you—" the clergyman interrupted, stumbling a bit on the change of wording. "Do you, Bennett, dare to take this woman Ida to be your lawfully wedded wife, to have and to hold, in sickness and in heath, in good times and woe, for richer or poorer, keeping yourself solely unto her for as long as you both shall live?"

"I dare." Bennett felt the truth of his words in his entire body.

The clergyman turned to Ida, who grinned as she waited for him to repeat the same words.

"I dare," she said in a voice loud enough to be heard at the back of the church.

Epilogue

Sometimes the most daring adventure is at home.

LADY IDA'S TIPS FOR THE
ADVENTUROUS LADY TRAVELER

*Y*ou're not—?"

Ida glowered. "No, I am not," she said, swatting Bennett's hand away from her midsection. "I probably just ate too much at breakfast. Just because my two sisters had babies practically within moments of their weddings does not mean I am like them."

"You are nothing like them, wife," Bennett said, kissing her shoulder. "You are only you. *Ida.*" As always, his touch made her shiver, and he chuckled, a deep knowing sound that made her want to drag him off somewhere and strip him naked.

But since it was the morning, and they were on their way to visit Della and Mrs. Wattings at the Society for Poor and Unfortunate Children, she couldn't very well take time out to have her way with him.

Or his way with her, to be honest.

She very much enjoyed making love with and to her husband. Bennett was willing to be flexible in all such matters, sometimes taking her hard and ruthlessly, other times letting her take the lead, giving her a gloriously powerful feeling.

What was always consistent was that she found her pleasure, and that was a wonderful thing.

"This afternoon, hedgehog," Bennett said, because apparently he had become a mind reader.

"Speaking of which," Ida said, picking up a letter from the tray, "I've had an odd letter from Della." She held it out to him. "She says not to worry about whatever news might surface about her, but doesn't say what it is." She looked up at him. "What could be worse than running off with the dancing instructor?"

Bennett took the letter and scanned it, handing it back to her when he was done.

"It seems as though your sister might finally be finding her own adventure. Perhaps she'll dare as well?" He shook his head in mock disapproval. "The Howlett sisters are quite disgraceful, aren't they?"

Ida grabbed the back of his head and drew him down for a kiss. "That they are."

**And now
check out a sneak peek of Megan Frampton's
next in The Duke's Daughters series**

Never a Bride

Coming next spring from Avon Books!

Chapter 1

Report from Africa

The H.M.S. Albert, steam sloop, Captain
Griffith Davies, captured a valuable slaver,
based in Brazil, off the coast of Monrovia on
17 February of this year. The slaver attempted
to evade its captors through nefarious deception,
but the brave and courageous sailors aboard the
man of war noticed the ship's suspicious activity
and boarded after exchanging a volley of
shots. None of the British crew was wounded,
although two of the slaver's sailors were slightly
wounded. Captain Davies and his crew liberated
the men on board and brought the ship's
captain and crew to the Brazilian authorities in
Monrovia for judgment. It remains to be seen
if Captain Davies will be reprimanded by the
British authorities since he did not follow proper
procedure.

April 30, 1851
London, The Mermaid's Arms, a not so respectable
pub on the dock serving mediocre porter

"*I* think we should get some more ale," Griffith said to his first mate, Clark, as he downed the rest of his drink. "*That's* proper procedure," he snorted ruefully.

Proper procedure in this pub meant that he would get more beer. But proper procedure, at least according to Her Majesty's government, meant that innocent people would likely die, caught in the conflict between nations. Proper procedure meant that women and children would live in a ship's hold for months, with meager provisions and unsanitary living circumstances.

So he'd acted improperly, according to the Naval authorities. It smarted, being told he'd done wrong. But he had acted entirely properly when it came to Griffith's own law, which demanded that people be free to live as they wish, not kept in captivity.

It was one of the many reasons he'd run off to sea when he was sixteen—he'd seen the inequity of his family's situation, that they were blessed with wealth and land and power, and the families that worked for them were entirely dependent on their largesse. He would not stand by and benefit merely because of the lucky circumstance of his birth. Especially if he could do something about other people's unlucky circumstances.

Also there was the truth that he and his parents did not agree on anything. They wanted him to follow in the footsteps of all the Davies sons before him, which meant getting the best education and then forgetting entirely about it since it wasn't seemly to appear too intelligent.

Not that Griffith believed himself to be too intelligent—school had been difficult for him. He wanted to be outside all the time, moving his body rather than sitting in a wooden chair for hours.

Although after several months at sea, this chair in the pub felt quite comfortable.

"Clark?" he said again. "Another drink?"

Clark did not answer. Likely because Clark had already had enough and was currently sleeping on the table.

"More!" Griffith called as he downed the rest of his drink. One of the barmaids nodded.

"Excellent service, don't you think?" Griffith asked Clark. "Very proper procedure," he couldn't help but add in a low aside.

Clark snored softly in reply. Not even appreciating Griffith's wit.

Griffith shrugged, adjusting Clark's head so he was lying more comfortably. That was one of the secrets behind being a well-respected captain: making certain your crew was taken care of.

He'd taken such good care of Clark that his mate was getting some well-deserved rest. Albeit in a pub, his nose pressed against a wooden table.

He didn't see the point of being sober either if he was on land, but unfortunately it took a lot for him to get drunk, since he was so large—he towered over everyone on his crew and couldn't get comfortable below deck. His jackets always felt a bit snug, too, since it seemed tailors did not actually believe that a person's shoulders could be as wide as Griffith's.

The curse of the Davies family.

The barmaid placed another glass on the worn wooden table in front of him. "You need one for your friend here?" she asked.

Griffith shook his head no and tossed a few coins to her, which she caught handily. "Thank you," he said as he took a long draught. The porter was fair to middling at best, but it was *beer*, so that made it all right.

They usually ran out of beer aboard the ship sometime around the second month of the voyage, and this most recent voyage had lasted over ten months. Too long without alcohol. Or a woman, to be honest.

He did feel slightly fuzzy around the edges, which was good. It also had the benefit of disguising the quality of the alcohol. And the lack of female companionship.

He might've attempted some sort of discourse with one of the barmaids, but several ships had docked, it seemed, so the pub was full to bursting and the women were scurrying about with no time for flirtation. Despite their bosoms full to bursting delightfully out of their bodices. He enjoyed the view at least.

While he'd engaged in anonymous couplings in the past, he found the idea distasteful now. He wanted something more, although he had no hope of finding more for the short time they were ashore. So he'd resigned himself to looking—discreetly, so as not to cause distress— and consoling himself with beer and sleeping in a bed long enough for him to stretch his entire body out.

That was heaven for him. Even if it was a solitary heaven.

Plus, there was Clark to consider—it would be downright rude to leave his first mate here alone. Even if Clark was currently unconscious, so perhaps not the best company.

"It's you and me, love," he said to the glass, which was already nearly empty.

He, Clark, and his crew had made shore only that morning, and after filing the ship's paperwork with the authorities, he had told his crew to do whatever they wanted for the next forty-eight hours. He presumed they were scattered around

London, doing exactly what he was doing, give or take a few ales and women.

Or, like Clark here, getting some well-deserved rest.

He took the last pull from his glass as he saw the door to the pub open. His mouth dropped open as he saw who had walked in—not that he knew the lady. How could he? Just that she looked like a glorious angel, a vibrant, dark-haired woman wearing a dark cloak. The glimpse he got of her face indicated she was truly stunning. And was entirely out of place in this dingy dockside pub.

"I wish you were awake for this," Griffith murmured in Clark's direction. "And I'm reconsidering my stance on anonymous couplings. Although she is clearly a lady, so that would not be possible." Too bad, he thought. For him, not for her. He didn't think a lady would wish to have anything to do with someone like him.

The female wore an enormous bonnet on her head, making her have to turn her head to glance around her, a newspaper tucked under one arm, while in the other she was brandishing a—a tiny sword? A poker for the fire?

Oh. A *hatpin*. Of course. Because young, beautiful ladies often ventured into disreputable establishments carrying only a newspaper and an accessory.

"The fool," he muttered, shaking his head as

he watched her movements. He felt his body tighten in an unconsciously protective position. He wished he weren't so determined to rescue anybody who seemed they might need help, but that was what had propelled him thus far, so he supposed it wouldn't stop just because he was off duty. He shrugged, taking another drink as he accepted his own inability to stay uninvolved.

She held the hatpin in front of her, clearly apprehensive. As she should be. The only women in the pub worked here, and they were definitely not ladies. The noise had been growing steadily in the short time he'd been inside. There had even been a few scuffles, although there hadn't been any full-fledged fights. At least not yet. She glanced around, her gaze, from what Griffith could see of it, intent. As though she were looking for someone or something. She picked her way over to the bar, a few tables away from where Griffith sat and Clark slept.

Griffith rose slowly from his chair, now relieved he hadn't had more to drink. This lady had no idea what she was walking into, or she would have at least brought a Derringer pistol.

"Pardon me," he heard her say to one of the barmaids in what was obviously a cultured accent, as though her clothing didn't give her status away. But she wasn't able to finish, mostly because the barmaid she'd inquired of was too busy handing out the ales at the other end of the bar.

The noise in the room began to subside as the occupants heard and saw the lady. Griffith grimaced as he heard the low hum of talk that wasn't the rowdy conviviality of a few moments earlier. This conversation held a tone of suspicion and interest. Damn it. It seemed likely he would have to interfere.

"Who's this, then?" The voice came from behind Griffith, and he turned, seeing the man wobble up to his feet, a predatory tone in his voice.

It wasn't one of Griffith's shipmen, unfortunately. If it were, he could command him to sit back down. To ignore one of Griffith's direct commands meant immediate dismissal.

"I am looking for someone," the lady said, raising her chin—and her hatpin—as she turned away from the bar to face the man.

The man walked toward the bar, a lewd grin on his face. "Looking for me, I'd say. How about we grab a drink and get to know each other? I've always wanted to have a la—" But he stopped speaking as she raised her arm, sticking the hatpin into the man's chest, making him yelp as he took a few steps backward.

"I am looking for someone," she repeated, punctuating each word with a poke as the man grimaced. "And I suspect it is not you."

Griffith had to admire her even as he anticipated how the man, and his companions, would
react.

Sure enough, the man's table companions rose,
their postures clearly indicating violence. There
were far too many of them to take out just with
a chair. He'd have to try diplomacy. If that failed,
he'd upend a few tables.

"Now, gentlemen," Griffith began, walking
toward the scene as he held his hands out in
a placating manner, "there's no need to make a
fuss. The lady—"

The man grabbed the hatpin and pushed it
back toward her, even as she struggled to keep
it pinned in him. It must have hurt, Griffith had
to admit.

"Stay out of it," the man interrupted without
glancing at Griffith.

"I cannot," Griffith said, stepping up and
grasping the pin, yanking it out from the man's
hand. Well, diplomacy and his own size and
strength. "I will see to the young lady, and help
her find who she's looking for. There is no need
for you to bother yourself any longer." Sometimes there was a benefit to forever championing
the underdog in a lopsided fight. Now he could
get a better look, see if she was as beautiful as he
thought.

The man opened his mouth as though to argue, then looked up—and up—at Griffith's height and breadth and apparently thought better of it. He nodded at his companions, all of whom lowered themselves slowly back down into their seats.

Griffith exhaled. It wasn't that he was dreading a fight, but it would be a shame to waste some of his precious free time busting sailors' heads.

"And who are you?" she asked in a haughty tone of voice, turning her gaze to Griffith. Unlike the man, she didn't seem intimidated at all by his size. That was a surprise; most people at least blinked twice when they saw him. Plus, he had just rescued her from an unpleasant situation. The very least he could expect would be some gratitude.

None appeared to be forthcoming.

She was as beautiful as he'd suspected; dark hair swept up underneath her hat, a few enticing strands falling down around her face. Her eyes were dark also, with delicate eyebrows that were raised in question. Her nose was perfect, and her mouth—her lips were full and red, and she had a mole to the right of her mouth that seemed, to Griffith, at least, a visual marker for where his own mouth should start kissing her.

Griffith took his hat off, sweeping low into a bow,

as genteel and respectable as he'd been taught so many years ago. "Captain Griffith Davies, at your service. I would be glad to assist you if you can tell me who you're looking for?"

Her expression was puzzled, and then it cleared as she whacked him hard on the arm. He was definitely not expecting that reaction. "You're Lord Viscount Whateverhisname! You're the person I'm looking for!"

Griffith hadn't heard anyone reference his title in so long he nearly opened his mouth to deny it. Then realized he couldn't, because it was true.

She was about to speak again when the door opened and a phalanx of men poured in, all wearing the garb of the Royal Navy Police.

Griffith did not think they were here for the ale. He positioned himself in front of the lady in an unconscious need to protect her. Was she wanted by the authorities? Was that why she was here, attempting to hide out?

"Captain Davies!" one of the policemen said, sweeping his gaze over the pub's inhabitants. "We need to speak with Captain Davies."

"You need to speak with me?" Griffith said, his tone skeptical. Because while he suspected they weren't here to drink, he hadn't thought they might want *him*. But perhaps this was the day when everyone came to this pub looking for him.

Maybe Queen Victoria herself would show up

eventually. And he'd have a word with her about ensuring there was enough beer on board her ships. Not to mention discussing what proper procedure should be.

Two of the men went to either side of him, taking his arms. Hm. They did not want him for a polite conversation, then. Unless they were determined to have his full attention. And he could have told them a full pitcher of beer and a large soft chair could have done just as well.

He glanced from one to the other, considering whether he should shake them off. He could do it, but it would likely just be postponing the inevitable. And he'd hate to wake Clark up just for something like this.

The man who'd spoken pushed through to step in front of Griffith, his face blanching as he looked up. "You're Captain Davies?"

Griffith bowed, at least as much as he was able to, given that his arms were being held. "At your service. What's this about?"

"You're being arrested by the authority of Her Majesty's Royal Navy. If you'll come with me?"

"As though I have a choice," Griffith muttered. His improper procedure must have drawn the ire of Her Majesty's Navy. He'd like to have a word with Her Majesty even more. It was unfortunate the Queen wasn't waltzing into disreputable pubs brandishing hatpins.

He glanced toward the lady who had done just that, nodding in her direction. "Perhaps we can schedule another time to speak, my lady. As you can see, I am somewhat busy at the moment." He winked as her eyes narrowed.